LUKE IRONTREE & THE LAST VAMPIRE WAR

Book 0 - The Centurion Immortal
Book 1 - Dark Fangs Rising - March 22, 2022
Book 2 - Dark Fangs Raging - April 19, 2022
Book 3 - Dark Fangs Descending - May 17, 2022
Book 4 - Blood Empire Reborn* - August 23, 2022
Book 5 - Blood Empire Avenged* - September 20, 2022
Book 6 - Blood Empire Burning* - October 18, 2022
Book 7 - Blood Empire Collapsing* - November 15, 2022
Book 8 - Ancient Sword Falling* - February 7, 2023
Book 9 - Ancient Sword Unyielding* - March 7, 202
Book 10 - Ancient Sword Shattering* - May 9, 2023

The Luke Irontree Historical Adventures
Rise of the Centurio Immortalis - April 5, 2022
Fall of the Centurio Immortalis - May 31, 2022
The Moonlight Centurion* - December 27, 2022
The Highway Centurion* - April 11, 2023

*Forthcoming
Titles and release dates may be subject to change.

FALL OF THE CENTURIO IMMORTALIS

A LUKE IRONTREE HISTORICAL ROMANCE

C. THOMAS LAFOLLETTE

FALL OF THE CENTURIO IMMORTALIS
C. Thomas Lafollette

A Broken World Publication
13820 NE Airport Way
Suite #K395495
Portland, OR 97251-1158
Fall of the Centurio Immortalis
Copyright © 2022 by C. Thomas Lafollette
ISBN 978-1-949410-58-7 (ebook);
ISBN 978-1-949410-59-4 (paperback)

Cover Design: Ravven
Developmental Editing by: Suzanne Lahna
Copy/Line Editing: C.D. Tavenor
Proofreading: Amy Cissell

All rights reserved. No part of this publication may be reproduced, distributed, or transmitted in any form or by any means, including photocopying, recording, or other electronic or mechanical methods, without the prior written permission of the publisher, except in the case of brief quotations embodied in critical reviews and certain other noncommercial uses permitted by copyright law. For permission requests, write to the author at editors@brokenworldpublishing.com.

This is a work of fiction. Names, characters, businesses, places, events, and incidents are either the products of the author's imagination or used in a fictitious manner. Any resemblance to actual persons, living or dead, or actual events is purely coincidental.

CONTENTS

LUKE IRONTREE PREVIEWS

CONTENT WARNING

This book contains some gore as well as depictions of starvation. There are battle scenes and sword violence.

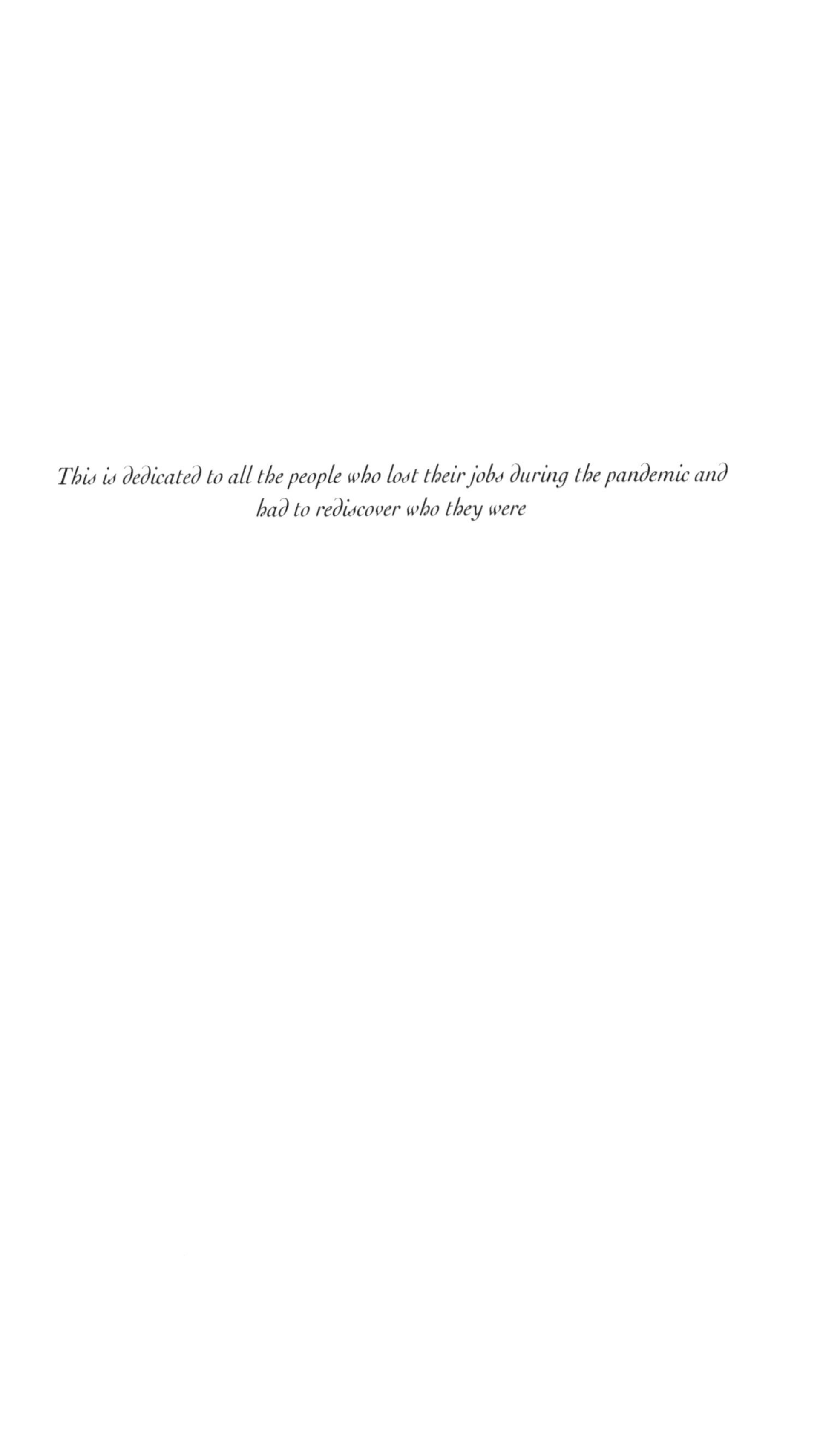

This is dedicated to all the people who lost their jobs during the pandemic and had to rediscover who they were

PRONUNCIATION GUIDE & AUTHOR'S NOTES

Pronunciation: Latin names and words are mentioned throughout the book and are intended to be read with the classical Latin pronunciation. For instance, "c" is always pronounced hard, like a "k." "U" is always a short "oo" sound. "V" typically sounds like a "w." There are plenty of resources on the internet if you wish to learn more about Classical Latin pronunciation.

- Lucius – Loo-kih-oos
- Silvanius – Sihl-wahn-ih-oos
- Ferrata – Fehr-rah-tah
- Marpesia — Mahr-peh-see-ah
- Aella — Ay-ehl-lah
- Pisakar — Pih-suh-kahr

Latin Words: Latin words are used for effect and to add to the "flavor" of the story, not to reflect Latin grammar/declensions/conjugations.

Anachronisms: It's nearly impossible to write historical settings without some anachronisms, especially when you're writing scenes set nearly 2,000 years in the past. Those used are done so intentionally for the purpose of story telling and to convey sentiments that would be recognizable to people then and now. Also, there are vampires.

ONE

THE CENTURIO IMMORTALIS half dozed in his saddle as they approached the bridge over the Danuvius River. He'd decided to push on and hit their fort instead of camping outside the empire's borders for another night. Although the day's march had been stiff, his men were in fine spirits as they approached the river that meant they were only a few more miles from their beds.

"Princeps Primus Centurio?" a young soldier asked.

"Boy, you don't need to use the full title," barked the grizzled officer riding next to Lucius.

"Sorry, sir. Centurio Ferrata. Legatus Pisakar is waiting for us just past the bridge."

"Hmm? What?" Lucius shook his head to clear the haze of his nap. "Pisakar? What's he doing here?"

"I don't know, Centurio. They just sent me back to inform you," the young man said.

"Just thinking out loud, Decanus…" Lucius searched for the name of the young man he'd recently approved for promotion to leader of his tent group.

"Martininius, Sir," Martininius said, aiding his Centurio.

"Decanus Martininius, thanks. Return to your station. Actually, hold. I'll join you and find out what Pisakar is up to myself." Turning to the Primus Pilus riding next to him, he said, "Tinkomaros, keep the men marching. You're in charge."

"Aye, Centurio," the gruff Gaul replied.

Between his nod of assent and the breeze, his long mustache tails fluttered in the wind. Although Lucius typically stuck to the shaved face and short hair in fashion when he joined the legions under the reign of Imperator Traianus, he'd let his hair and beard grow out longer than he had in ages, bordering on unkempt. He allowed his men a certain sense of freedom when it came to their grooming—as long as they were clean, they could wear their hair and facial hair anyway they liked as befit the Empire's elite legion. His men were allowed to have their quirks and eccentricities; they'd earned them.

Lucius rubbed his hand through his shaggy, dark brown hair and pulled his horse out of line and behind the decanus, the old gelding replying to his commands smoothly. They rode at a sedate pace along the line of Lucius's marching men, who nodded to their respected leader as he rode past.

"Remind me, son, where are you from?" Lucius asked his newly minted platoon leader.

"Massilia, sir," the handsome young soldier replied, his face still containing the softness of youth despite the intense training of the legions.

"What did your father do in Massilia?"

"He was a clerk, sir."

"Not a legionnaire?"

"No, sir," Martininius replied.

"How'd you end up in the legions?"

"I didn't fancy quills and parchment for a lifetime."

Lucius let out a bark of laughter. "Fair enough. My father joined so he wouldn't be forced to toil in the soil outside his village in Belgica." Lucius smiled fondly, remembering his father and his stories. "He said he moved more dirt in the legions than he ever would have as a farmer… Anyway, what do you think of the Lugii?"

"They seem a fine people, sir."

"Ah, politic answer. Certainly a safe option. Cautiously polite but interpretable as a small slight. Certainly a far cry from the people of Massilia."

The city on the Gallicum Sea had been a colony of the Hellenes before hitching its star to the Roman Republic five hundred years ago when they joined forces with Hannibal Barca.

"Yes, sir. Have you been to Massilia?"

"I've passed through a few times over the years. It's a whole other world than the forests of Germania."

"Yes, sir. The forests…" He seemed to be formulating a thought. "They're dark. Even in the full light of Sol. They're almost sorrowful."

The thoughtful and slightly poetic statement from the young soldier intrigued Lucius. Most of his men were there because they were the elite legionnaires of the empire, the best fighting men in the world. Lucius could understand why the young man's centurion had singled him out for his first promotion.

"Sorry, sir, if I spoke out of turn."

Lucius waved Martininius's concern aside. "Don't worry about it. Continue. Please."

"It was just… When I could tune out the sound of the march, the wind sighed through the branches. They almost seemed weary at our passing."

Lucius raised an eyebrow. "How much do you know about the history of this area?"

"Not much, sir."

"We're at a crossroads. These woods have known blood. The Getae, Dacians, Sarmatians, Macromannians, Vandals, Goths, Romans, Gauls, and probably hundreds of peoples I've never even heard of. We've all bled in these woods. All left the bones of our fallen in these woods. For centuries upon centuries. I've spilled my share of it over the years too, more than my share if truth be told.

"These woods know me. They've long stopped fearing my arrival, instead only greeting it with weariness for what I might do. They do feel sorrow. They'd prefer to drink of the spring rains. Instead, I feed them blood."

They rode in silence for a while. The dark German woods always made Lucius feel maudlin. The tall pines were nothing like the trees of his youth in faraway Belgica where the leaves rustled with laughter, forgetting the long-gone wars of Caesar's conquests of Gaul.

"Sir, why didn't the Lugii accept protection in the empire like the rest of the Vandals?"

"Some men don't want to bow to the Imperator. They'd rather take their chances and be free," Lucius replied.

The hooves of their horses clattered over the stone bridge as they pulled in front of the column. At the far end of a bridge, a giant of a man stood, holding the reins of his horse. He removed his helmet shaped like a roaring lion's head, revealing dark black skin and a shaved head. He raised a hand in greeting.

"Thank you for the conversation Decanus Martininius," Lucius said. "You may return to your unit."

The decanus banged his fist into his chest plate and extended a crisp salute to Lucius. "Yes, Centurio Ferrata." He wheeled his horse around and returned to his commander. Lucius nudged his gelding into a trot. The horse snorted and shook its head.

"Quit your complaining, Cicero. It's been easy duty this time around," Lucius said to his pony.

Pisakar, seeing Lucius trotting toward him, mounted up and waved his detachment to fall in behind them as they passed. "Hamilcar, bring the rest of the men home. You're in charge," he yelled over his shoulder as he brought his stout pony up next to Lucius. "What'd the free Vandals have to say?"

Lucius was quiet for a bit. "Ariaric and his Tervingi are moving south…in numbers."

"What does 'in numbers' mean?"

"Judging by the poorly contained panic of the Lugii? The whole damned tribe. Thousands upon thousands, Pisakar."

Pisakar whistled his dismay. "What drives them? It'll be soon winter in the mountains and steppes."

"Benetrax wouldn't say specifically, but that scared him most of all. Best I could surmise is 'demons in the night.'"

Shaking his head, Pisakar let rip a steady stream of curses.

"That's the job we accepted when we took our oath to the Black Legion."

"It's not that, Lucius. It's just a poor time for the Imperator to be calling you off the border."

Lucius perked up and turned his head to his friend and second-in-command. "What?"

"You didn't think I came all the way up here just to welcome you across the bridge? Constantius has deigned to acknowledge your existence after nearly thirty years. There's a messenger waiting for you at the castrum."

"When?"

"He and his entourage arrived four days ago."

"I guess we should go see what our Imperator wants."

"You mean 'Dominus Noster'?" Pisakar said, loading the title with sarcasm.

Lucius could hear his friend's eye roll. Like Lucius, Pisakar didn't care for the new stylings of the most recent breed of imperators. They'd shed the title of "Princeps," first among Romans, and sought to elevate themselves to nearly divine status while living.

"Yes. Let's go see what the servant of 'Our Lord' wants with the Black Legion." Lucius kicked Cicero into a canter. The horse grunted and kicked out behind him before responding to his rider's commands.

"Lucius, it's time to put that old bastard out to pasture."

"I'd watch out if I were you when we get back to the fort. He'll be aiming to bite you after that comment. He still does what's asked of him." Luke patted Cicero's neck fondly.

"Aye, he's a smart beast, no doubt, but it's getting harder for him. He's not immortal."

Lucius caught the pointed look his friend directed at him. He sighed and stroked the horse's neck. "You're probably right, Pisakar. He's probably as stubborn as I am."

"That he is, my friend, but it's time for him to rest and enjoy his days. I have a feeling we have some tough campaigning in our future, and I'm not sure the old bastard has another one in him. He'll soldier on until he drops, but why not let him enjoy some time getting fat on easy grass? He's done his duty; let him muster out."

The two men rode in silence, the only sound the beating hooves of their horses and the detachment of guards riding behind them at a discreet distance. Pisakar was right. Lucius had kept Cicero around longer than was standard for the war ponies his legion and its cavalry units maintained. Cicero was one of the smartest and most cantankerous horses he'd ever ridden in the two centuries he'd commanded his legion. The old bastard had been his friend and steadfast companion since the herd master selected him to be Lucius's prime mount nearly a decade earlier.

"He should have been retired years ago," Pisakar added.

"You could say the same of me."

Pisakar laughed; the deep rumbling sound always made Lucius smile. "You should have been dead almost two hundred years ago, my friend. But that's what happens when you put yourself in the way of the gods; they find a way to use you beyond your time."

Again, Pisakar was right. At nearly 245-years-old, Lucius had outlived everyone he knew and would probably bury all his current friends. Talk of his age did nothing to improve the mood the dark, lonely German forest inspired.

In contrast, the village of camp followers and the families of the legionnaires he commanded bustled with activity, laughter and yells filling the air as they rode through. While the men of the Roman legions couldn't marry during their time under the eagle, nothing prevented them from having a companion outside the legion. Some men even started families who followed them from post to post until they mustered out and could sign the marriage contract.

The glint of sun off steel caught his eye as a young man in armor wearing the black of Lucius's legion stepped out of a small hut, a woman following him. She pulled him back into her arms, laughing when he bumped into her, nearly knocking her down before wrapping his arms around her for a passionate kiss. Lucius sighed, letting his eyes linger on the young couple.

Over the two plus centuries serving under the eagle, he'd had his share of dalliances, but he'd never committed to anyone knowing his contract with the empire would probably never end. As his legion moved around the empire, if he met someone, he'd eventually have to move on when the empire's need to fight foreign enemies, living or undead, arrived.

Once they crested the last hill before their fort, Pisakar raised his arm and signaled to the guards behind them. Spurring their horses forward, they closed ranks around the leader of their legion and his second-in-command, one of them racing forward to alert the fort to their general's return.

Lucius straightened in his saddle. "Legatus Pisakar, inform our guest I'll meet with him first thing in the morning after I've broken my fast. I think I'll spend some time in the baths tonight. Have food and wine prepared for after. You can join me and update me on what's been going on while I was gone."

"Aye, Centurio Ferrata." Pisakar saluted and, when they passed through the gates of their fortress, split off from their detachment to carry out his orders.

After dismounting, Lucius handed Cicero's reins to his groom. The Sarmatian was one of the few people Lucius's gelding didn't try to bite or kick, probably because he was always slipping the pony treats.

"How did the old brute do, Centurio?" Marcellus asked.

"He grumbled a lot, but he responded."

Marcellus laughed. "So the usual?"

Lucius nodded. "Give him some extra grain tonight and mix in some honey and apples."

"Yes, Centurio." Marcellus led Cicero off to be groomed and rubbed down before his evening meal.

LUCIUS TOOK his time with his breakfast the next morning. He knew the Imperator's emissary was waiting, but he enjoyed the pettiness of forcing him to cool his heels after he'd passed up meeting with him the previous evening.

"Anything else, sir?" his valet asked.

"No. I've kept him waiting long enough." Lucius stood and walked toward his armor stand.

His valet lifted the lorica off the stand and held it open for Lucius. As he settled the segmented armor on Lucius's shoulders, Lucius wondered what the man who'd set himself at the top of the empire wanted of him after all this time. Flavius Valerius Constantius had risen to power under his father's auspices when Diocletian selected him to be one of his four co-rulers after dividing the empire in half for two co-emperors with two successors under them.

When his father died, his father's legions declared Constantius his successor and emperor of the west. Through several civil wars, Constantius had eliminated his co-emperors and competitors to perch himself and his family atop the empire's power structure, going so far as to establish a new capital in the east and naming it after himself—Constantinopolis. In all that time, Constantius had never called on Lucius and his Black Legion to join him nor sent so much as an emissary or letter acknowledging the existence of the elite legion charged with protecting the empire from the demons of the night—the drinkers of blood.

While it never put Lucius in the difficult position of denying the Imperator his direct support, he was still insulted at the lack of regard. He'd watched the borders of the empire for over two centuries, protecting Roma and her people from enemies both human and undead.

"I think the bear cloak, sir," the valet said after cinching the front of the armor closed.

"It's not that cold."

"No, but it's most impressive, especially with Marcus Aurelius Antoninus's seal on it."

Lucius nodded. With its bear hair running down the shoulders and upper back, the black cloak added more bulk to his already sizable appearance. While he hadn't grown as tall as his father—who was tall even for a Gaul—Lucius was six feet tall and broad.

Settling the cloak over his gladius, he took his helmet from the valet. Like Lucius, the armor, helmet, and gladius were antiques. He had a matching spatha, the longer sword standard for Constantius's modernized infantry, but he preferred the continuity the old weapon added to his appearance. He was the Centurio Immortalis; he needed to look the part.

When he approached the camp's headquarters, the legionnaires on guard duty snapped to attention, saluting crisply as he passed. Pisakar had selected some of the most decorated of the Black Legion to further display the Legion's prowess. Pisakar was the best second he'd ever worked with and a trusted friend. He always took care of the more bureaucratic or ceremonial details Lucius had grown disinterested with over time. Of all the Legionary commanders in the Empire, Lucius was probably the least formal, reverting to his "barbarian" upbringing as a Belgic Gaul growing up in the territory of the Nervii tribe some eight-and-a-half centuries after the founding of Roma.

Pisakar met him inside the door. "The new Imperator thinks he knows you and can woo you."

He always referred to the emperor as "new," refusing to acknowledge his nearly thirty-year reign until he paid proper respect to the Black Legion as emperors since its founding under Traianus and Hadrianus had.

Lucius saw what Pisakar meant as soon as he stepped through the door. A man with graying blond hair abruptly stood, saluting Lucius.

"Princeps Primus Centurio, Sir!" the man shouted along with his salute.

Lucius, before sitting behind his desk, gave the Imperator's emissary a once over. He was taller than Lucius and lean. The man had the bearing of a German. At some point, his nose had been broken and set poorly; it jutted off to the side about halfway down. Like Lucius, he favored the old-style segmented lorica. Few used it today; it had fallen out of favor over half a century ago. He held a helmet under his left arm, the crest of a Centurion running transverse. Constantius had sent a Centurion instead of a higher leader or diplomat. Something about his face tugged at Lucius's memory.

"Sit, Centurio."

Pisakar took up a position behind and to the side of Lucius, serving as guard and aid-de-camp during the meeting. And although one of the lower officers usually served in this capacity, Pisakar probably wanted to snoop. He cleared his throat to let Lucius know he was disappointed in him for not making the centurio stand for the meeting.

"Thank you, Princeps Primus Centurio," the centurion said.

Lucius nodded, acknowledging the man. "And please, address me as Centurio."

"Aye, Centurio."

"If you don't mind me saying, you look familiar. Have we met before, or is age blending all faces into the familiar?" Lucius asked, tone airy and bemused.

"I can't speak for your memory, sir, but in my case, it may be both."

Lucius cocked his head to the side, an eyebrow quirking up. "How so, Centurio? How are you called?"

"Segomaros, sir. It's a family name."

"That's a name I haven't heard in a while…" Lucius mused.

"I doubt you'd remember me, sir. The last time we met, I was a snot-nosed miles fresh out of training. I fought alongside the Black near Mongotiacum."

"That was about thirty years ago."

"Aye, sir. I've aged a bit since then."

"And the name?"

"It's a family name. An ancestor of mine served with you back when you were with the XXX Ulpia Victrix, sir."

"Shit, Sego? Gods, that was a long time ago." Squinting a bit to blur the edges of Segomaros's face, Lucius nodded. "You've got something about him in your face. The chin and the cheeks." He turned to address Pisakar. "Segomaros enlisted the same time I did. We went through training together. He got promoted to signifier when I was promoted to tesserarius."

"How old were you, Centurio?" Pisakar asked.

"Nineteen, I think. It was the first year of Traianus's second Dacian war. Sometime I'll tell you how I led, with the aid of Centurio Segomaros's great-great-great- however many times great-grandfather, a half centuria out of an ambush and rescued the Vexillation I was assigned to."

Turning back to Centurio Segomaros, Lucius smiled as the color drained from the Centurio's face. He could hear Pisakar's deep chuckle behind him.

"I don't think the Centurio quite believed why the Imperator sent him," Pisakar said.

Lucius chuckled. "And that brings us to the point of this meeting. What news from our Imperator, Centurio?"

Segomaros took a second to collect himself and reached into an oilskin bag, pulling out a sealed folio. Pisakar stepped from his position behind Lucius and retrieved it from the Centurio, inspecting it before turning it over to Lucius.

"I'm to wait for your reply and return immediately, sir," Centurio Segomaros added.

Lucius broke the seal on the folio and pulled out folded papyrus, again, sealed. He brought his pugio to hand and carefully ran the dagger blade along the papyrus's edge, popping the wax. Carefully, he preserved the Chi Rho surrounded by a laurel wreath, the symbol Constantius had used since his victory at the Battle of Milvian Bridge twenty years ago, earning his undisputed status as Imperator of the western half of the empire.

Lucius unfolded the papyrus and scanned the message from the newest self-styled "Dominus," Lord of the Roman Empire. "I'm to report to Constantinopolis to 'consult' with the Dominus on matters concerning the Goths and Sarmatians."

"When?" Pisakar asked.

"'At my earliest convenience,' it says."

"So, immediately?"

"Immediately," Lucius confirmed. "Legatus Pisakar…"

Pisakar drew up to full attention at the use of his title by his commanding officer.

"See to the comfort of the Centurio and his men for one more night." He turned to address the Centurio. "You'll depart at first light with your message for Dominus Constantius."

The centurio stood up and saluted. "Sir!"

"Centurio Hamilcar," Pisakar called. When a man wearing a centurion's crest stepped into the office, Pisakar issued his orders. "See to Centurio Segomaros and his men. Have their supplies restocked and ready to march out at first light."

Hamilcar saluted and stepped out of the office; Segomaros followed.

Lucius turned around and pulled out a large roll from the storage cabinet. Setting it on his desk, he unrolled the large map of the northern region encompassing the territory along the Danuvius.

"Pisakar, I want you to take the legion to…" He ran his finger over the blue line of the river. "Oescus. I want you close in case I need you. That's central enough so we can go east or west before crossing the northern border into wild country."

Piskar looked over Lucius's shoulder, checking out the small mark on the northern border of Dacia, near the western border of Moesia.

"You don't think he'll send us north from here?" Pisakar asked.

"I'm not sure. I don't know the man, only what I've seen him do. I'd rather not gamble and have you out of place if we need to hurry. I'll need a proper escort."

"Two Cohorts?" Pisakar asked. "The First Cohort and the Eighth?"

"Yes. Give me the First…" Lucius hesitated, considering which other cohort he'd want to take. "And the Sixth."

"The Young Men?" Pisakar sounded doubtful. "The Eighth is a good match for the First…"

Lucius looked up from the map. "It's our job to season them in all aspects of legionary duty, including kissing the ass of Imperators. Besides, I don't want to take both of our best cohorts. I want to make sure you're manned. While I'm thinking about it, I'm going to give you an order to grab a couple cohorts from I Adiutrix at Brigetio. Also, send to the II Italica at Lauriacum for two, and…" His finger settled on another dot. "Two from the IV Flavia Felix at Singidunum. And, take two from the XIV at Carnuntum. Don't take everyone's best, but don't let them palm off their weakest men. I'm going to need to trust their abilities where I suspect we're going."

"I know the drill. They're going to be underpowered either way. These new 'Domini' have been siphoning off the cream of the crop from the border legions for half a century now. Do you want me to notify Quietus that you're leaving Vindobona?"

"Organize and train them as you see fit. You know I trust you to make those decisions." Lucius scratched his jaw. "I'll take care of Quietus. It'll give me a good chance to try out the new horse they want to replace Cicero with."

"He's not going to be happy about you moving out of the neighborhood. The X Gemina is a fine legion with a storied history, but they've grown complacent with you stationed here."

"It'll give them a chance to get some exercise. Quietus is a good man. He'll be able to organize this section of the border. The other legion commanders will listen to him."

Pisakar nodded, rubbing a hand from front to back over the deep brown skin of his bald head. "If there's nothing else, I'll make preparations."

"Actually, you haven't filled the open position for my secretary, have you?"

"Not yet."

"Detach Decanus Martininius from his current assignment and move him to my staff. Looks like he won't quite escape quills and parchment yet."

Pisakar raised an eyebrow but didn't seek clarification. "Martininius?"

"The scout who was escorting me to the bridge."

"Ah, I'll see to it." Pisakar was used to Lucius's sometimes odd orders and rarely asked questions unless it mattered or he was curious. This seemed to qualify as neither.

"That'll be all." Lucius pored over the map in front of him and didn't notice when Pisakar left to fulfill his orders.

TWO

LUCIUS STOOD STIFFLY outside Dominus Constantius's throne room in his finest black tunica, his armor polished and swords' hilts gleaming. Like when he'd met with the imperator's emissary, he wore the bulky cloak decorated with black bear fur, the insignia of Imperator Marcus Aurelius blazoned in gold on two medallions joined by a chain.

He carried his helmet with its flowing, black transverse crest under his arm. Behind him and to each side, two of his more decorated legionnaires stood sentry, holding signa, one with the legion's emblem and one with Lucius's personal emblem. On the legion's banner, the various commendations the legion had earned dangled thickly and nearly to the ground. Lucius's banner, similarly decorated, displayed all the personal commendations he'd earned from Roma's various imperators. And though he'd served many, he always kept the first ones he'd earned under Traianus and Hadrianus at the top.

Those he'd earned before taking on his true life's mission.

He wasn't alone in waiting on the man who'd styled himself the empire's lord. A small entourage of armored men, Sarmatian by gear, hovered around two women in Roman dress. However, unlike

Roman women, their arms were covered in long, elaborately woven sleeves. The one who seemed to be in charge based on everyone else's bearing, wore sleeves with a black and white zig pattern dancing over her arms.

From her ears and neck dangled intricately designed gem-encrusted gold jewelry. Her brown hair had a slight red cast when she shifted her head, light skipping across her slightly wild curls that was barely contained in the combs and chains scattered across her head.

Across her aquiline nose, she had the straight line of a scar silvered with age. Laugh lines creased her cheeks, radiating out from the slightly upturned corners of her mouth. Even now in the cool light inside Constantius's new palace, she squinted slightly as if riding across the sunny steppes. Faint wrinkles spread in a small burst around the corners of her dark gray eyes, as if her squint reflected the sun's own rays.

A soft soled boot peeked out from the hem of her dress, the leather intricately embroidered in a riot of colors. Despite the Roman dress, he could practically feel the winds of the steppes coming off her. He guessed she probably had a dagger or two scattered about on her person, and based on her escort and how she held herself, the right to carry them in the presence of the Imperator. He doubted she was one of the tame Sarmatians the various imperators had allowed to settle in the empire and provide troops to the legions.

She caught his eye as he stared at her. Face flushing, he studiously found something else to look at. As he turned his head, he thought he saw a smirk cross over her face.

Lucius was glad he'd allowed his valet to fuss over his appearance today. His lightly oiled beard and hair were neatly trimmed in the traditional military fashion. The hair at his temples had a light salting in his dark brown hair, the short, oiled curls on top rising like cresting and breaking waves.

His eyes, dark brown, were surrounded by the same wrinkles as hers, only a bit deeper. Unlike her, the skin near his mouth lacked the telltale wrinkles created by a sunny disposition. Nor were they marked by the lines of a sour or dour temperament. His eyes drifted back toward the Sarmatian woman and her entourage.

He struggled to identify their tribe—they could be from any of the tribes orbiting the western region of the steppes closest to the Empire's border. Most Sarmatians favored using stags and birds of prey as their emblems. He didn't recognize the wolf abundantly adorning their decorations and insignia.

Again, his gaze settled on her face. She radiated power and danger, both in the small movements of her body and in the body language of those standing around her. He chalked up his interest in them to boredom or the light reflecting off their abundance of gold ornamentation.

The woman must have felt his eyes. She turned her head slowly to the side, making eye contact with him and quirking an eyebrow in challenge.

He was saved when one of his legionnaires coughed to draw his attention to the bureaucrat standing in front of him.

"Centurio?" the man said.

"Princeps Primus Centurio," barked one of his legionnaires to both ensuring Lucius's attention and to remind the official to use Lucius's proper title. His men would brook no disrespect to their commander.

The man, his eyes shifting nervously to the two legionnaires flanking Lucius, bowed deeply. "Princeps Primus Centurio Ferrata? Dominus Constantius will see you now."

Lucius nodded, but he couldn't help looking back toward the band of Sarmatians. He was disappointed to see they'd disappeared the minute the officious little man had distracted him. He turned back and gestured for the man to lead the way in. The official bobbed his head, a flash of metal catching Lucius's eye. The man wore a Chi Rho on a chain around his neck—the symbol favored by the Dominus and those who followed their Christ god. As he walked to the grand doors leading into Constantius's audience chamber, he gestured toward the guards blocking the closed door.

After speaking with one of the guards, the bureaucrat turned to speak to Lucius. "My apologies, sir. The other delegation is being announced at the moment. The Dominus will let us know when he's ready for you."

Lucius nodded, standing rigidly, glancing over to where the Sarmatians had been only moments earlier. The sound of the doors opening drew him back to alertness. The official nodded at the guards as they stepped to the side, pushing the doors open the rest of the way.

Lucius's legionnaires snapped to attention, sending their gear and banners jingling under the heavy decorations. He followed the bureaucrat. When the official stopped a respectful distance from the imperator, Lucius's escorts both took a couple more steps forward, placing them one step in front of Lucius.

The little bureaucrat turned to Lucius. "Shall I announce you?"

"I will announce him," Optio Pertinax said.

The bureaucrat nodded. The optio rested the base of his banner near his foot.

"Princeps Civitatis, Princeps Senatus, Imperator Constantius, may I present Princeps Primus Centurio Lucius Silvanius Ferrata, first among centuriones, leader of the Black Legion, beloved of Mithras, a soldier of Sol Invictus, and Luna's lone spear against the darkness." The optio's voice boomed throughout the audience chamber—and probably throughout this quadrant of the city.

At the naming of Mithras, Luna, and Sol Invictus, a man with wild hair and a shaggy beard standing in the position of an advisor bristled. Constantius's face was inscrutable. Lucius, when the optio had finished his list, bowed respectfully.

At the base of the dais, the Sarmatians fanned out around the women they'd shown deference to in the waiting room. Her soldiers stood behind her, arrayed a safe distance away but still close enough to protect their mistress. A platoon of the imperator's guards stood sentry near the foreigners in case they were needed. The other woman was seated next to her mistress, but slightly back in a position of subservience.

"Dominus Constantius, it is a pleasure to be called before you. May I apologize for my optio's impertinence? Those of us in the

Black Legion are an old-fashioned lot. How may I serve the empire?"

Lucius had chosen to use Constantius's preferred title while allowing his optio's display to inform the imperator the Black Legion was respectful but not servile. The second Sarmatian woman spoke quietly to her mistress, translating what she'd heard.

"Old-fashioned, indeed?" Constantius chuckled. "You come before me wearing antique armor, wielding antique weapons, using antique titles."

"I am an antique, Dominus," Lucius said.

"He lies, Dominus," the hairy man whispered harshly, loud enough to be heard by Lucius, his men, and everyone else.

The jangle of the banner to his left alerted him that the arms of the legionnaire shook with anger. Lucius casually held up his left hand to remind his men to be calm. He'd have to speak with the optio about who he selected for such duties in the future.

"On occasion, but never about my accomplishments, Dominus," Lucius replied crisply to the imperator, an edge seeping into his voice.

He ignored the man standing behind the leader of the Roman Empire. The advisor wouldn't have spoken out in such a manner unless he knew it would be condoned. Constantius was testing Lucius and his temperament. He maintained eye contact with the imperator, studiously avoiding the burning gaze of the zealot.

Constantius chuckled at a Lucius's response. "Indeed. My advisor, Eusebius of Nicomedia, believes you're an impostor. No man can live for two hundred years."

"Two hundred and forty-five, I believe. I lose count sometimes. It's been a long time."

"He comes to spread lies about false gods, Dominus." Again, Eusebius hissed his whisper for the room to hear.

"I never lie about whom I serve, Dominus."

"Do you serve me?" Constantius asked, an eyebrow raised.

"I serve Roma, Dominus."

Constantius laughed, waving Eusebius back for the moment. "A good answer without committing too much."

Constantius stood slowly and walked toward Lucius and his men, a guard drifting behind the imperator at a respectful distance. The man who'd spent sixty years walking the empire now did it with a bit of a limp. Lucius couldn't tell if it was an old injury or simply age. The imperator had spent most of those years leading Romans against other Romans to secure the empire for his sole rule.

"I've heard some of the tales about Princeps Primus Centurio Ferrata." Stepping to the side, Constantius looked over the banner held by the optio, inspecting the commendations and trophies attached to the legionary banner. He made an impressed noise and stepped toward the tesserarius to inspect Lucius's personal commendations.

"Ah, here it is. Traianus? Dacia, correct?"

"Yes, Dominus. His second war against the Dacians. I earned two promotions and three phylarae and my appointment to the cohort that would become the Black Legion under Hadrianus."

"Ah, yes. I see his here." He looked back to his throne, addressing Eusebius. "If he is an impostor, he's got his details down."

Lucius kept a neutral expression on his face. He'd been in the presence of too many imperators of various degrees of respect and belligerence to allow himself to betray his annoyance at Constantius's nearly thirty years of disrespect.

"Not too many from my predecessors of the previous century."

"Most weren't imperator long enough to bother calling on me," Lucius replied.

"I'm surprised they didn't try to win you to their cause," Constantius said.

"When I swore my oath to Hadrianus before forming the Black Legion, I gave my word to never take part in the internal wars of imperators. Besides, I had more important duties."

"Ah, yes. The mysterious di inferi you swore an oath to Mithras to defeat."

Lucius nodded.

"I'm not sure if I should admire your steadfast devotion to your duty or wonder you an imbecile."

Lucius blinked, his face a marble carving.

Constantius continued, "The 'immortal' man. Feared by many, beloved of the legions—you could have marched your legion to Roma, and they'd all joined your banner. You could have been imperator."

"I never wanted to be," Lucius replied. He held the imperator's gaze, keeping his face a mask of calm. He let a bit of his neutral mask slip as his grew more displeased with the imperator's line of thought.

The sound of a woman's laughter broke the tension. Turning toward the sound, Lucius saw the Sarmatian woman laughing. The free sound of it lifted a smile to his lips as their gazes locked. He gave her a nearly imperceptible nod.

"Ah, our guests," Constantius said. Turning his back to Lucius, he returned to his throne but didn't sit. "Centurio, if I may address you so to save the extra words?"

Lucius nodded. "As it pleases you, Dominus."

"May I present the ambassador from the Roxolani chief, Marpesia, her translator, and her honor guard."

Her name was Marpesia. The sound of her name rolled pleasantly into his ears. She rose and bowed toward Lucius. She spoke in her dialect of the tongue the Sarmatians shared. He only caught a few words of it, knowing mostly the dialect of the Iazyges tribe residing near the borders he'd haunted off and on for decades and not even knowing that terribly well.

"Before I speak to you the words of my mistress, may I ask your preference for Latin or the tongue of the Hellenes?" the translator asked in heavily accented Latin.

"I speak both with facility. Please choose whichever is your better language," Lucius replied.

The translator nodded and switched to Greek. "My mistress is most pleased to meet an illustrious warlord and leader of men such as the 'Centurio Immortalis.'" She used the unofficial Latin title most knew him by inside and out of the empire. "She knows of your reputation with the gladius and as the commander of warriors, but didn't realize you were also a man skilled at not showing offense at the insults of both imperators and little, prattling men."

Eusebius audibly scowled at the Sarmatian's leader. "Impertinent witch…" he mumbled too loudly.

Marpesia slowly turned her attention to him, leveling a withering glare before dismissing him and returning her attention to Lucius. "If we can avoid the buzzing of blow flies, perhaps I may continue," the translator said. "To you, Centurio Immortalis, I bring the respectful greetings of the Roxolani people."

Marpesia bowed deeply before continuing.

"We bring word of your ancient enemy, the enemy of the living, the enemy of the light—the drinkers of blood."

Eusebius grumbled but kept his tongue in check. The powerful Sarmatian woman intimidated the man.

Marpesia held Lucius's gaze. As a cloud shifted outside, a beam of sunshine fell on her, setting the red in her hair afire. He thought he could see blue-green flecks in her gray eyes. His optio, clearing his throat, alerted him that he'd gotten lost for a moment, not hearing the words the Imperator had said.

"…anyway, they say these 'drinkers of blood' are behind the movement of the Goths toward our border."

Recovering, Lucius feigned a light cough, covering his mouth to give himself a moment to collect himself. Now was not the time to be distracted by a pair of pretty eyes, no matter how intensely they held his gaze. He'd seen many in his day, including on beautiful women, though he rarely did more than look. His men joked his only woman was the Black Legion.

"I've heard similar news from the free Lugii, Dominus. Just before your emissary invited me to Byzantium… My apologies, Dominus. Constantinopolis. He said Ariaric is bringing the whole tribe south."

Marpesia listened to her translator as she translated Lucius's Greek. Her jaw set, she nodded rigidly at Lucius then Constantius.

"My mistress says this matches what news she's obtained from our northern tribes and contacts."

Constantius, having returned to his throne, spoke up. "The Roxolani wish alliance with us against the Goths, but only on the condition I send the Black Legion to fight alongside them against the creatures they claim drive the Goths into their lands."

Lucius nodded respectfully to Marpesia. "It's a small price, then, Dominus, since you've little use for the Black."

Constantius chuckled. "Indeed, a small price. Centurio Ferrata, you and your legion will accompany the Roxolani out of the empire where they'll escort you through their lands. You and the Roxolani will form the hammer to my anvil."

Hearing his name and the tone of command, Lucius straightened to attention and bowed when he received his orders. "Yes, Dominus."

"You're dismissed. My Magister Militum will send for you when he's ready to discuss strategies." Turning to the Sarmatian delegation, he addressed their leader. "Marpesia, you have your Black Legion. We will finalize our negotiations at a later date."

Waiting for the translation, her steely gaze held Constantius's, her face tightly guarded against revealing anything. She nodded, standing. The rest of her delegation came to attention. Marpesia bowed and turned to her people, issuing a few curt orders.

Seeing that the emperor had already forgotten them, Lucius saluted, turned, and walked toward the massive doors, his escort following at a respectful pace. As he approached, the doors opened, and he marched through without stopping. Once he was out of sight of the throne room, he swept a hand through his hair, loosening his jaw muscles before he broke a tooth.

"Your orders, sir?" Optio Pertinax asked.

"Back to the barracks for now," Lucius said.

"Yes, sir."

"And find me a legionnaire who's fluent in Sarmatian, preferably the Roxolani dialect. I'm going to need my own translator and someone to teach me." He had a few people of Sarmatian origins in his legion but couldn't put a name to one at the moment.

"Sir."

They stepped out into the courtyard where the rest of his escort cooled their heels in the shade. Seeing their commander's sharp step betraying his annoyance, his men snapped to attention and readied themselves to escort him wherever he wanted. Lucius pulled his helmet onto his head and was reaching for the leather thongs to strap it into place when he heard his name called.

"Primus Princeps Centurio Ferrata!"

Turning, Lucius saw the translator walking quickly to catch up with him. He pulled his helmet off and bowed to the woman, allowing time for her mistress and her entourage to catch up.

"My mistress wishes to speak with you before you depart."

Lucius nodded. "I'm at her immediate disposal. How are you called?"

"Aella, Centurio."

Lucius nodded, waiting with the woman. Aella's hair was dark, tending toward black, and although it had some wave, nowhere near as much as Marpesia's. Aella had the look of a Persian or Parthian or one of the other peoples closer to the southern border of the great steppes.

Marpesia emerged with her escort into the courtyard. She strolled, unhurried. Now that she wasn't in the presence of the imperator, she'd allowed her face to display her annoyance. When she saw her translator, she changed course. When her eyes fell on Lucius, the clouds cleared from her gaze as she drew her face into a friendly expression.

Marpesia, keeping her eyes on Lucius, spoke to him, her translator speaking the words as hers in Greek. "Primus Princeps Centurio Ferrata, I wish to invite you to a banquet in your honor at our palace tomorrow evening."

Lucius replied, "I'd be honored."

"Excellent. I shall send an escort tomorrow evening at two hours before sunset. Then we can share food and drink and discuss matters of importance."

"I shall be ready." Lucius bowed respectfully.

Marpesia returned it, but unlike the quick one she'd sketched for the imperator, she bowed deeply with grace and respect.

"Until tomorrow, Centurio."

THREE

LUCIUS RELAXED, leaning back in his chaise, sipping the high-quality wine they'd served him. It was a nice change, although living in forts around the border had rendered his taste in alcoholic beverages less picky. If he wanted a drink, he drank what was available. He was enjoying watching his officers and the assembled Roxolani interact, especially as the drinks flowed. The laughter and good cheer were doing more to lighten his mood than anything. When he saw Marpesia and her translator approach, he sat up, standing when they stopped in front of him.

"Are you enjoying yourself, Centurio?" Aella asked.

"Yes. I don't get much cause or time for revelry. It's a nice break from the routine. Thanks for hosting this banquet."

Once Aella translated his words, Marpesia replied, adding a bit of invective to her words. Aella replied, an uncertain, questioning look spreading across her face. Marpesia answered firmly.

"My mistress says it's the least we can do to show proper respect to our honored guest and ally. She knows how to show respect to great leaders, unlike certain others who neglect the resources they have available to them."

He chuckled. Apparently, his treatment at Constantius's hand had offended the leader of the Roxolani clan he was about to be allied with.

He shrugged. "I appreciate the sentiment. The courtesy you've shown means more to me than the thirty years of being ignored by certain others." He gave a respectful half bow.

"My mistress would like to know if you'd accompany her on a tour of the palace Constantius has lent us for our stay. It's quite wonderful."

Lucius nodded. "I'd like that." He smiled at Marpesia.

She returned his smile. His breath hitched at the twinkle in her eyes and the broad, open expression. The sound faded from his ears as the rest of the room disappeared from his awareness. Aella's subtle cough drew them both back to the moment.

"Please, Centurio, whenever you're ready."

Lucius nodded, keeping his gaze focused on Marpesia. He couldn't take his eyes off her. Marpesia gestured for Lucius to walk beside her. Aella fell in behind them, close enough to translate but not on top of them.

Seeing that Lucius was about to leave, Tinkomaros called out, "Would you like an escort, sir?"

He waved his centurion off. "No, I think I can manage."

Marpesia laughed, speaking.

"Are your men afraid a couple women could harm the great Centurio Immortalis?" Aella translated.

He turned around, looking Aella over in her scale armor with axes poking over her shoulders. "I'd hardly call either of you harmless. I know what hardened fighters look like. How they carry themselves. You both know your way around combat. My men are always cognizant of my safety, mostly unwarranted. It's like having five thousand little mothers looking after me."

"Does your age bring you fragility?"

"No. The age you see me as now is basically where Mithras has locked my body. I wish it had happened a few years earlier. I put a lot of mileage on this body. It's supremely annoying to live for over two hundred years and wake up each day with the same aches and pains you had before the change happened."

Marpesia chuckled after Aella translated his small diatribe.

"She says, 'I'm not nearly as old as you, but I have old scars and the twinges that go with them. It's not a soft life we lead, warriors, soldiers, and leaders of people.'"

"True."

They stepped onto a balcony overlooking a large garden. The huge estate was one of the older ones not torn down in Constantius's orgy of building when he took over Byzantium to make his new capital. Green-hued bronze and marble statues were scattered about the mature landscaping.

"My mistress says if you'd like, she can show you the wonderful statues some other time when there's the light to do it properly."

"I'd like that very much." He smiled at Marpesia again, pleased at the offer to spend more time with her. He liked art and statues, always seeking the softer signs of civilization when he arrived in a city. It reminded him what he fought for.

"Do you like art, Centurio?" Aella asked.

"I'm quite fond of it, actually. I've never been struck with the impulse to create for the sake of beauty, but I can appreciate the drive in others and love being able to witness their work."

"Our people don't make many statues, at least those of us who still keep to the old ways. They're hard to carry when you're riding over the steppes. They're too heavy and take up too much space in our wagons."

"What do Sarmatian artists make then?"

"They stick to things we can carry with us. They work in metals." Marpesia held up her wrist, showing an elaborately engraved and constructed gold bracelet.

A series of wolves chased each other's tails as they ran around her wrist. The lead wolf's head arched up, a howl frozen in time, tiny red gems sparkling in its eyes. With that hand, she ran her fingers over the gold and bejeweled ornaments dangling in short chains from the diadem circling her brow. The ornaments twinkled under the flickering flames of the lamps, although the sparkle in Marpesia's eyes rendered them dull and gauche.

"We also have wood carvers who decorate our wagons and talented weavers create pleasing designs in our textiles."

She touched the sleeve of her tunic to demonstrate. The black base was covered in white stars of various sizes and shapes. She wore matching trousers under the tunic.

"My favorite, though, are the tattoo artists who decorate our bodies." Marpesia pulled up her long sleeve, revealing a stunning stylized wolf tattooed over her forearm. She rolled her arm around so Lucius could see the whole thing. Against Marpesia's rippling muscles, the wolf almost appeared alive, howling at a moon that wasn't there.

Once he pulled his eyes away from the pale skin of Marpesia's arm, he made eye contact. "Your artists are truly talented."

Marpesia nodded and left the balcony, taking Lucius's arm at the elbow to direct him back down the hall.

"My mistress would like to show you some of the beautiful stone floors and painted walls."

Lucius walked alongside Marpesia in silence, simultaneously relaxed, enjoying his proximity to the woman he'd just met, and tensely alert, watching her body language to gauge her opinion of him. They stepped into a large, mostly empty room. It didn't look like it had been cleaned and pressed into service. The oil lamp Aella had grabbed from the hall cast a dim flickering light into the room.

The walls were a riot of reds and blues and greens, depicting a massive ocean scene with dolphins and sirens and other creatures from Greek and Roman stories. He looked around to see if Odysseus might be floating about somewhere in the scene. The same aquatic theme continued on the tile mosaic floor.

"It's a shame they didn't make this room available for your use. It's beautiful," Lucius said.

Aella, picking up on the tone of her mistress, added the note of scorn from Marpesia's voice. "I don't think they wanted us barbarians fouling their artwork."

"I'm not terribly sure my imperator respects the empire's neighbors."

"He views us as people to be used or conquered, mostly both. He longs to make us Romans and send our warriors across his empire to fight for his glory. He doesn't see us as free people," Aella translated.

"You're being awfully open with me. I'm one of his subjects. A leader of a legion."

"What can he do to us? We are free Roxolani."

"He could deny your request for the Black Legion."

"He won't. This presents too many conveniences for him. He can use us to defend his borders and send you out of his empire." Marpesia stopped, looking him over. "Besides, you have a reputation beyond Roma's borders as a man of honesty and fair dealing with 'barbarians.' I do not think you'll betray my confidences to an emperor who does not respect you."

"No, I wouldn't," Lucius replied. "My emperor has pledged my aid to you. We need to trust each other if we're going to make it out of this alive. The Lugii say the whole tribe of Goths is moving south, and if you're right about what's driving them, it's going to be a difficult task to come out of this intact on the other side, one legion and your clan."

Marpesia, her expression growing serious, nodded, a delicate frown tugging at the corners of her mouth after she heard the translated words. His eyes lingered on her full lips, wishing they'd return to the smile she'd worn so freely around him.

They turned down a dark hallway, making for another one of the large rooms. "My mistress wishes to show you the room of the Amazons."

The room wasn't as large as the hall they were using for their banquet or the aquatic themed one, but it still left plenty of room for frescoes of Amazon warriors fighting Greek heroes from antiquity. The mythical warrior women looked suspiciously like Aella and Marpesia in their tunic and trousers, their pointed axes flying toward nude Greeks with their shields and helms.

"Do you know the story of the how the Sarmatian people came to be, Centurio?" Aella said, translating Marpesia's question. Marpesia faced him, her eyebrow lifted.

He shook his head. "I'm afraid not."

"Would you like to hear it?"

Lucius nodded, staring into Marpesia's gray eyes. At the mention of Amazons and Sarmatians, there was a wildness contained inside her gaze he couldn't look away from.

"Please, sit. We brought in chairs for your comfort," Aella said, gesturing toward two chairs facing each other.

Lucius gestured for Marpesia to sit first. Once she relaxed into the cushioned wooden chair, Lucius joined her while Aella walked around the room, lighting other oil lamps. The two chairs were angled slightly so they could look over the room while also facing each other. When Aella finished, she took up her post behind their seats so she could translate without blocking their view.

Marpesia started speaking, the cadence and tones of a practiced storyteller filling her words with gravitas.

"Our story begins on the south shore of the Euxeinos Pontos, in the ancestral home of the Amazons. The Greeks had invaded our lands, seeking to conquer us as they did to any who lived where their ships could reach. They captured many of our warriors, loading them on boats to take them back as slaves.

"Our ancestors were fierce women and took over the ships they'd been herded onto. And although they were dangerous warriors, they weren't sailors." Marpesia shifted to the side, leaning more toward Lucius and letting her wool covered knee come into contact with his bare knee.

The sudden touch caused him to startle slightly in his chair, the contact sending tingles throughout his body—confusion at his own reaction joined the tingling sensation. He worked to calm his breathing, not wishing to show the effect caused by the simple, accidental contact.

She continued on as if she didn't notice his reaction, although the faint trace of a smile on her face betrayed her. "Eventually, their ships washed up on the far northern shores of the Euxeinos Pontus. On foot, the Amazons wandered into the land of the horse people known as the Scythians by the Hellenes of old, before the Romans conquered the lands of the Hellenes and even before Alexandros stretched out his arm to the far lands of the east."

Reaching out to lay her hand on his forearm, Marpesia leaned in even closer. Lucius swallowed, the skin under her fingers burning from her touch. The playful glint in Marpesia's eyes persisted.

She continued, leaving space for Aella to translate. "Our horses often run free, not fully tamed. The Amazons found a band of horses wandering the steps, letting the free wind flow through their manes and tails. They captured the horses, befriending them and making them their companions.

"The Scythians who lived in the lands the Amazons were roaming feared and admired the fierce warriors and wished to integrate the women into their community, to strengthen their bloodlines, and grow their power by adding the fierce warriors to their ranks. They sent out a band of their young, fierce warriors, men and women, to seek out the Amazons and woo them to join their tribe.

"Wherever the Scythians showed up to speak to the Amazons, the Amazons disappeared into the steppes, not understanding the words called to them over the broad distances they kept between themselves and the band of Scythians who pursued them. One of the Scythians, wiser than most, suggested a change to their tactics."

Lucius stared into Marpesia's eyes, engrossed with her story.

"They followed while keeping a safe distance so as not to spook the Amazons into riding away yet another time. One night, as one of the Amazon women swam in a river under the stars and moon, a Scythian approached, speaking soft words. The Amazon found the Scythian attractive. Soon, they sat under the stars together, seducing each other under the watchful eye of the moon goddess." Marpesia's eyes sparkled with mischief.

"The next night, each of them brought a friend to introduce. Soon, the two groups were spending much time together, teaching each other their languages and exploring each other's bodies with all the vigor of youthful warriors until there were no longer two groups but one. However, the Amazons didn't want to become part of the Scythian tribe and give up the ways of the warrior, nor did their Scythian lovers want to see their Amazons diminished, having fallen in love with their fierceness."

Marpesia, her hand still on Lucius's forearm, sat up straighter. "Instead, they formed their own band to roam the steppes. And as they grew and prospered, they split off and coaxed more Scythians away from their tribes to join the bands of warrior men and women who became known as the Sarmatians. And thus, our people were born of the blending of the mighty Amazon women and Scythian peoples."

"Thank you for sharing this with me." Lucius bowed his head appreciatively. "May I ask a question?"

"Marpesia welcomes the words of the great Centurio Immortalis."

Lucius chuckled. "You may refer to me in private as Lucius, the name my mother gave me. Centurio will suffice in front of my men."

Marpesia smiled broadly, nodding at the courtesy.

"Why would the Scythians leave their people to join with a people who are separate from their tribe?"

"It is the way of our people, the way of the steppes. We don't mate within our own clans. Clans are our family. Our peoples often gather at the borders of our territories to trade in the spring. We celebrate the gathering. Those who are inclined may select a mate from the other tribe. Some women will find a man to father a child with and leave him if they're not interested in bringing the man with them, or she may choose to join his tribe."

Aella was resting her hand on Marpesia's shoulder. Marpesia reached up and affectionately squeezed Aella's hand, rubbing her fingers over the back of her hand. This time, Aella spoke as herself. "I am from a different clan than Marpesia's wolves. I joined the wolves after Marpesia and I met at such a clan meeting."

Aella translated her words for Marpesia who nodded in agreement. She added, "I left my father's clan to form the wolves. I wasn't particularly interested in the man he wanted me to marry. He was not thrilled I wished to continue bearing axe and shield, wishing me to be a docile clan chief's wife. I didn't want that, so I challenged my father's proposed suitor to a fight. I refused to marry any man who couldn't best me in a duel. He failed to put me on my back, so I refused to go onto it voluntarily for a man such as him. Though after that, he wasn't much interested in me either and called off the betrothal." She looked up affectionately at Aella. "So I seduced his pretty cousin and took her with me, then took my friends and left my father's clan. I prefer to be free to pursue my own destiny.

"My father named my cousin as his heir, and he's welcome to it. He's a far better choice to lead the combined peoples of the Roxolani. He lets my wolves wander where we want, and we respond to his call when he needs my warriors or support with the other clans." She let go of Aella's hand and leaned closer to Lucius.

"That's why I'm here. He needed someone he could trust and who had dealings with you southerners." Seeing the look of confusion on Lucius's face, she added, "I like to bring my wolves along the Euxeinos Pontus to the borders of your empire to trade."

Lucius nodded, letting her words and story sink in. He found his eyes wandering over her relaxed body as she sat in her chair. She'd returned her hand to the hand of her lover and translator. Then he looked at her hand still resting on his arm, feeling a new surge of warmth spreading over his body, his confusion doubling.

He decided to rescue himself. "We should probably get back to the banquet, or my men will wonder what you've done with me."

Marpesia gave a courtly nod and stood up. Lucius stood, rolling his neck around to loosen it up after watching Marpesia's face while she told the history of her people. Disappointed in himself for breaking the magic moment, he could have listened to her melodious voice all night. After fighting the empire's enemies for nearly two hundred and thirty years, he'd been routed by a feminine touch.

FOUR

WHEN THEY STEPPED out of the room of the Amazons, Lucius held his hand up, halting them. He'd felt a twinge he didn't like. A twinge that said his enemy was near, too near. They shouldn't be here, this far beyond the border. He leaned over and whispered into Marpesia's ear, "Quiet, the blood drinkers are near."

When he stepped away from her, she smirked and shook her head, running her finger along his jaw and sending shivers through his body. She tipped his face toward Aella, who likewise had a smirk on her face. He'd spoken to Marpesia, not her translator. Blushing, he repeated his whisper to Aella, who translated it to her mistress.

They both grew serious at his words. Blowing out the lamp, Aella set it aside and pulled the two axes from her back, handing one to Marpesia. Lucius slid his gladius from its scabbard and stalked forward on quiet feet, the slippers he'd been offered rendering his feet quiet—if somewhat less sure-footed than his hobnailed caligae would. Aella and Marpesia fanned out behind him, Marpesia to the right and Aella to his left. Together, they crept down the dark halls.

When they passed a lighted junction heading back to the main banquet hall, they ran across one of Marpesia's Wolf Clan. Marpesia issued a series of hand signals and sent him scurrying down the lighted corridor as they turned into the darkness.

They continued the slow progress, keeping silent to preserve the element of surprise and to give their eyes more time to adjust to the dark. After a couple more turns, they moved through a dark and dusty portion of the estate. Lucius held up his left fist, stopping. He could feel a handful of the demons not far from where they stood. They were up the corridor and to the left; he couldn't see far enough in the darkness to determine if it was another corridor.

With his hand still in the air, he folded his thumb in to indicate he thought four of the blood drinkers were nearby. He pointed down the corridor and to the left. The Sarmatians nodded.

He stalked forward. He could hear the blood drinkers' hushed voices arguing tensely based on their tones, but he couldn't quite make out what language or what they were saying.

When he saw one of them backing around the corner, he darted into the doorway to his right, pulling Marpesia with him. Aella responded instantly, jumping into the doorway on the opposite side of the hall. Marpesia and Lucius huddled together against the short wall to the side of the door. A tantalizing scent kept sneaking into his senses—spices, conifers, and something he couldn't quite grasp. He shook his head and pulled his attention back to the task at hand.

The voices grew louder as the blood drinkers—the di inferi— continued their argument, nearing where the two Sarmatians and the Centurio hid. He felt a strong hand slide into his empty hand. Marpesia's grip was firm, her hand calloused from her weapons. When he heard the creatures, he pushed back into Marpesia, ensuring he wouldn't be seen as they walked by. The even closer proximity to Marpesia's scent nearly overwhelmed him. When the sound of their talking receded, Lucius knew they'd passed by.

He gave Marpesia's hand a squeeze and stepped away from her, creeping into the doorway. She let go of his hand and followed him out. He spotted Aella peeking from her alcove and waved her forward to join them. When one of the blood drinkers turned to say something, his eyes went wide as he saw the armed warriors suddenly appear behind them. They should have been paying attention and using their senses. Lucius used it as the cue to attack. He sprinted as best he could in the soft slippers and skidded to a halt with his gladius outstretched, taking the first creature in the back.

The monster seized up and nearly pulled Lucius's gladius from his hand. Marpesia had already separated the head of the creature nearest her. Aella took an arm off at the elbow as the third monster reached for a sword, then followed up by planting the spiked backside of her axe into his skull. The fourth blood demon turned and tried to run, but Marpesia was already pursuing him. She managed a low slash that caught him in the back of the leg, dropping him to the ground.

The di inferi Lucius stabbed sloughed off his blade into a pile of dust. The two with head wounds lay still on the marble floor. The last writhed on the ground, cradling its cut hamstring and trying to pull itself away from Marpesia as she stood poised, axe ready. Lucius pulled the wooden rudis from its scabbard and walked toward the one still moving.

When he approached and drew back his gladius to strike, Aella grabbed his wrist. "It's a man. He can be questioned."

"He won't answer. Even now his wound is closing. Look at his leg, he's regaining control. Trust me."

She hastily hissed his words to Marpesia, still holding onto his wrist. Marpesia looked firmly at Aella and directed her, with a curt gesture of her head, to pull back. Aella let go of Lucius's wrist.

Stepping forward, Lucius kicked the creature's hand out of the way, then opted to just lop its arm off. He dropped to his knee, plunging the rudis through the chest of the blood drinker and into its heart before pulling it out. The body turned into a thick pool of reddish-black goo. Lucius jumped up and back to avoid getting his feet wet. Marpesia and Aella backed away with him.

He turned and walked over to the other two remaining bodies. The hole Aella had put through the forehead of the one she'd neutralized was closing up, the blood flow already stemmed.

"Do you recognize either of these two?" Lucius asked.

"What's happening to his head? It's healing," Aella's voice trembled.

"He is a creature of the night. He is the walking dead, a monster of darkness suffused with the bleakest of magics. Soon he will be awake. If he held his arm in place, it would reattach itself. Do you recognize him, Aella?" He looked at Marpesia, her face troubled and thoughtful. "Marpesia?"

Using her name pulled her out of her thoughts. She requested a translation of what was said.

"No. I've never seen him before, although he looks like a Goth, even in those Roman clothes. His face is raw, and you can see the white of his skin where the beard used to cover the whole face."

Lucius shoved his rudis into the creature's chest, leaving it there. The hole in its head ceased its healing. He stepped over the body Marpesia had beheaded. He prodded the head over with the flat of his gladius to turn its face into the dim light. When they heard running feet, they turned toward the sound, weapons at the ready.

Seeing a few of his men's faces in the group of Sarmatians running toward him, he relaxed. The Sarmatian they'd seen had brought reinforcements, although too late. The deeds had been done.

"Centurio, do you need any assistance?"

"No, Tinkomaros. We've got it covered. Although we could use that lamp over here. I want to see if anyone recognizes this last one."

"Aye, sir." Tinkomaros took a lamp from a legionnaire and brought it to Lucius.

He tipped the head so its face was in the light. Aella gasped, turning away. Marpesia's face hardened, her jaw clenching.

"I take it you recognize him?"

Aella turned back around, studiously avoiding looking at the face. "Yes. We recognize him. He was a close companion of Marpesia's cousin."

Marpesia started speaking, Aella translating. "He was one of the scouts sent out to trail the Goths and determine if the rumors about the blood demons were true. The scouting party split up to follow different leads. His party never returned. Well, at least he didn't fail at his task."

Lucius stood up, facing Marpesia. "Did the other group return?"

Aella said, "They did. That is the information we brought with us to your imperator."

"Centurio, what next?" Tinkomaros asked.

Lucius looked at Marpesia. "We should sweep the building."

"My mistress agrees." Aella stared at the face of the Sarmatian she'd met, probably many times.

"If you don't mind my suggestion, we should probably mix the groups. I don't have enough of my men on hand and your people aren't as familiar with the dangers and signs of these creatures. They were men once and know how to blend in."

Marpesia nodded.

Waving everyone forward, Lucius squatted down next to the detached head. He set his gladius on the chest of its body and held it still with one hand. With the other, he carefully drew back the top lip, revealing the elongated, needle-sharp fangs where a human's canine teeth would be.

"These fangs are the only way to tell one of these creatures from a human. This is how they access your blood. They can also shift their fingernails to claws. They are faster and stronger than even the largest of warriors. Your best bet is to stab them through the heart with wood or silver. Failing that, take their head until you can finish them off. Removing limbs will buy you time. Understand?"

Aella was rattling off his instructions to the Roxolani in their dialect. When she finished, they looked around at each other and finally settled their gazes on Lucius, nodding their understanding.

"My men all have a rudis, a wooden sword, they carry with them at all times. At least one of them should be in each group. They know what to look for and what to do."

When Aella finished talking, Marpesia turned to face Lucius, Aella translating. "We don't have enough people right now to do this properly. Let's pull back and we can plug the approaches to the banquet hall and organize everyone else and then push out and sweep the halls."

Lucius nodded. "As you wish, that's probably a better solution. These four could be the advance party. Tinkomaros, head back to the banquet hall. Organize the men, send two back to the fort and tell them to bring the rest of First Cohort here. The Sixth should be on high alert and make sure we've got the barracks secured."

Tinkomaros nodded. "I'll see to it, Centurio."

"Aella, if you can take Marpesia back to the banquet, I'll be along shortly. I need to send these vampires on their final way."

Aella nodded, translating, and took Marpesia and guided her to the cluster of warriors. Lucius turned back to the bodies. He retrieved his gladius and plunged it into the heart of the headless body, turning the Roxolani into a pool of ooze. He picked up the tunic of the night demon he'd killed first and wiped his gladius clean before returning it to its scabbard.

Standing beside the body with his rudis sticking out of its chest, Lucius knelt next to it, wrapping his hand around the hilt, and laid his forehead on the pommel. He closed his eyes and spoke the incantation to activate the rudis. A white light slithered down the hilt and onto the blade, working its way over the silver filigree covering the wooden sword and down silver and steel alloy cutting edges. The light disappeared into the chest of the di inferi and reemerged, winding its way back up the silver to disappear into Lucius's forehead. The creature started dissolving as soon as Lucius removed the rudis from its chest, joining its companions in the spreading pool of reddish-black sludge on the dusty white marble floor.

Lucius sighed, feeling the monster's energy filling his veins. When he stood up and turned, he saw Marpesia standing alone, staring at him. He shook his head, knowing she'd ordered everyone back to the banquet hall so she could watch. She had questions according to her expression, but they'd have to wait until they found someone who spoke more of the Sarmatian language than the smattering of words he'd picked up over the years. He really needed to learn the language if he was going to effectively communicate with Marpesia and his new Sarmatian allies.

He wiped the rudis down with the tunic he'd used earlier but kept it unsheathed in case he needed it. He approached Marpesia and gestured for her to proceed down the hall back to the rest of their people. When he reached the lighted juncture in the hall, he called out his approach. After giving the day's passcode for the fort, they let him through their line. He assumed the Sarmatians knew the passcode, but it was best to pass it along in whispers in case there were more blood drinkers about with their excellent hearing.

When they returned to the banquet hall, the room was a hub of activity as Tinkomaros organized the remaining men with Aella's help to translate for those Roxolani who didn't know Latin or Greek.

"Tinkomaros, I'll hold things down here and keep an eye on the Sarmatian emissary. Take charge of the sweep. Aella, do you have someone who can translate for my centurio?"

"Yes. Dorgolel, go with him."

"Alright, Aella," Dorgolel replied in Greek.

While Lucius organized the few men he'd brought and helped Tinkomaros get their sweeping parties finalized, Aella helped Marpesia into a coat of stunningly beautiful scale mail. Each steel leaf was edged in polished bronze, creating a shimmering display of silver and gold as the light reflected off the armor. The mail dropped to her waist, split once down the front center and twice in the back to form a tail and two sides, falling to just above her knees. Draped across a horse's flanks, it would provide extra protection to horse and rider. She kept Aella's second axe, but she strapped on a sword belt at her waist. It was a longer blade than his gladius. It looked like the spatha he carried with him for cavalry work.

Unlike his gladius, his spatha wasn't enchanted by Mithras to bring the final death to the drinkers of blood, but he preferred it for more than just its magical properties. It had been a gift from his father, specially made for Lucius by the finest swordsmith in Belgica, and had been with him from his first day in the Legions of Traianus through two hundred years of wars and monster slaying. He'd purchased the spatha, ensuring it was of highest quality, when he'd been transferred to the I Auditrix and started training with horse and lance and longer swords. He was fond of the weapon, but it wasn't his gladius.

Aella, finished helping her mistress into her armor, approached Lucius. "We are ready to assist, Centurio."

Marpesia nodded.

"We'll stay here and provide a central command point until my

First Cohort arrives. For now it's best if we stay here so our people know where to find us." He turned toward Marpesia. "Also, from this point, it's my duty as a soldier of Roma to protect the ambassador of the Roxolani people." Turning away from Aella and Marpesia, he found his centurion. "Tinkomaros, make sure the corner where the remains are is left undisturbed. I want to look through their effects when we have enough men here to secure the compound.

While they waited, Lucius prowled around, feeling naked without a full legion. Marpesia, his eyes constantly drawn to her, seemed as nonplussed as always. She was chatting quietly with Aella, her eyes periodically drifting toward him. He heaved a sigh of relief when he heard approaching horses, lots of them.

A man with black hair shot through with gray entered with several legionnaires. The grizzled veteran, spying Lucius, saluted and approached his leader. "Centurio, I can't seem to let you out of my sight without you finding trouble. Good thing you have us here to bail you out."

Lucius chuckled. "Well, I wouldn't want you to get bored, Optio. Secure the perimeter, then coordinate with Tinkomaros to organize teams to sweep the halls and grounds. Will six centuria be enough?"

"This is a pretty big building, but I think we can manage."

"Good, I want to move the Roxolani ambassador to the barracks where we can provide proper protection. I'll send the four centuria back when we're behind the gates."

"Very well, sir.

Aella, who'd been listening and translating, drew Lucius's attention back to Marpesia. "My mistress says she would prefer to stay here."

Lucius shook his head. "I'm afraid I must insist in this matter. There could be who knows how many more in here just waiting for you to fall asleep. There could be an army waiting in the darkness. This wasn't a random house they wandered into. This was an attempt to infiltrate your sanctuary and target either you or me. There may be more, many more. I can do a reasonable job of ensuring your safety behind the stout walls of the barracks we're using."

"Secure this place."

"It's too big and has too many nooks and crannies. My sincerest apologizes, but we're going to need to move your people to safety. There's plenty of room in the barracks. The quarters aren't as luxurious, but you may take mine. They're the nicest."

Marpesia held his gaze, the gray of her eyes turning steely. After a few moments, she shook her head in annoyance, then nodded and issued orders to her Roxolani.

While she organized her people, Lucius grabbed a handful of men to escort him back to the scene of the incursion. The site of the banquet turned into a hornet's nest of activity, yet Marpesia glided through it untroubled, elegant, and deadly.

When Lucius started down the corridor, she and Aella joined him. "Shouldn't you be packing up?"

Aella shrugged. "My mistress knows how to move out quickly. She wishes to learn more about the attackers who've rousted her from her comfortable palace."

"Very well, let's go. The quicker we get this done, the quicker we can get you settled." He gestured for them to follow.

Marpesia, increasing her stride, caught up and joined Lucius at the head of the group, Aella following just behind. When they reached the remains, Lucius's legionnaires fanned out, surrounding the scene and allowing him, Marpesia, and Aella space with the remains. He searched through their clothes and the few belongings left behind.

He found a bag full of coins, too many of them heavy gold bearing the face of Constantius. Beyond an assortment of daggers and small weapons, the only other curiosity was a small stoppered glass container. Lucius worked the stopper out and sniffed it—belladonna. He pulled back and took another sniff.

He shook his head, making a gesture against evil, and stood. "Poison, I think."

Marpesia's relaxed visage sloughed off, replaced by a mask of anger and concern.

"They were armed, sneaking into my space, and brought poison along with a bag full of fresh Roman gold," Aella translated. "Were we the targets? Would your imperator so easily sunder the alliance and treaty he made with our people?"

"It's possible, I guess, but unlikely. This is clumsy, amateurish. Constantius seems nothing if not professional and thorough. This is likely someone else. I don't think he'd throw away a key alliance along an important stretch of the border when he's about to go to war against such a large force. It's possible I was the target. It's obvious I'm not terribly popular with either the imperator or his pet Christian. I'm not entirely ruling out Constantius, but it doesn't feel right. It doesn't fit."

Lucius bent back over to finish sorting through the intruders' effects, finding nothing else of note. Turning to one of his men, he ordered everything gathered up and bundled for later inspection if needed and sent off another man to get cleaning supplies to clean up the evidence of the failed assassination attempt.

Even though Marpesia wore the soft soled boots favored by her people, the hard stamp of her feet betrayed her annoyance and anger; the motion caused her wild, curly hair to bounce with a life of its own. He didn't sense any blood suckers around, but he kept his hand on the pommel of his sword, his eyes scanning every bit of space in front of him.

When he returned to the banquet hall, he led the men he'd grabbed earlier to Marpesia's room to provide security as she and Aella packed their clothing. When they finished, Lucius led them to the courtyard where Marpesia's Roxolani already had their horses saddled and ready.

They formed a column with the Roxolani riders and wagons in the center and his I Cohort arrayed around them. Lucius joined Marpesia in the center of the column with a detachment of his men to provide an extra ring of steel between her and any interested parties. As they worked their way through the stone streets of Constantinopolis, the streets empty due to the late hour, he thought he felt a few twinges of nearby di inferi, but he wasn't sure. Only once did he get what he thought might be a positive feel of at least a few, probably watching them pass from the nearby shadows.

They made it back to the walled barracks they'd been assigned and sorted out the Sarmatians, doubling the watch on the walls in the process. When he finally fell into the bed of his new quarters, it was entirely too close to morning. For now, he'd take what sleep he could. The emissary was safe. He could ruminate over the possible assassination attempt with a fresher brain in the light of day.

FIVE

AFTER THE INITIAL flurry of activity upon Lucius's arrival in Constantinopolis, the dominus left them cooling their heels in their fort while they waited for his summons to the planning session. In the meantime, Lucius used the time available for a project he needed to work on. One of his optios had found a legionnaire who knew the Roxolani dialect and assigned him to his personal staff as translator and tutor.

"Thank you, Optio, dismissed," Lucius said crisply. "What's your name, miles?"

"Katokas, Centurio."

"Where'd you learn Roxolani? I thought most of the Sarmatians in our ranks were from the Iazyges."

"Aye, sir. My father was of the Iazyges. My mother was Roxolani and taught me her dialect."

"And you're confident in your Roxolani?"

"They're not too far off, Centurio. The Roxolani like to come down through the northern mountains to trade. I'm confident I can translate for you and ensure the words you're getting from their translator are honest."

"Good, I'll add you to my staff with its commensurate pay raise.

Let's go walk around the barracks. You can teach me the words for things while we stretch our legs."

"Aye, sir, thank you, Centurio."

Lucius dragged Katokas around, asking him to teach him the words for their implements of war as well as the actions they could perform, thus learning some rudimentary commands in Sarmatian.

It wasn't until eight days after the initial meeting with Constantius that Lucius and Marpesia were summoned to discuss matters of the coming campaign. When the message came from the imperator, Lucius brought Katokas along as one of his personal escorts. He met Marpesia and her retinue at the gates of the barracks. She waited with her steppes pony, wearing full armor.

"Greetings to the Centurio Immortalis on this fine sunny day," Aella said, bowing as he walked up, Katokas behind him holding both their ponies.

"Greetings to Marpesia, leader of the Wolf Clan and her companion Aella. Are you ready to go discuss war with Constantius and his Dux Belorum?"

Marpesia rattled off several lines, clipped and annoyed sounding. Lucius waited for Aella's translation. "My mistress is ever ready to hear the inspired words of the great Constantius."

Katokas coughed behind him. Lucius thought he was covering a laugh, although he didn't need his own translator to tell him Aella had cleaned up her clan chief's words. Marpesia's tone and delivery had made her meaning more than clear. Like Lucius, she was not happy being shunted aside on such an important mission for her people, forced to cool her heels while Constantius and his generals discussed whatever it is they felt was more important than meeting with the leader of the Black Legion, their Sarmatian allies, and their emissary.

"No Roman dress today?" Lucius asked as he signaled for the gates to be opened.

"She wishes to remind them of who she is and why she's here," Aella supplied. "And if you don't mind me adding my own opinion, she is peevish at her treatment and wishes to annoy those for whom a woman in war gear is viewed as an abomination."

Lucius laughed. He was fortunate to catch Marpesia's face, the scowl lifting from her face under the sound of his laugh. Not taking the care to guard his expression as he usually did except around the few he counted close, he smiled warmly at her before turning to lead his pony out the gate. When their small detachment cleared the gates, they mounted up.

"Form around our guests!" he called. "Let's deliver them to his shining lordship."

He still wasn't sure about the gelding the horsemaster had picked out. The horse didn't complain much, responding to his commands easily, but he lacked that *something* he'd gotten used to after riding Cicero for so many years. His new horse hadn't tried to bite anyone or kick. In the miles they'd put in together since leaving Vindobona, he'd not come up with much of an impression of the beast; its four legs carried him to the place he needed to be efficiently enough but that was all. The animal was still nameless. He sighed.

Marpesia asked Aella something.

Aella, riding between him and her mistress, turned to Lucius. "Why such a big sigh on a beautiful warm day?"

"Oh, it's nothing really." He let the silence hang. "It's this pony."

Aella looked it over. "It looks an adequate mount."

"It is, but it's not my pony. I had to retire my previous mount. He's too old for what we're about to do, but Cicero was a cantankerous bastard." He sighed again. "This horse is like plain porridge."

When his words were translated, Marpesia favored him with a laugh. The rich, vibrant sound brought a smile to his face as the sun glinted off her dark auburn hair. Seeing his smile and catching him admiring her, she winked before saying something to Aella.

"My mistress thanks you for lightening her mood. It's often hard to hold one's tongue when annoyed, and she feels she'll need that ability in the coming meeting."

"It was my pleasure." Truth was, her smile and laugh had done more good for his disposition that day than the sun, even though he knew he was likely riding into the north as winter approached, and he should soak up the sun while he could. He was just as annoyed about the situation as Marpesia.

TABLES SCATTERED about a large room greeted Lucius and Marpesia when they were escorted into the presence of Constantius and his warlords. Surveying the maps, Lucius saw two strategies laid out, depending on the movement of the enemy. If they went through the passes and to the west of the Montes Sarmatici, their attack would likely fall somewhere in the land of the Lugii and Iazyges along the Pannonia border. If they chose the eastern route, they'd come out on the Pontus Euxine and down into Thracia.

As he stared at the maps, Marpesia standing over his shoulder, someone stepped up behind them. "What's your assessment of the situation, Centurio? Will it be east or west?"

Lucius heard Aella whisper the words to her mistress. Not looking up, he pointed to the mountains deep outside the Roman borders, moving to the range to the farthest northwest of their area of concern. "I don't know if you've ever seen the Carpates and this section where they join the Montes Sarmatici, but it's rough—the mountains are tall, although the range is thin at this point. Further west, there's lower ground, but it's a long journey in winter. Then you're coming up against the Noricum, and nobody wants to attempt those mountains in winter."

Aella cleared her throat before speaking. "My mistress agrees with the Centurio's assessment. Based on our last dispatches, the Goths have been steadily angling east."

Lucius nodded at Marpesia and Aella. "I think east seems the most likely option. Based on the reports I've heard from my contacts across the border, the Goths are traveling with their full tribe, not just warriors—men, women, children, elders, everyone. The east is the easiest path in winter. Thracia is the likely target. Marpesia, what do you think?"

"Word from our northern tribes and our allies is that winter is already harsher than normal years. They will make for the least arduous path south and into the sun. East along those mountains is where you'll find the Goths," Aella translated.

"That is my assessment was well."

Lucius turned after giving his opinion and quickly bowed. "Dominus."

Constantius continued. "We're marshaling my forces here, near Nicopolis." He pointed to the map.

"It'll allow you the flexibility if we've guessed wrong," Lucius said. He'd sent his men to Oescus, north of Nicopolis, for the same reasons.

Constantius turned and looked at Marpesia. "Now, my Roxolani Chieftainess, how do you propose to get around behind the Goths? Shall we load you on boats and ship you across the Pontus Euxinus along with the Black Legion?"

Marpesia shook her head, reaching for a rolled up leather Aella held for her. Lucius stepped out of her way, allowing her to unroll the leather onto the table. Printed on the leather, a map depicted the southern mountains. The mountains he'd marched through over two hundred years ago. The mountains he'd fought and bled in to bring the Dacian province into the empire.

"I wish we had some of Traianus's or Hadrianus's old maps of Dacia," Lucius commented offhandedly. Lucius had seen those maps and their details, including the varying passes through these mountains. He'd been young and didn't remember most of them from his first journeys there. Judging by these and their less than stellar details, those maps might have been lost or not available here. Constantinopolis, despite being built on an ancient city, was still new as a capital. The resources that were available in Roma might not be here yet.

Marpesia was about to explain her ideas when she was unceremoniously shouldered out of the way by a skinny kid in an elaborate leather cuirass with Roma's eagle spread across its chest, its shoulder armor and cloak attached with the Chi Ro symbol favored by the Dominus and his Christians. The boy had a Greek nose and a prominent chin on a round face. He looked to be in his mid-teens, still not quite able to fill out his armor.

"Ah, Princeps Primus Centurio Ferrata, this is my eldest son, Flavius Claudius Constantius Caesar," Constantius said. "Flavius, this is the man who styles himself the Centurio Immortalis."

Marpesia's jaw clenched, and she looked daggers at the boy who'd shoved her out of the way. Aella's hand landed on her mistress's arm, and Lucius saw her hold Marpesia back.

Clearing her throat, Aella said, "My mistress says the world knows him as the Centurio Immortalis; he does not need to style himself anything, his reputation does it for him."

"Apparently your pet barbarian has taken a liking to him," Flavius commented to his father.

"The Roxolani are our allies. We should show them respect," Constantius replied, although his indulgent tone belied the meaning of his words.

The boy's rudeness had used up what laughter Lucius had created for Marpesia. Lucius's eyes narrowed and his face hardened as he stared at the whelp. He wasn't sure if it was arrogance from his position, the cocksure attitude of youth, insecurity because of his age and inexperience surrounded by hardened warriors and leaders, or a combination thereof. Lucius, though, would do what he'd always done when dealing with the arrogance of Roma's rulers—grit his teeth, be aloofly polite, and maintain his independence.

Lucius tore his stare away from the boy and turned to the Roxolani emissary. "Marpesia, I believe you were about to show us your plan to put your forces and my legion behind the Goths?"

Aella squeezed Marpesia's arm, harshly whispering Lucius's words into her ear. Finally, Marpesia shook her head and made eye contact with Lucius. He tried to fill his gaze with calm reassurance and support. She was to be his ally for the coming campaign, and he needed her to trust him. Flavius had been rude and continued to be so. Lucius didn't blame Marpesia for her anger with the arrogant whelp and was himself annoyed on her behalf. Annoyed with the boy himself, he backed up further, making more room for her.

Marpesia kept his gaze as she stepped forward, letting her hand brush against his, her fingers dragging across the back of his hand. Lucius inhaled sharply at her touch but tried to keep the noise contained. Despite having space to step closer to the map, she kept her body close to Lucius's. Reaching down, she put her finger on a section of the southern mountain range. Lucius leaned over her shoulder to look at it. She pulled her map toward her.

Aella started speaking, but Lucius lost the thread of her words when he inhaled through his nose; Marpesia's scent—herbs, spice, and evergreens—wiped his thoughts clean.

"Centurio? Centurio?"

The sound of Aella speaking his name finally drew Lucius back to the moment and their meeting. He felt heat suffusing his cheeks as he flushed with embarrassment. When he brought his gaze level with Aella's, he could see the knowing look in her eyes, the friendly laughter at his distraction.

Aella only let him dangle over the precipice for a moment before throwing him a lifeline. "My mistress wishes to move our combined forces through this pass in the southern mountains. Once through, we'll head east through the highlands until we get to the eastern mountains. The passes there aren't as easy as the southern pass, but it's one our people have used many times. It'll put us out on the plains here." Aella pointed to the hills and lowlands that lead down to the Pontus Euxinus.

Constantius looked up from the map, looking toward Lucius. "Centurio, are you familiar with this territory?"

"Aye, Dominus. I spent three years campaigning through this area under Traianus. I've passed through a few times after, before the province was lost. I think I'm familiar with the southern pass our Roxolani allies want to use. If it's the one I remember, it'll serve our needs nicely." He looked at Marpesia. "May I?"

She moved slightly, giving him enough space to lean over and point to the map. "We'll come out here on the highlands she mentioned. It's a good spot. If it turns out the Tervingi have gone west instead of east, we can harass their forces and slow their advance until you can bring your main force to bear. If they go to the east as our intelligence suggests, this pass should be easy to defend against a larger force. If we can't get all the way behind, we can hopefully keep a large portion of their warriors occupied. It's a good, well thought out plan, Dominus."

"Very well, Centurio. You'll coordinate your legion with the Roxolani. Draw what stores and gear you need."

Lucius stood straight, saluting. "Aye, Dominus. It shall be as you've ordered. We'll try to keep messengers running to Oescus as long as we can to keep you appraised of our progress."

The rest of Constantius's war leaders had gathered around the table. Nodding at the map, Constantius straightened up and called the room to order. "Everyone is dismissed for now. Centurio, you and the Roxolani are free to proceed to the border. When your forces are marshaled, move across the Danuvius and engage the enemy when the time is right."

Everyone, save for the Roxolani, snapped to attention and saluted their imperator.

"Centurio, I'd like to speak with you after the room clears," Constantius added before walking toward an ornate chair on the far side of the room. His son followed him. "Someone send in Eusebius."

Lucius stood by the table as everyone filed out. Marpesia and Aella waited by Lucius.

"Aella, please tell Centurio Tinkomaros to form up. As soon as I'm finished here, we'll retire to the barracks."

Aella nodded, passing his words onto Marpesia. She nodded at Lucius, smiling before following Aella out of the room. Once everyone else had left, the wild-eyed fanatic entered, eyeing Lucius disdainfully as he stalked across the room to stand to the left of Constantius. Flavius stood to his father's right. Lucius stopped in front of Constantius, bowing with his fist over his heart.

"How may I serve you, Dominus?" Lucius asked.

"You may serve me by executing this mission successfully, then you will serve the empire no more."

Lucius's breath caught in his chest, his eyes blinking as he tried to work through what Constantius might mean. To give himself time, he let his eyes drift to Eusebius. The zealot looked positively gleeful, his smile a triumphant sneer. On the other side of Constantius, Flavius smirked cruelly, trying to look haughty.

"I beg your pardon, Dominus?" Lucius asked, the words barely louder than a whisper.

"Your time under the eagle has come to an end, Centurio. The empire no longer needs your services to fight monsters from false gods. When you cross the border, you may never return across it under penalty of death. If you return, you shall be declared a traitor and an enemy of the state." Constantius stared at Lucius, his face molded into a stern visage.

"My...my men..." Lucius breathed shallowly, trying to understand what was happening. Two hundred and twenty-nine years...

"Your men may return to the empire and retire. Those who wish to remain in the legions will be dispersed to various units at their current rank and the commensurate standard pay to serve the remainder of their term."

"But...my service to the empire?" The muscles in his jaw twitched, his brow furrowed.

"It has come to the end and is no longer needed. Some suggested you be executed outright to prevent you from fomenting a rebellion, but in honor of your service, you will be allowed to live under exile. You are dismissed."

Lucius snapped his jaw closed, straightened, and saluted. He turned crisply and marched toward the door, the triumphant sneer of Eusebius and Flavius's laughing eyes etched into Lucius's brain. When he approached the door, the two guards yanked them open, fearing Lucius might walk right through them.

As he marched through the halls, people scattered out of his way, his face filled with thunder, driving those before him. When he reached the courtyard where his men waited, he yanked his skullcap out of his belt pouch and pulled it on. A legionnaire waited, holding his helmet while another held the reins of his gelding. Yanking the helmet from the inoffensive man's hands, he pulled it over his head and lashed it tight, leaping onto the back of his horse. Once he had his reins, he kicked his horse into motion, everyone else responding.

He kept his eyes forward, all sound missing his ears, his back straight and rigid. He thought Marpesia and Aella might have brought their ponies up beside him, but he didn't bother checking. He held his reins and let the gelding follow the rest of the horses back to their barracks. Seeing anger sketched vividly in his face, Lucius's men didn't speak to him, carrying out their orders as always.

When they got back to the barracks, Lucius slid off the back of his horse, tossed his reins to his waiting groom, and trudged to his quarters. He took his helmet off, lifting it by grabbing the cheek guards. The guards were damp, as were the back of his knuckles. Reaching up, he ran the tips of his fingers over his cheeks, finding tear tracks. He set his helmet on the edge of the desk, missed; the helmet clanged to the ground.

Looking at his hands, he didn't recognize the tremble. He tried backing away only to run into a chair and sag into it when it shoved his legs out from under him. Letting rasping gulps of air fill his lungs, he tried to control himself and failed. Finally giving up, he let his head fall into his hands as tears streamed down his cheeks, falling from his face to land on his legs and onto the floor.

After serving the empire with loyalty and distinction for almost two hundred and thirty years, the Centurio Immortalis was no more.

SIX

LUCIUS AND HIS TWO COHORTS, along with Marpesia's Sarmatians, set a solid pace marching to Oescus, arriving in eighteen days. Along the way, they picked up the rest of Marpesia's escort, bringing the number of Sarmatians up to two hundred and fifty. At first, Lucius kept to himself as much as possible, brooding about Constantius's orders and his banishment, the latter of which he told no one. He'd met with Marpesia, Aella, and his centurions to plan their march north and to pilfer what they could from Constantius's stores. If he wasn't needed, he rarely left his quarters, even when invited to dine with Marpesia. When they'd finally left Constantinopolis, they departed with a far longer train of pack mules and horses than they'd arrived with, carrying the winter gear and stores they'd need to survive campaigning in winter in the mountains.

Once they were on the road, he avoided his men even as they surrounded him, drawing a shell of aloof authority around himself, but he couldn't avoid Marpesia and her translator. Whenever he found his eyes on Marpesia's face, and they always seemed to seek her out, her expression was filled with concern over the turn in his humor since the strategy meeting with Constantius.

Eventually, they drew him out, although he could only push his dejection away for so long. When he felt the worst, his mind dipping into hollowness, he'd seek out Marpesia with his eyes, watching the sunlight reflect off her hair, teasing the red tones out or the gestures she made as they rode north—filling his emptiness with the flash of her smile or the bright tone of her ringing laughter. When Marpesia and Aella joked together, Lucius let his placid gelding drift toward them, yearning for the sound of her voice and the soft smile it brought to his face.

By the end of the first week out of Constantinopolis, Lucius had managed to compartmentalize his despair and the anger it was turning into, enjoying the company of Marpesia and her translator, seeking it out as much he could on the march. He even joined in the laughter as they approached the end of their first journey and the rest of his legion. Yet, when he was alone inside his tent at night, the darkness outside joined with his own inside. He even thought he saw her silhouette in the light of the moon outside his tent. He'd recognize that form anywhere. Maybe she'd sneak into his tent, and he could see her face in the light of the moon.

When Lucius's two cohorts and Marpesia's small band of warriors crested the shallow hills overlooking the Danuvius and the town of Oescus, Lucius was fighting two battles—the depression and rage at being kicked out of the empire and his unexplained fixation with the Roxolani leader. Off in the distance to the east of the town, the footprint of the legionary fort appeared much larger than he'd anticipated, even for the eight extra cohorts Pisakar was supposed to pick up.

Lucius held up his arm. "Halt."

"Sir. Send up the call?"

Lucius nodded. Knowing it was the last day of their march before rejoining the Black Legion, his legionary cornicen had assembled his carnyx, the ancient war horn of Lucius's Gallic Celt ancestors. The long neck curved up from the mouthpiece above the troops and forward again, capped by an intricately engraved and sculpted bull's head, a wide gash engraved in the neck, symbolizing its slaughter by Mithras. As the symbol of the Legion's divine patron and Lucius as

Mithras's knight on earth, the bull carnyx was always allowed first call to announce the return of Lucius into the embrace of the Black.

The cornicen, having an audience of foreigners, decided to show off, using the magic of the carnyx to its fullest potential, with its reverberation chamber and the always moving tongue that sang with the horn. The bull carnyx call, though standardized for practical purposes in marching and battle, allowed the player to embellish and play around the dimensions on special occasions.

Today, the call chilled Lucius. The cornicen gave all the rage and pain of a bull wrestled into submission before having its head yanked back so Mithras could slit its throat. Lucius, having witnessed the Mithraic scene in person in all its divine intensity, thought the cornicen captured the emotion of the scene perfectly.

Everyone waited for the return call from the fort, though if Pisakar didn't know he was coming already, notified by his scouts, Lucius would need to have a severe talk with his second. Pisakar had claimed the elephant call as a Kushite who'd grown up in Aegyptus, and right on cue, the elephant carnyx sent back its call, letting Lucius know Pisakar was in fort.

Lucius started his men marching toward the fort, their dinners, and rest. When Lucius breached the gates, he was surprised by the density of Legionnaires packed into the fort. After his groom took his pony, Lucius had the First Cohort hold to stand watch over their Roxolani guests, sent the Sixth to their billet, and walked into the command building. Pisakar stood when Lucius was announced, stepping from behind his camp desk to clasp Lucius's hand.

"It's good to see you, Centurio."

"You too, my friend. Why are we so crowded around here?"

"Vexillations have been drifting in from the west for days. Constantius must be draining the border forts. He'd better hope no one notices how thin and brittle the border defenses are. Gods know I picked them clean on the way through."

"What did you get?"

"I've got, all told, eight cohorts worth of men. Half of them can probably be turned into men we can rely on."

"What about the other half?"

"They know which end of a shovel to hold."

Lucius chuckled. He appreciated his second's sardonic sense of humor. "We'll need trenches dug at some point, always need spare dirt warriors."

Pisakar filled the small space with his deep rumble of a laugh. "Theirs is not to question why, but to dig and let dirt fly. What of these Roxolani?"

"They look competent, more than competent. They're the chieftain's personal escort, so they're most likely the elite, but the whole Wolf Clan has a fierce reputation in the steppes." When Pisakar raised his eye, Lucius added, "I found some people that'd been up that way, deeper into the steppes away from the Pontus Euxinus. Word I gathered was they prefer not to fight, but are fierce and brutal when called to."

"We've fought beside people with far less for reputations. So what's going on? Your letter was sparse on details."

"The short story is we're going to cross the Danuvius with the Sarmatians. They will lead us into the Montes Sarmatici, back through the heart of the old province of Dacia, and out a pass into the east where we will strike the Goths in the rear."

Pisakar sat forward in his chair. "Through the mountains?"

Lucius nodded his head jauntily. "Yes."

"You do realize were coming up on winter, right?"

"Correct."

"You do know it gets cold in the mountains in winter, right?"

"I have heard such before."

"I guess we'd better ensure we have enough winter gear.

"That we had." Lucius shook his head, not looking forward to another winter spent in the mountains of Dacia. He wasn't as young as he was the first time he'd had to do it. "I raided the imperator's stores pretty thoroughly, but we'll want to sort through it all and make sure we augment it before we get into the mountains. I don't want to lose half our men to frostbite and freezing. We'll also need to send out riders to see when the rest of our allies will be here—messages were sent to them when I sent yours. They should be marching along the Danuvius to meet us here. We'll want to get moving north before Constantius decides to reclaim the men I pilfered."

Pisakar nodded along, taking notes as Lucius spoke. "I'm assuming we'll need to find billeting for the Sarmatians you brought with you?"

"Aye. The emissary will want to get her people settled."

"Her?" Pisakar asked.

Lucius nodded. "Apparently, I was requested by name. She believes it's our old enemies driving the Tervingi out of the north."

"And Constantius wants us to put our small force at the tail end of thousands upon thousands of Goths being driven by hordes of monsters powerful enough to do that? Fuck."

"That sums it up perfectly. Did you happen to dig through our maps and bring any of the old maps of the Dacian province?"

Pisakar ran his hand over his bald head. "I think so, I tried to grab any that might be relevant. We're not going to rely on getting through the Dacian mountains in winter with only old maps, are we?"

"No. Fortunately Marpesia and her Wolves know those mountains pretty well. She has her own maps and has traveled the passes often enough to be confident of our course. We won't need to rely on old maps nor on my old memory." Lucius ran his hands through his hair, shuffling about his growing curls.

Pisakar scoffed. "If you've forgotten anything, it's likely the first time. I'd rely on your memories over most maps, and that's the truth. So, what do you think of this Dominus?"

"He's sharp, confident, competent. It's more his son and advisor I'm concerned about."

"The boy fall a bit too far from the tree?"

"Possibly. He might mature out, but then again, his arrogance might get him killed young. I nearly thought Marpesia was going to take him apart."

"What about this advisor?"

"He's a Christian zealot. If he has his way, the old gods' time in the empire is drawing to an end." Lucius sighed, shaking his head.

"That's a lot of gods to offend, gods who've taken a special interest in the doings of the Roman Empire."

"The Romans and their old gods conquered all the land and seas from the end of the world in the west to Syria. Now an eastern god is conquering the Romans." Lucius sat up straighter, clenching his jaw, exhaling sharply. "Well, I've left our guests for long enough. Where can I put two hundred fifty horse warriors? And arrange for a place for me. The Roxolani emissary will be taking my quarters."

"Aye, Centurio. Take them to the southeastern corner. I've prepared some space. But we may want to think about moving some of our people across the bridge and establishing a camp on the other side. Might be a good opportunity to get some additional training in with the new men, and it'll free up space for those who need it."

"And it'll put those men slightly further out of reach of the Dominus should he decide he would rather have them."

"Now that you mention it…" Pisakar laughed.

Lucius stood up, sighed, nodded to his friend. "I'll be back when I'm done with our allies."

"I'll follow you out. I'm curious to meet our new friends."

Lucius strode out of headquarters, Pisakar behind him, and waved to Marpesia and Aella. "We have a spot for you to bed down for now. Marpesia, I've assigned my quarters to you."

Lucius waited for Aella to translate Marpesia's words. "My mistress says you don't need to abandon your quarters again on her behalf."

"It's only polite to allow our respected ally and their revered emissary to have the best quarters available. It would be rude to put you in lesser quarters."

A sly smirk spread across Aella's face as Marpesia boldly held Lucius's gaze. "She didn't say anything about putting her in lesser quarters."

Lucius's brows furrowed in confusion. "I don't understand."

Pisakar let off a loud laugh. "She's saying you're welcome to share your quarters with her." Pisakar slapped Lucius on the shoulder, knocking him forward half a step.

Blushing furiously at the innuendo and his missing it, Lucius coughed to cover his embarrassment. "Pisakar, this is Marpesia, emissary of the free Roxolani and leader of the Wolf Clan, and Aella, her companion and translator. Pisakar is my second-in-command. If you can't find me, he'll be able to take care of anything you need. Pisakar, if you'd be so kind as to show them where we've got them billeted and then show Marpesia to her quarters, I'd appreciate it. I need to take care of a few things."

Before anyone could say anything else, Lucius turned and walked back into the headquarters, sinking into the chair he'd abandoned just moments ago. His cheeks burned as he shook his head. With nothing to do at the moment, he spaced off into his mind, trying to hide from the disgrace of being exiled from the empire—but failing.

He wasn't sure how long he'd sat there until Pisakar returned, his deep chuckle pulling Lucius back into the room.

Pisakar sank into his chair across from Lucius. "I don't think I've ever seen you routed so effectively and quickly, Centurio. And she did it through a translator."

"Yeah. She did." Lucius shook his head.

"She's a pretty woman. You could do worse than taking her up on the offer."

"No."

"What, you don't find her attractive?" Pisakar's thick eyebrows lifted away from his eyes.

"No, it's not that. I think she's very attractive." Lucius was getting flustered again, unsure why the turn in conversation bothered him. It wasn't the first time he and his friend had talked about women who looked admiringly at Lucius.

"Not into the warrior women?"

"No, she's a fine warrior. Together, we killed a quartet of vampires that had sneaked into the palace she was borrowing in Constantinopolis." Lucius fought to keep a smile from spreading across his face and betraying his thoughts about the Sarmatian warrior.

"Well, if that's not it, what's going on?"

Lucius sat stiffly, his eyes narrowed. "It would be inappropriate to sleep with an ally, especially before heading beyond the border into wild country."

"Suit yourself," Pisakar said, shrugging.

SEVEN

LUCIUS AND PISAKAR sat in the command building, a table covered in maps separating them, when Pisakar looked up, clearing his throat. "Will you be visiting the Mithraeum while we're here? The pater patrum visited as soon as he saw the Black marching into view of Oescus."

"Yes. It would be rude not to pay my respects."

"And foolhardy to offend a priest and a god before a dangerous march," Pisakar said.

Lucius chuckled. "If I give offense to the pater patrum, it's not like he can do anything about it; I outrank him. But you're probably right. I doubt Mithras will take the time to smite me, then find a replacement, but no need to make our life harder. Did he say when my presence is requested?"

"At your leisure was the implication."

"Tomorrow should suffice."

"I will let him know. I'll arrange your escort." Pisakar rose. "No time like the present."

Lucius nodded and went back to scouring over the maps. After a while, the lines blurred into incomprehensibility, so he pushed back in his chair. In a few days' time, he was supposed to cross the border, never to return—a lifetime of service and duty wiped away with a span of stone bridging a river. For over two hundred years he'd kept the empire relatively free from the blood sucking demons Mithras had charged him to destroy; now they'd have free rein and access to all the wealth and power assembled behind the borders of Roma.

As he closed his eyes, resting his head in his hand, a pit opened beneath him, gently sucking him down into its depths. It would be so easy to just give in, let the pit draw him into its abyss, but instead, his mind pulled him somewhere else. Her face. The face of the Roxolani woman. Marpesia.

Like a lifeline, the image of her face in his mind kept him from falling deeper, yet he feared to hold too tight to it, afraid that instead of pulling him free, he'd only drag her down with him. Thus, he floated, suspended, drawn in two different directions, and there he stayed, in the silence of the empty room until Pisakar roused him later that afternoon.

"The local pater patrum says to be there on the early side of sunset. I informed him we'd be bringing seven in addition to you. I'll be bringing your new secretary as an initiate to the corax," Pisakar said.

"Very good," Lucius replied.

Pisakar stared at his friend for a few moments then squeezed his shoulder before leaving Lucius to his privacy. He decided to take a turn around the camp instead of sitting and moping; the fresh air would do him good, as would the simple interaction of walking among his legionnaires. After he made a circuit of the fort, he headed to his new quarters for a quiet dinner by himself and an early bed, trying to store away sleep before the exhausting intensity of crossing the mountains in winter then a hard campaign.

PISAKAR COLLECTED Lucius with plenty of time to spare. Pisakar took the lead, allowing Lucius to ride in the middle of his escort and contemplate the coming visit to the Mithraeum. As the only man in the empire given an eighth rank in the mysteries of

Mithras by the god himself, Lucius was the de facto leader. He was known as the Dux Belorum Mithrae—the warlord of Mithras—though for simplicity's sake, he preferred everyone refer to him as pater patrum, Father of Fathers. Out of respect for Lucius and his position, when he was in attendance, no other pater patrum used the title, going by the standard title of Pater instead. He even stood above the imperators when they still adhered to Mithras and his ways, though out of courtesy, Lucius had deferred to Roma's leaders if they were attending the same Mithraeum at the same time.

Seeing the banner of the leader of the Black Legion, the guards at the city's gates snapped to attention and admitted Lucius's small party. Pisakar led them through the winding streets of Oescus toward the wealthier district until they turned into an alley next to a large manor and stopped in the middle of the narrow street. Pisakar issued a series of orders, and the Princeps Primus Centurio's guard formed up, blocking the entrance of the Mithraeum to anyone. If anyone invited for tonight's ceremony was late, they could only be escorted in by the Mithraeum's pater.

The pater greeted Lucius and Pisakar, bowing deeply before escorting them down the stairs under the manor and into the entry way. Pisakar instructed Martininius to sit on the bench in the entry way; he'd be summoned later when it was time for his initiation. With that handled, the pater led Lucius and Pisakar and the five other men into an antechamber where they could change into their regalia.

"I am Quintus Antoninus Tullius, Pater Patrum of this Mithraeum. Your presence here humbles us, Pater Patrum." He bowed again.

"My thanks for allowing me the honor of visiting," Lucius replied with a respectful nod.

Quintus turned to Pisakar and bowed again. "Pater Pisakar, do you wish to take the role of Sol this evening?"

"Thank you, but I'll defer to you, Pater Tullius."

Quintus seemed pleased with being allowed to perform the ceremony with Lucius. "Thank you, Pater. Pater Patrum, we shall begin when you are ready." He bowed again and left the antechamber.

Lucius pulled his caligae off and traded them for an elaborate pair of sandals. His men followed suit. Lucius felt slightly ridiculous in the luxurious sandals while dressed in his full battle regalia, but he didn't want to damage the marble and tile floors he'd glimpsed. Normally, one wouldn't wear armor to the Mithraeum, save for the fact his armor and swords were themselves religious artifacts, given to Lucius and enchanted by Mithras himself. They were the costume of his rank. Once Lucius pulled his travel cloak off and replaced it with the embroidered black cloak, a giant sun in yellows, reds, and oranges taking up the majority of the back, Lucius's mind drifted, a faraway look taking over his vision.

"Pisakar," said one of the men, pointing to Lucius.

"Right. It's going to be one of those nights." Pisakar pointed toward the door, leading the men out of the antechamber and into the Mithraeum.

Lucius, Mithras's call filling his awareness, barely noticed his men leaving. The tension drained from Lucius's body as he stood silently in the antechamber, waiting until his master called him. It was always this way—the calm before the storm, the breath before the plunge.

"Sit with me, my brave soldier," a gentle feminine voice said from behind Lucius.

Even though he wasn't expecting someone to be in the room with him, the voice didn't shock or startle him. When he turned around, Luna—Selene in the Hellenic tongue—goddess of the moon, stood resplendent in a simple Hellene gown, gathered at the shoulders and waist with ornate silver belts. Gentle silver light suffused her being, bathing the room in its delicate glow and caressing Lucius inside and out. She indicated the bench, then sat; Lucius joined her, sitting to her right. Taking his left hand in both of hers, she gave it a squeeze.

"What troubles you, my brave soldier?" Selene asked.

Lucius sighed, lowering his eyes. "I'm to be banished from the borders of Roma under penalty of death."

"What do lines on maps mean to the light of the moon? My eyes do not see borders, only the earth that lies under them and the people who walk above them. What do the ones who pervert the will of the gods care for borders?"

Lucius nodded.

"Your task, as it ever was, is to find and end those who destroy the essence, the souls of humanity. What line they exist on is of no matter. Besides, a single man may cross any border and go unnoticed where an army cannot."

"I understand," Lucius replied.

Selene stood, as did Lucius, and smiled softly. "Not all changes are bad, and in this there is one constant. You are still and always will be my champion of the night." She put her hand on Lucius's armor over his heart where she'd placed her symbol all those years ago in that Mithraeum in Antiochia. "This too shall heal in its proper time. Now go. My brother and the wanderer await you."

"Thank you, My Mistress." Lucius bowed and kissed the back of her hand.

"I will walk with you, if you please."

Lucius extended his arm. Selene placed her cool hand on his forearm and let him escort her out of the antechamber. When they walked through the doors, the room flooded with the silvery radiance of the goddess. Everyone stood to bow to Lucius as he entered, but upon feeling the presence of the goddess, fell to their knees. Lucius's men were more controlled, sinking to one knee and bowing their heads. When they passed Pisakar, the goddess extended her left hand and placed it on Pisakar's bald head briefly.

As they reached the end of the benches jutting out from the wall, Lucius stopped. Selene patted his arm, then continued forward, taking her place to the side of the Mithraeum's altar. Lucius couldn't make out the details of the Mithraeum, the goddess's glow muting all things save for her beauty and the soft touch of her light.

Instead of Sol Invictus, the unconquered sun, and Mithras joining Selene, the altar at the end of the room disappeared, becoming a black void extending into infinity as far as Lucius could perceive. The sounds of the devotees faded as did everything in his peripheral vision until only Selene, the void, and himself existed. In the far distance, a point of light formed in the center of the void.

It moved toward him, gradually growing larger, the sound of beating hooves making their way to his ears. Reaching down to his left hip, he pulled his gladius from its scabbard with his right hand, then freed the rudis with his left hand. Finally close enough to see some details, the monstrous speck resolved into a massive bull, horns wide and sharp gracing its lowered head.

The thundering of the bull's hooves shook the ground but failed to shake Lucius. He crouched, coiled—ready to strike. So focused was he, he wasn't even surprised when the bull, finally closing the last of the distance that had separated them, melted mid-stride and turned into a snarling demon, razor sharp fangs gleaming and eyes boiling with hatred for Lucius and for all humankind.

Instead of taking the impact, Lucius sidestepped and stabbed down into the back of the monster as it glided by, taking it in the heart. The monster crashed into the ground, returning to its previous shape. The wounded bull tried to stand but fell to the ground. Leaping onto its back, Lucius grabbed its chin and hauled back on its head, exposing its neck for a killing stroke. Under him, the mythical beast shuddered before slumping to the ground dead.

Breathing heavily, Lucius dismounted from the bull and pulled his rudis from its back, planting a foot against its side to aid his pull. As the blade left flesh, the bull turned to stone. When Lucius looked down, his blades were clean and polished, brighter than new.

Lucius looked up when he heard the fall of feet, then bowed when the bright figure of Sol Invictus formed out of the black void. Sol returned the respectful gesture with a nod. From the center of the void, Mithras appeared, standing in front of the stone bull. He shook Sol's hand, renewing their association and covenant after the killing of the bull. Lucius bowed deeply, then he shook Mithras's offered hand.

"Father of Fathers," Lucius said.

"Well met, my son," Mithras replied.

Sol and Luna stepped forward, standing on either side of Mithras, just off his shoulders.

"What news of Roma's masters, my son?" Mithras asked.

"Little good. A new god comes from the east, one god who is also three but still one. The one called Christ. The imperator pays his honor to him now."

"Is Roma breaking its covenant with me?" Mithras glowered, storm clouds shading his eyes.

"I fear her imperators do, but there are many who still honor you and pay their respects accordingly." Lucius held his master's gaze.

Mithras nodded. *"Then for now, they shall have my renewed blessing while they still pay me respect. Do you come to renew your covenant with me, Princeps Primus Centurio?"*

"I am and shall always be your servant, my master." Lucius gave him a half bow.

Sol Invictus stepped forward and shook Lucius's hand. "May my strength continue to flow through you."

Selene stepped forward next. Instead of taking his hand, she leaned in and placed a kiss on each of his cheeks. "Thus do I renew my gifts to you and give you my blessing."

Looking into the infinite depth of Mithras's eyes, Lucius shook his hand and sealed the covenant he'd first agreed to two hundred and fourteen years ago in the mountains of Armenia.

Mithras, who was not so subtle or gentle as Selene, finished the handshake with a manacle and chain appearing around Lucius's wrist, attaching him to the stone bull that had appeared as one of the di inferi only minutes before. Not only had Lucius accepted the renewal of the task, but Mithras reminded him that his acceptance bound him to Mithras's mission. When the last link fell into place about the neck of the bull, it looped back around and up to link Lucius's other arm, binding him completely. When the manacle captured his other wrist, he shrank in on himself slightly.

Lucius knew better than to get involved with gods. It never worked out for anyone who did, whether they angered the gods or joined in their causes. Mortals were such limited beings compared to the gods who walked among them. Odysseus had gotten off lightly with only twenty years of his life chiseled off after stepping into weighty matters above his station. Lucius's debt to Mithras had lasted ten times that length of time—and then some—with no sign of it ending anytime soon.

Finished with Lucius, Sol stepped into the air, walking up and to the left until he mounted his sun chariot. Selene, likewise, rose in the air until she stepped into her moon chariot. Nodding at Lucius one last time, Mithras turned and walked back and away from him, eventually disappearing into the darkness whence he came. When the altar returned to its previous state of static stone, the chains tying Lucius to the bull disappeared back into nothingness, freeing him.

The crack of stone reported through the room. Looking down, Lucius saw a ragged line appear through the neck of the bull; from it dripped a dark, thick red substance. He turned around. The entire room, save for the six men he'd brought down into the Mithraeum, knelt, some falling onto their hands and bringing their heads to the floor while others even wept at what they'd just witnessed. Lucius was unsure how much of what he'd just done had been viewed by the room. The gods could control everyone's perceptions. Even Martininius had fallen to his knees, wonder filling his eyes. Lucius reached back and dragged his finger along the crack, scooping the red substance onto his finger.

Pisakar made eye contact with Lucius, who gave a nearly imperceptible nod in return. He stepped forward, strolling down the center aisle of the Mithraeum sedately. When he passed one of his men, they stepped out of their row with military precision and joined Lucius, following behind him. When he came to Martininius, Lucius stopped. The young man looked up. Reaching out, Lucius steadied Martininius by gently taking his chin in his hand, then with the finger covered in the bull's blood, he drew a line down the center of his secretary's head followed by two squiggly lines. They joined with the straight line to form the symbol of the caduceus and marking him as the first rank of Corax. Giving Martininius a brief nod, he continued down the aisle and out of the main chamber of the Mithraeum, through the entryway, and up the stairs.

Lucius silently mounted his gelding and nudged him forward, letting the rest of his men catch up with him. A few moments later, Pisakar slowed once he drew next to Lucius. The two men exchanged a look, then wound their way through the streets of Oescus and out the gate to return to their fort.

PISAKAR SENT two cohorts to escort the rest of Marpesia's Wolf Clan warriors to Oescus, along with a few volunteers from the warriors who'd come with her. Lucius, eager to get moving, left the First and the Sixth in Oescus to rest from their march while he and Pisakar organized the rest of his cohorts and the eight new ones pilfered along the border.

Their advance forces had already gone across the bridge, seeking a campground to lay down the plans for their temporary fort. Lucius's third in command was in the process of getting the borrowed cohorts over the bridge, leaving Pisakar and Lucius with the last four cohorts of the Black Legion and Marpesia with her small force.

When they reached the new fortified bridge Constantius had dedicated three years earlier, Lucius pulled his horse out of line and rode out of formation, Pisakar following him to the top of a nearby hill. Together, they watched the long line of men stretch out from the bridge to the fort.

Lucius took in a deep breath, holding it, and let it out explosively. "This is my last campaign, Pisakar."

"What?" Pisakar whipped his head around to look at Lucius, but he kept staring out toward the bridge. "You're being relieved of command?"

Lucius let out a harsh bark of a laugh. "You could say that."

Off in the distance, the sun glinted off the silver and bronze of Marpesia's armor as she pulled her horse out of the line and walked it toward Lucius and Pisakar. Seeing her, he relaxed into his saddle a bit, a soft smile winning out over his dour expression.

"I'm being exiled. Once I step across that bridge, I can no longer to return to the empire under penalty of death." He sighed, letting his eyes drift back to Marpesia as she drew near.

Pisakar let off a string of invective-laced curses in his native tongue. He apparently was digging deep into his vocabulary, finding words he'd never taught Lucius. When he finally calmed himself, he spat onto the ground.

"And you're going to go through with it?" Pisakar asked.

"Do I have a choice?"

"Well, you could—"

"I have neither the will nor the desire. My place is not ruling an empire, but to hunt the monsters who feast on humanity."

"You'll continue hunting the fanged demons?"

Lucius tore his eyes away from Marpesia and met his friend's gaze. "It's why I'm still alive after all this time. Just because a new god pushes out the old gods doesn't mean Mithras will let go of me. His grip is too strong; he renewed it at the Mithraeum, further binding me to his cause."

His smile reemerged as he returned his eyes to Marpesia.

Pisakar made a curious noise, changing the subject. "Your eyes never leave her."

"What?"

"Whenever Marpesia is in view, you can't stop watching her."

"She's in my line of sight." Lucius replied matter-of-factly. She was, but if she were to his left, his head would turn that way.

"She always seems to be."

Lucius barely heard what his second said. He nodded toward Marpesia and Aella as they crested the hill.

"Come up here to admire the bridge?" Aella called, stopping in front of Lucius and Pisakar.

"It's a lovely bridge," Pisakar replied. "Although, apparently not the most interesting thing happening on this hill."

Aella chuckled. "Ah, yes."

Marpesia scowled playfully at her friend, riding next to Lucius and turning her horse around to watch the line of legionnaires and her few Sarmatians making their way over Constantius's Bridge. Aella and Pisakar drifted away from Lucius and Marpesia and quietly conversed.

Marpesia's horse drifted closer until their legs bumped. Lucius kept his eyes on the line of men moving north when he felt a finger whisper across the back of his hand until it snagged under the edge of his palm and pulled the rest of his hand into Marpesia's. She squeezed it, rubbing her thumb over the back of his hand. For the first time in weeks, he felt warmth spread through his body.

He sighed, squeezing her hand back. By the time the sun set, he'd no longer be a part of an empire that had dominated his life since before he was even born. He'd complete his mission because he'd committed to it, but beyond that, his destiny was empty. Aella and Pisakar allowed them their time, although Lucius didn't recognize the gesture nor what was happening with Marpesia. He just knew the touch of her hand felt nice and right, somehow.

Pisakar pulled his horse up next to Lucius and sat quietly for a while, but as the sun worked its way west and the tail of men crossing the bridge across the mighty Danuvius River shortened, he cleared his throat. "Lucius, are you ready to cross the bridge?"

Lucius knew the question was loaded. He wasn't ready to cross the Danuvius. But today wouldn't be the day he crossed the Rubicon.

"Does it matter whether I am or not? I am not Julius Caesar." He let go of Marpesia's hand reluctantly. "Let's get the rest of our people into camp and get them bedded down. I want this over with."

EIGHT

PISAKAR HAD STARTED the process of turning the borrowed cohorts into real soldiers. Like many of the men stationed on the border under Diocletian and his successors, they'd been ignored as the men who called themselves "Dominus" concentrated their forces behind their borders under their new policy of being able to send them to the border where needed. In reality, the men had been used in their internal struggles while the borders were neglected.

More oft than not, Lucius and the Black had been holding back raiders more than hunting vampires as others fought for the power. Pisakar had done a good job selecting units to integrate into Lucius's forces. His centurions and the optios were doing quick work getting them in shape, refreshing their training and turning them into a reliable fighting force that could hold the line when called to. They were using the quiet before the storm to get their borrowed cohorts into shape. They needed to rely on these men for their lives in the coming weeks; they were going to use every moment to gather the last of their supplies and train their men before the rest of Marpesia's people arrived.

Lucius had been watching one of his optios run his new men through some drills, engaging with some of the more promising swordsmen. The man the optio was currently working with had caught the optio flatfooted and was driving him back.

"Fuck, halt!" the optio cried after the trainee shoved the optio's shield back and into his face.

Making sure the trainee had halted, he propped his scutum against his leg and reached up and felt his nose, drawing it back covered in blood.

Lucius did his best to hold his laughter. "Looks like he got ya there, Optio. Go see the medic. I'll keep running them through their drills."

"Aye, Centurio," the optio said, sounding muffled with his hand holding his nose.

Lucius took the wooden training rudis from the optio so he could take his scutum with him. "Martininius?"

"Centurio?"

"Mind taking my cloak?" Lucius asked. He unclasped the black cloak, handing it to his secretary, and turned to the trainee who'd gotten the better of his optio. "What's your name, miles?"

"Decanus Naram, Centurio."

"My apologies, Decanus. That was excellent work. Can you repeat the series of moves that caught my optio off guard?"

"Aye, Centurio."

Lucius twirled the rudis and rotated his shoulder, warming up his muscles before stepping in to work with his new men when he saw Marpesia and Aella approaching.

Lucius held his hand up to signal a brief halt and stepped toward the two Roxolani women. He nodded respectfully, giving a half bow. "How may I serve you today?"

Aella translated for Marpesia, waited for her answer, and turned to Lucius. "She only wishes to watch the mighty Centurio Immortalis train his warriors. Please, continue."

Lucius nodded and turned back to the patient Decanus, taking an en garde position. "Ready? Begin."

Lucius countered the decanus's moves with the standard options, wanting to see where his optio had tripped up. It wasn't until after the first several moves that the decanus started modifying things.

"*Interesting,*" Lucius thought. The decanus had come up with some ideas that tweaked the standard moves and caused the counters to fail.

His optio had been working through the standards to ensure everyone had a proper base and had grown complacent. He'd have to inform his junior officer how he'd been bested. When the decanus launched the victorious move, Lucius easily countered it, turning the move back on the decanus. The decanus's wooden sword flew into the air, and Lucius paused with his blade against the neck of the soldier. Like his optio who'd expected the standard moves, the decanus had grown used to beating his compatriots with it.

"Excellent move. If you'll fetch your rudis, I'll show you how I turned it."

The decanus nodded respectfully and fetched his implement as his comrades snickered, apparently happy to see his tricks turned against him. Once the decanus recovered, Lucius ran him through his paces, showing him several ways to recover and use his skills and how a Goth might counter his moves. By the time he was done, Lucius held every eye as they dissected the lessons.

As Lucius taught his clinic on sword fighting, he'd gathered a crowd of Sarmatians and some of his upper officers, including Pisakar, who was standing next to Aella and Marpesia.

"My mistress would like to know if the Centurio always works with his common soldiers," Aella asked.

"Quite regularly. He's the finest hand with a sword I've ever fought beside," Pisakar replied, his deep voice carrying.

Out of the corner of his eye, Lucius checked out the scene. Aella was busy conversing with Pisakar, occasionally translating a sentence or two from Marpesia. And although Marpesia engaged with Pisakar through her translator, she wasn't moving her eyes off Lucius.

He waved over one of his officers. "Baranis, mind running these men through some more drills?"

"Of course, Centurio."

Lucius nodded and walked toward Pisakar and his Roxolani guests, wiping a sheen of sweat from his brow.

"Ah, Centurio. Our guests were wondering why you still train with your men."

Aella nodded at Pisakar.

Marpesia's eyes challenged him, her face an inscrutable mask. He addressed her, letting Aella carry his words to her.

"There's nothing common about my soldiers. They're the finest fighting men anywhere. I work with them to ensure that stays true and to hone my own abilities. The skills I've developed and refined keep me alive when I'm fighting my true enemy. The blood drinkers are fast and strong, and every one I've crossed has met its end at my hand." He waited for Aella to translate his words.

Marpesia's reply was much shorter. "Finest fighting men? Would you care to test that supposition?"

"How?" Lucius asked, cocking his head to the side, his eyebrow quirking up.

"My mistress would offer a challenge to Roma's greatest warrior," Aella translated.

Marpesia stripped off her cloak, revealing her ornate, bronze-edged steel scale mail.

Lucius turned to Aella. "Excuse me. I don't understand."

"My mistress wishes to challenge you to a friendly contest. She says you may have the finest men, but you've left out half of the world's people."

Lucius looked at his friend. Pisakar was doing his best to hide his grin and to keep from laughing. He gave Lucius a smirk and a nod. Flipping the rudis so he held the dull blade in his hand, Lucius offered the handle to Marpesia. She looked at it and sneered.

"My mistress says she does not play with children's toys."

Marpesia reached to her back and pulled free her pointed battle axe. Lucius had fought against the weapon many times in his two centuries of war, although he doubted he'd seen one as fine as Marpesia's. The crescent blade had a stylized antelope leaping, his round belly at the center of the blade, its exaggerated legs leaping out into the top and bottom corner. The head tilted back at the perfect angle so its impossibly long antlers formed a pointed spike on the opposite end of the blade.

Lucius nodded, handing the rudis off to an empty hand. He didn't see who, his gaze captured by the challenge in her mesmerisingly gray eyes. They sparkled mischievously, a question in them Lucius couldn't figure out.

"Very well. Helmet and shield."

She nodded.

"Martininius? If you'd be so good as to fetch my scutum and my helmet."

"Yes, Centurio."

Marpesia called to one of her warriors, sending him off to fetch a helmet and a shield. He'd learned enough of her tongue to know that much. As he jogged off, she turned her gaze back to Lucius, eyeing him up and down and saying something to Aella he couldn't translate.

"My mistress says you're big for a Roman."

"I'm not a Latin Roman. I'm a barbarian from Belgica in Gaul, from the Nervii tribe. There aren't a lot of Romans from Italia in the Black. Pisakar?"

"Barbarian from Napata in Kush."

Lucius looked at the grizzled Centurio of the I Cohort. "Zyraxes?"

"Thracian, Centurio."

Martininius came jogging back, Lucius's Scutum in one hand and his helmet in the other.

"Martininius, tell the Roxolani emissary what variety of barbarian you are."

"Barbarian, Centurio? I'm of Hellene and Roman descent from Massilia, sir."

Lucius chuckled, knowing the serious young man would answer stiffly at being called a barbarian. "We're all children of Roma's conquests. Except Pisakar—no one has managed to conquer the Kushites yet, Egyptian, Hellene, or Roman." Lucius took his helmet with its transverse crest made of long black horse hair. While the standard centurion's crest was short and spiky, and stuck straight up, his was long and swept down the back of his helmet and over his shoulders. He let Martininius hold his scutum, the surface painted black to match the legion's official color save for Selene's moon painted in white at its center. He waited for Marpesia's warrior to return with her gear.

A few moments later, he returned carrying a wicker shield and a bronze and steel helmet. Marpesia handed her axe to Aella and grabbed a knit cap out of the helmet and tucked her hair up, arranging it into a pile on top of her head. Grabbing her helmet by the cheek guards hinged onto the crown in a similar manner as Lucius's Gallic helm, she pulled it over her head, tightening the straps. It had a smaller neck guard than Lucius's wide, deep plunging neck guard. Unlike Lucius's helmet, hers had a nose guard jutting down from the rim. A long tail of golden horsehair was attached to the top, sticking up before arching back and falling down behind her. On each side of her helmet, bronze decorations featured the stylized wolf—her clan's symbol.

She took her crescent-shaped wicker shield then her axe and ran through a few slow movements to warm up her body. Lucius took his scutum, watching Marpesia's fluid movements, admiring her economy of motion while Pisakar backed everyone into a broad circle to give the combatants plenty of space. As word spread throughout the camp, the crowd grew. Lucius suspected a large amount of betting was already under way.

He strolled across the circle, tuning out the noise of those who'd showed up to watch. The only warning he got was the slight scrape of Marpesia's soft-soled boot on a hard patch in the dirt as he turned around. A smear of silver arced toward his head.

He raised his scutum hastily, shoving the cut to the left. He pivoted, swinging an awkward slash toward her midsection, but she'd already danced back out of the way, sliding around his slash and knocking it around with her shield. Knowing the axe would be coming in toward his right shoulder, Lucius stepped into his failed slash and yanked his scutum around as he spun, catching the axe.

He pivoted, trying to reach a place where he wasn't desperately responding to the lightning-quick and graceful arcs of Marpesia's axe. Back pedaling to open enough space to get set, he moved around looking for an opening. When his heel caught on something, tripping him slightly, Marpesia darted in with a low cut aimed at his legs. He turned it aside with the flat of his blade, but she was already changing direction, catching the edge of his scutum with the long spike on the back of her axe. Her axe's momentum pulled Lucius off balance, allowing her to finish pushing his shield out of the way with hers, exposing his side. Pivoting around, she caught the back of his knee with her foot and scooped the leg forward, darting out of the way as Lucius crashed onto his ass.

Wind wheezed from his lungs as he rolled to the side so he could shove himself up. He yanked his scutum upward, positioning it between him and where he thought Marpesia was. Once the blood rushing through his ears calmed some, he could hear the laughter filling the circle. He'd never hear the end of it from his men.

Marpesia seemed content to let him set himself, having made her point. He unwound his body and stood up, tipping his head to one side, then the other to stretch his neck after the crash. She quirked an eyebrow. Lucius nodded, ready.

As she lifted her axe back into position, Lucius twirled his gladius around in his hand and launched a stab toward her stomach. She directed it out of the way with her shield, using the momentum to spin and strike out toward his head with a backhanded slash. Lucius caught the blade and moved it aside as she completed her spin, shoving into his shield with hers, trying to force him back. He was prepared and met her shield, pushing back with his. Instead of knocking him back, she adjusted and used the combined force of their shields to leap back, nimble as a gazelle.

She was bold and innovative as a warrior. Her moves, if deployed by a less-skilled person, would likely get them killed. She used the lightness of her wicker shield to her advantage, keeping herself quick and mobile. She couldn't get into a hacking contest with Lucius and his scutum. It could likely take more damage, although an axe on wood was nothing to sneer at.

He kept trying to catch her off guard, off balance, to finesse his sword inside her guard and land a blow, yet he couldn't find an opening as she either deftly danced away or blocked and countered. She was fast, although not as fast as Lucius if he pushed himself to full speed, aided by his godly powers and those he drained from the di inferi. But she could practically feel his movements, predicting his next move as he launched it.

Dancing back and forth, all sound blocked from his ears, a smile spread across his face. Lucius was enjoying the fight. She was the finest fighter he'd crossed blades with in ages, perhaps ever. Marpesia's eyes squinted, wrinkling the corners as she took in every movement of his body preparing her next move. Beyond the first attack when she'd tripped him to the ground, she'd not pressed the advantage, either willing to wait or unable to find the right opening to turn the engagement.

Curious, he gave her an opening, letting a slash carry just enough too far to open an opportunity to counter. She took it. Pressing him back, she rained blows toward his shield and body with both blade and spike, using her shield to block or attack where opportune. It was an impressive display, and it nearly put Lucius on his back for a second time until he halted her momentum, returning to the previous status quo.

Without the opening he'd given her or the element of surprise, she couldn't get past his attack and defense. Deciding to see how hard he could press her, he turned up his speed and power, tapping into the well gained from draining the fanged demons.

His focus sharpened, the smile falling off his face as he pushed forward, stabbing out or delivering slashes faster than he'd shown her so far. Her eyes widened as each block she made became a little more desperate and almost too late.

Lucius had her firmly on her heel when he saw his opening. He caught her axe on his scutum and launched the shield up, knocking her back, her axe tumbling out of her hand and through the air to land behind her. Bringing his scutum back in, he shoved forward, catching her in the side with the shield and knocking her to the ground.

He backed up and relaxed, although he didn't lower his scutum or gladius entirely. He stood up straight, taking deep breaths, sweat dripping down his face.

Marpesia lay on the ground, her scale armor rising and falling heavily as she worked to catch her breath. Balling up her first and lifting a boot clad foot, she punched the ground with the heel of her fist, stomping the sole of her boot into the ground at the same time.

"Fuck!" she yelled in Sarmatian.

Although Lucius was still learning the rudiments of Sarmatian, he'd long known most of the swear words. Lucius shoved his gladius into its scabbard and walked over to her axe, picking it up and transferring it to his left hand so he grasped it with the hand holding his scutum. He stepped closer to her and leaned down, offering his arm.

She squinted, pursing her lips, and hesitate. He gave her a closed-mouth smile, spreading his fingers to reiterate the offer. She reached up, grasping his forearm and planting her feet, ready for Lucius to help her up. On her feet, he returned her axe to her and stepped back, unsure if they were still engaged or done.

She barked an order over her shoulder. Aella stepped out of the crowd, walking toward her mistress, and nodded respectfully to Marpesia before acknowledging Lucius. Marpesia looked at Lucius, a smile on her face. She called off a string of Sarmatian that Lucius couldn't catch at his early stage of learning.

Aella gave half bow to Lucius. "My mistress congratulates you on a fine display of your martial skills. She is most impressed."

"I'm likewise impressed with her skills," he replied to Aella.

He turned his gaze to Marpesia. She'd tossed her shield to one of her warriors and shoved her axe into her belt so she could remove her helmet. Her face glistened with sweat, her reddish-brown curls plastered to her forehead. Her smile broadened as she watched him looking her over. The combination robbed Lucius of his next words as his heart, finally calming, skipped a beat and picked up its pace under her bright eyes.

Addressing her directly, he bowed respectfully before her magnetic gaze drew his eyes back to hers. "You're one of the finest warriors I've ever exchanged blows with. I look forward to fighting by your side."

She bowed her head, acknowledging his sincere compliment after Aella translated it. Looking toward some of her warriors, Marpesia called out to one of them. "Kumis!"

He tossed her a leather skin. She caught it and pulled the plug from the neck and drank deeply, sighing happily after. She closed the distance to Lucius and offered him the skin.

"She wishes to share a drink to celebrate the excellent fight," Aella translated.

Not wishing to be rude, and also quite thirsty, Lucius took the skin and tipped it to his lips, drinking deeply. He wasn't sure why the Sarmatians looked so eager, almost appearing to be holding back laughter. As soon as his mouth filled with the sour, fetid liquid, he got the joke. Thick and tasting of cheese left in the sun, he quickly shoved the skin back to Marpesia as he stepped back, trying to keep from gagging.

Failing, he bent over, shielding himself from view behind his scutum, and heaved up the kumis and everything else in his stomach. Marpesia howled with laughter, breaking the dam as Roman and Sarmatian alike guffawed as the greatest soldier Roma had ever produced unleashed his lunch upon the hard dirt, defeated by the unknown fermented substance. Once he got himself under control, he kicked some dirt over his mess and stepped away from it.

Marpesia, raising her arms to the sky to call everyone to quiet, called out, "And thus have I breached the great Centurio Immortalis's defenses, defeating him two blows to one!"

Everyone howled with laughter. After a few moments, when Lucius realized what she'd done and said, in only a slightly accented Hellenic, he started laughing too. Catching her gaze, he smiled at her and bowed, acknowledging the defeat.

Marpesia walked back over, smiling broadly and kindly, and offered him the skin again.

"No, thank you."

"This one is just water. Rinse your mouth out," she said, offering the skin again.

He took it and did as suggested, spitting the water into the dirt. "Thank you. What is that awful stuff?"

"Kumis? Fermented mare's milk. It's the lifeblood of our people. You'll get used to it, but it's always a nasty trick to play on southerners when they've never tried it before."

"What if I'd had it before or liked it?"

"Fortunes of war," she shrugged, chuckling and patting his steel-clad shoulder.

"Your command of the language of the Hellenes is quite good."

"I speak Latin too, if you please." She gave Lucius a saucy bow.

"I'm afraid my command of your dialect is much more rudimentary. Why the ruse?"

She tipped her head to the side and shrugged. "Letting Aella play at translator gives me time to think, to formulate answers. It lets me watch the room. It gives me an advantage when I'm only thought of as an uneducated barbarian. Come, let us go drink and speak of matters. I'll teach you to speak a proper tongue."

The crowd was dissipating as officers shouted orders, getting men back to work or training after the afternoon's entertainment. Marpesia turned and strode away. Lucius's eyes fell to her hypnotically swaying hips under the three-tailed coat of scale armor.

She turned over her shoulder and smirked, knowing she'd scored a third strike with her hips. She gestured for him to follow. "Come."

NINE

WHEN WORD of the approach of Marpesia's remaining warriors arrived, Lucius and Marpesia rode out from their camp to the north of Constantius's bridge to greet the arriving forces. Pisakar sent a century of troops to escort their Centurio and the chieftain of the Wolf Clan. Keeping a respectable distance behind the two leaders, they'd be able to plug the bridge if called to hold it in case of a double cross from Constantius and his troops filtering west. Although they didn't expect anything, it was best to be prepared.

Since Marpesia had revealed her ability to speak directly with Lucius, he found himself in her company almost constantly during the daylight hours, and often in the evening as they planned out their campaign through the mountains of what used to be the Roman province of Dacia and the Dacian Kingdom before that. If they weren't looking over a map and checking supplies, she'd often invite him to dine with her in private, ostensibly under the guise of more planning, but in reality, they mostly talked about the small things—the places they'd seen, the people they'd fought against, the dangers of the fanged demons.

Lucius, whose eyes had followed her constantly, found his feelings toward the pretty warrior deepening and growing more confusing, more complicated. He'd been attracted to women before, indulged it even on occasion, but he'd never had the depth of feelings Marpesia generated, never wanted anyone the way he wanted Marpesia. And while he wasn't experienced with women like some men he'd known in the past, he thought she might be attracted to him too. She'd been less than subtle thus far.

He couldn't help feeling the man she was attracted to, the Centurio Immortalis, was no more, that he was living a lie stripped of meaning, posing as his former self for the sake of propriety. Yet he couldn't push her away—he craved her attention, her company.

As they waited by the side of the road as the first of his remaining cohorts crossed the bridge and continued to their temporary fort, a rider leading a magnificent, tall golden horse split off from the column of Roxolani, making a line for Marpesia. As they drew nearer, Lucius was overwhelmed at the beauty of the animal.

Its soft pale coat shone brightly, as if it was coated in gold leaf, and its golden mane flew out behind it. Lucius admired the sleek lines and power of the horse; it was taller than the ponies the Romans rode and the steppes pony Marpesia sat on now. The horse seemed to catch the light of the sun and reflect it out more power-fully. A noise from Marpesia drew his eyes to her face and the look of profound longing in her eyes.

"Marpesia!" the rider called out, saying something else in the tongue of the Roxolani.

"He says he's brought an old friend for me," Marpesia translated, sliding off her pony. She strode toward the rider and the golden mare, wrapping her arms around the horse's neck before letting it go and taking the bridle in her hands. She looked into the animal's eyes while she stroked its cheek. "Come, Centurio, meet my... I guess her name would translate to Day Star."

Lucius slid off his gelding and walked over to Marpesia. The man who'd brought her offered to take the reins of Lucius's pony as he had Marpesia's.

"I've missed her," Marpesia said as Lucius reached out to stroke the other cheek of the horse.

"Why didn't you ride her to Constantinopolis?"

"Your Roman imperators are greedy, seeking to take that which doesn't belong to them, always grasping for more. I would not bring a temptation like this with me. She is too precious to me."

"I've never seen a more beautiful horse. What breed is she?"

"She's a Sogdian. I got her in Sogdiana." Marpesia rested her cheek against the horse's.

"Raiding?"

Marpesia laughed. "No, I traded for her and a few others of her kind. I want to breed them. I don't like fighting if I can avoid it. I love my Wolves and don't wish to shed their blood in needless fighting."

"Yet, here you are, about to march with me through dangerous mountains in winter to attack a far larger force."

She sighed, hiding her face in her mare's mane. "With the Romans and Sassanians to the south, the Alans to the east and Goths coming in from the west and north, soon there will be no land left for my people to roam free. Joining with the Romans is our only hope of staving off the Goths and preserving my people's way of life for a little longer."

The truth of her admission and the honest assessment of the potential doom of her people cut Lucius to the quick. His people had been largely Romanized by the time he was born, creating a Romano-Gallic culture. More immediately, his own way of life had been destroyed by Constantius. His heart ached for his loss and the loss Marpesia saw for her people.

Taking her hand, he guided her gently into his arms, her scale mail rattling against the steel bands of his lorica. He wrapped one arm around her waist and slid his hand under her thick mane of hair, cupping her neck as she lay her head against the bear hair on the shoulders of his black cloak. When she looked back up at him, her eyes shined bright with tears she was holding back in view of every-one., he saw the tracks her tears had traced against her soft cheek. Smiling gently, He brought his hand up ran his thumb along her cheekbone.

Looking deep in her eyes, he found a question he didn't know how to answer surrounded by vulnerability. In that moment, he wanted to lower his head and brush his lips against hers. He was about to give in to his desire when her mare snorted and lipped at her hair, pulling a laugh from her throat.

Marpesia pulled back and let her horse rest its head against her shoulder as she reached under its head and rubbed its cheek. "She misses me and wonders why I pay attention to another. They're a very loyal breed. Strong, fast, and they can run for days." She sighed and took a deep breath. "Centurio, I need to ride, to feel the wind in my hair. I need to feel free for a little while. Will you ride with me?"

"Do you need to settle your people in?"

"No, Aella can manage that for now."

Lucius nodded and took the reins of his gelding, leaping into the saddle. He trotted over to the century who had escorted him out. "Watch the bridge. I'll be back later."

"Aye, Centurio!" The centurion saluted and issued the orders to move the men closer to the edge of the bridge.

Marpesia was waiting a short distance away. He trotted over to her, and she guided her horse alongside his, trotting for a while until they rode far enough away so they could play. With a playful whoop, Marpesia kicked her mare into a gallop. Her joy at the simple pleasure of riding washed over Lucius, inspiring a carefree laugh from his lips. He watched her race away before nudging his nameless gelding to follow.

The Sogdian was indeed fast, elegant in a full run, agile as Marpesia turned the mare, dashing off in a new direction. They were a pair in flight, working as one. Marpesia's mane of auburn hair flew behind her, the golden mane of her mare flicking her in the face. Lucius didn't try to catch up or match her. He knew his mount was adequate for his needs, yet still untested in battle. He contented himself with watching her. Though she had never seemed reserved, he felt like this was Marpesia in her truest essence — at one with her surroundings and free.

He had to assume his horsemaster knew his business when selecting this mount for him, but the animal didn't inspire love the way Marpesia's did. As she galloped left then right in a long zigzag, Lucius kept his horse on a straight path to keep up with her, more interested in witnessing her skills as a rider and the power of the animal under her than pressing his placid gelding to stretch for all he was worth and keep up with a superior beast. He envied her and her openness, wishing he didn't feel so trapped by his obligations. Wishing he could break out of the I he and time had constructed.

When Marpesia slowed to a trot to cool her horse, Lucius rode up beside her. "She's a fine horse."

Marpesia, breathing heavily but with a broad grin splitting her face, laughed and directed her horse to the side then back again. This time she walked her horse forward, the horse lifting its forelegs high and setting them down as if marching on parade. Marpesia continued dancing her horse around Lucius, showing her off—showing off for him. He smiled wistfully at her antics. He'd give anything to be with her, but doubted he had anything worth giving.

Inside, he knew he shouldn't indulge her. He didn't want to lead her on, didn't want her attaching herself to his dying star. Yet he couldn't resist the smile on her face as she displayed her skills with her horse, only achievable through great practice and a close bond to the animal. When she'd turn and catch his gaze, the smile in her gray eyes drove away his anger and melancholy, bringing a genuine smile to his lips.

When she'd finished her display, she trotted over to Lucius, sliding off her horse. "Walk with me for a while?"

They headed back toward their fort, strolling quietly in the early fall afternoon, enjoying the mild sun and cool breeze. After a while, Marpesia angled toward him until her shoulders bumped into his, their armor clanging lightly. He turned his head to meet her gaze, returning her gentle smile. She slid her hand into his, intertwining their fingers.

He closed his eyes while they walked, a content smile on his face, and basked in the breeze and sun, enjoying the feel of Marpesia's hand. When he opened his eyes, they walked toward a small copse of trees. Marpesia picketed the horses so they could crop at the grass, before sitting on a fallen tree, the tail of her scale coat flopped over the back of the log.

"Come sit by me, Centurio."

"You should call me Lucius."

She tipped her head to the side, smiling up at him, and patted the spot next to her. He nodded and sat.

"I'd much prefer to lie in the grass on my back, but then I'd have to clean my armor," Marpesia said, returning her hand to his.

Lucius chuckled. "Indeed."

"You know what? Soon we'll be climbing into the mountains and the sun will not warm our faces."

She stood up and unbuckled the sword belt around her waist, leaning it against the log. She pulled the axe off her back and set it next to the sword. Tugging the leather straps that ran down the seam under her left armpit, she unbuckled her scale mail.

"Help me off with this, please?"

Lucius stood and held the shoulders while she slid out of it. She took it from him and spread it carefully over the log.

Looking him up and down, she smirked. "You're overdressed, Lucius."

He thought better of stripping down to his tunic in what wasn't technically Roman territory. If his men were to see him, he'd look ridiculous. It would be beneath the Centurio Immortalis's dignity to lie on his back in the grass. Then, he reminded himself—the Centurio Immortalis had dignity, but he no longer existed. Waffling between feeling dejected and rebellious, he chose rebellion.

He removed his cingulum militare and laid it over the fallen tree, then pulled off his baldric and gladius, setting them beside Marpesia's weapons. He pulled the leather thong from the front loops and shoved it in his pouch, then pulled his lorica off, resting it on the log.

It was an unusual feeling, being out in the world without his armor on. It had become his skin over the last two centuries, constantly wrapped about him. He took a deep, slow breath, letting the air expand his chest and stretch the muscles of his torso. He let it out slowly, taking in another breath.

Marpesia held her hand out to him. "Shall we?"

He took her hand and followed her out into a small clearing sprinkled with a few late blooming wild flowers. She let go of his hand and flopped onto the ground, lying on her back in her three-tailed coat and striped leggings and tunic, the toes of her ornately embroidered boots pointing toward the heavens. He lowered himself to the ground, stretching out beside her, the grass tickling the bare skin of his calves.

Thinking back to the last time he'd done this, over two hundred and twenty years ago, he smiled fondly at the warm memory and sighed.

Marpesia's hand sought his, seemingly unable to be away from it for long. "I haven't done something this frivolous in ages."

"I was just remembering the last time I lay in the grass like this. It was a long time ago," Lucius replied, feeling more relaxed than he'd felt in a while.

"When was that?"

"Oh, I'd just come home after Traianus's second Dacian war. I'd been promoted to Optio and had a furlough. I walked home from our fort on the Rhenis back to the village where I was born. My parent's house no longer felt like my home, so I found myself wandering like I used to as a boy. I ended up in the forest by our village."

He smiled at the memory. "In the spring, bluebells bloom, and I'd caught them at their peak. I used to escape my chores in a clearing among the bluebells looking for monsters in the clouds. So I found a clearing and laid down. Eventually my father came looking for me and joined me as we looked up into the sky."

"How long ago was that?"

He hummed as he did the math. "Two hundred and twenty-two years ago, I think."

"You really are that old?"

"I am."

They lay in silence, her warm hand in his as clouds passed above, until the sound of birds returned to the copse. After a while, she took her hand back and rolled onto her side, looking down at him. She reached across him and caressed his cheek, tipping his head toward her. He wasn't quick enough to hide the nervousness in his eyes as his breathing quickened.

"Lucius, why do you keep fighting with yourself?"

He cleared his throat. "What do you mean?"

"I know you want me. I see the way you look at me."

"How do I look at you?" His licked his lips, his mouth going dry.

"It's… It's equal parts fear and longing. Like you're seeing something you've never wanted more, yet fear what it'll do to you."

"You've keen eyes. I fear what wanting you will do to me. I feel old. Used up. Too old for one such as you."

"I know what I see in you, and those things are not what I see. I've seen into your eyes. My eyes may be gray, but yours are dark, haunted. I know what I see, and I know I want you to stop fighting with yourself."

She ran her hand through his hair along the side of his head, bringing her hand forward under his ear, onto his cheek. The warmth of her palm against his face felt hotter than the sun of the Syrian desert. His breaths grew shallow as she lowered her head, her eyes closing as she drew closer.

The first brush of her lips over his was tentative, soft to see if the kiss would be accepted and reciprocated, sending warmth surging though his body as his stomach lurched. When he didn't say stop or turn his head, she continued. Lucius's resolve melted under the soft insistence of her lips, her intensity meeting its match in his as he responded. Reaching up, he ran his hand down her side, letting it rest on the swell of her hip. When her tongue teased against his lips, he parted them, letting his tongue meet hers.

As she pulled back, he opened his eyes, looking up into hers. His breath came in short gasps through his nostrils as he kept his lips clamped shut, afraid of what words might spill out. While he could control that, he couldn't control the fear and longing Marpesia had recognized pouring out of his eyes. In hers, he saw his salvation but knew it would be her damnation. His only future was hunting the monsters who prayed on humanity, drinking their blood.

"Why do you look at me like that, Lucius?" Her eyes widened, her brows pinching together slightly.

Lucius warred with himself, wanting her, wanting to push her way. "Marpesia, I…"

She stopped his words with her lips, and he lost his war with his better sense and gave in to his desire to feel the heat pouring through her lips into him. If he'd died in that moment, he would do so happily to avoid the consequences of giving in to his longing for Marpesia.

When she pulled back for a second time, he was left wanting, his lips grasping for more. After a moment, when his mind returned to thought, he caught the sound that had interfered with their kiss. Someone was calling his name.

He sighed, shaking his head. It was probably for the best that someone had interrupted them, but he still wished for all the world they hadn't. When his eyes met Marpesia's, he could see the frustration in hers. She didn't seem torn about her attraction to him. She was winning her campaign only to be interrupted before completing the victory.

"I suppose we should return to camp before they turn out everyone to look for us." It was a reasonable suggestion, but Marpesia still frowned at having to admit it.

They stood up, helped each other into their armor, and grabbed their horses, walking out of the copse back into the open grasses. When Lucius spotted the giant form of Pisakar dwarfing the pony he rode, Lucius raised his hand and waved to his friend, hating him just a little bit for pulling him back to reality. Before they mounted up, Marpesia reached out and squeezed his hand, then leapt into her saddle, trotting off to join Pisakar and the few dozen Roman and Sarmatian horse soldiers he'd brought with him.

When Lucius and Marpesia merged with the small band, Pisakar pulled his pony beside Lucius's. "I hope I didn't interrupt anything special."

"You did," Lucius said, kicking his horse into a canter so he could pull to the front of the group, ending his conversation with Pisakar before it could even start.

TEN

ONCE THE SARMATIANS WERE CAMPED, Lucius and Pisakar gathered in the command tent with Marpesia, Aella, and several of her war chiefs to discuss the next stage. Since Marpesia owned the map they were using and the strategy to go with it, she led the discussion.

Pointing to the eastern edge of the mountains and the pass they planned on using to exit and attack the Goths from, she cleared her throat. "When we agreed on our strategy with your Dominus, I sent riders with dispatches on the ships he sent north. They were ordered to move our wagons and herds across the plain." She traced her finger along a gap between the Euxeinos Pontos and the mountains. "By the reports we had, we should have had enough time to get them safely across and moved into the high valleys where they'll be safe from the eyes of our enemies."

Lucius, pulling his eyes away from the graceful lines of her fingers and hand, caught her attention. "Will you know for sure if they made it?"

"I hope so. I have teams of messengers coming through the mountains along our planned path, as well as south and west along the southern edge of the mountains. One or both should reach us to let us know their status. With the wagons and supplies we have, there is plenty to get through the mountains feeding both beast and soldier, although by the end, we might be on dried rations. The wagons and herds will get us fresh supplies and meat."

Lucius nodded his head. "Excellent. Can your wagons make it through the mountains easily enough?"

"They have before. What good is visiting our Iazyges cousins if we don't bring goods to trade with them? My Wolves are very capable of moving swiftly through mountains or the steppes."

"I didn't realize your clan was so large," Lucius replied.

"We're not the largest, but we're a free people and many come to join if they wish. Also, my cousin has loaned me a sizable force of warriors and wagons. The majority of those in the mountains will be his people. They'll be scouting the movement of the Goths. I don't expect any of Constantius's messengers to get through to us once we get into the mountains." When she said Constantius's name, her lips rose into a bit of a sneer, saying his name with an annoyed bite.

Lucius's eyebrows lifted at her vehemence. "Do you doubt the competence of the Dominus Noster's troops?"

"I'm not sure if it's his competence or his lack of interest in this part of the campaign."

Lucius nodded, ceding the point to her. He was quite sure it would be a bonus for Constantius if Lucius and his legion died of exposure in the mountains or were wiped out by the Goths. Sighing, he asked Marpesia to continue.

"That's it, really. It's a simple plan. The difficulty comes in executing it. We're going to need luck if we don't want to get snowed in while we're in the mountains."

He smiled and nodded, turning to Pisakar. "How are our supplies looking?"

"Food and fodder are solid. I'm concerned about winter gear. We're a bit thin on heavy woolens."

"We can provide those," Marpesia interjected. "Aella?"

"The sheep were very prosperous this year. We'd planned on bringing cloaks, tunics, leggings, and other wool goods to sell along the border this fall. We have a very good supply available."

Luke nodded appreciatively. "Pisakar, please coordinate with Aella. Ensure we have a full accounting so we can compensate them. Dye everything black."

Aella looked the tall, broad Black man over, an impressed look on her face. Lucius turned back to Marpesia, who hadn't been watching her second making eyes at Lucius's Kushite friend, but had been watching Lucius's face instead.

Lucius nodded. "How are your people doing after the long march here, Marpesia?"

"Give us three days' rest and we'll be ready to go. We've been putting our horses on their winter feed to get them fattened up, so they're in good shape, but they could use a few days cropping fresh grass."

"Alright, unless anyone has anything to add, we move out in four days."

The Sarmatians filed out of the room, leaving Pisakar and Lucius.

Pisakar looked over the map. "She's very competent."

"I noticed," Lucius replied, pacing back and forth on the other side of the table.

"I noticed you noticing. What's going on with you two? She's always watching you. Even when she's talking, her eyes track your movement."

"I don't know, Pisakar." He stopped pacing, looking at Pisakar. "We kissed the other day."

"I thought you said it would be inappropriate to dally with an ally?" Pisakar gave him a saucy look.

"She seems to be of the same opinion as you, that I should stop fighting with myself. If you hadn't interrupted, I might have."

"I'm sorry, Lucius."

"It's probably for the best. The Centurio Immortalis is no more. Once I crossed that bridge..." He gestured in the direction of Constantius's bridge. "I accepted my banishment and all it implies."

"I've seen how men and women look at you, Lucius. I've seen the hero worship in their eyes, the adoration at an idol. You're the incorruptible servant of Roma, the great warrior, the protector against the dark night. You could have bedded hundreds seeking to have a moment with a celebrity of your stature." Pisakar walked around the table so he stood directly in front of Lucius. "You've only taken up with a couple people in all the years I've known you. And the looks they gave you weren't empty-headed worship."

Pisakar rested his hand on Lucius's shoulder. "I think she's genuinely attracted to you. She may have gone to Constantinopolis to gain the Centurio Immortalis as an ally, but she left looking to grow closer with Lucius Silvanius." Pisakar dropped the honorific "Ferrata" Lucius had earned in the legions to hammer home the point. He thought Marpesia was pursuing Lucius because she was interested in the man, not the legend.

Lucius started pacing again. "Maybe… But what's left of me? In a few months, my legion will be no more. The only home I've ever known will be denied to me. My name will be erased from Roma's history." He stopped, turning to look at Pisakar. "I may have never wanted to be an imperator, but I didn't want to be a nobody either. I wanted to make my mark on history."

"And you have. Every village you've saved, every fanged monster you've killed, the thousands of evil creatures your legion has sent to their final rest. How many people are alive because of you? I know you're hurting, my friend. You're grieving a profound loss. But I also know you're tired of being the Centurio Immortalis. It's become a part you're playing. It's as much a piece of armor you put on at the beginning of the day as your actual lorica. Now, it's been stripped from you and you feel naked without it. You feel adrift without its purpose to guide you, but you still have that purpose. Mithras isn't letting go of you just because the Roman Empire has."

Lucius sighed and flopped down in a camp chair, putting his head in his hand. "You always speak truth, Pisakar."

"Does she know?"

"Know what? That I'm attracted to her? That I can't stop thinking about her?"

Pisakar laughed, the deep rumbling sound filling the room. "No. I mean, yes, I'm sure she does know that. Your eyes never leave her. I meant does she know about your banishment?"

Lucius shook his head. "At least I don't think so. I haven't told her." He thought back to all his interactions with her since Constantius had placed his doom upon Lucius. "I don't think it was mentioned around her, even before I knew she could understand Hellenic and Latin. I kept it to myself on the march to Oescus and told none of the men. As far as I know, you're the only one who knows."

"Maybe you should," Pisakar suggested.

"I don't know. That's a lot to put out there." Lucius thought of several reasons he shouldn't tell her, mostly the fact they didn't know each other very well, and he still had no idea what his life would be in the future. "What does it matter for now? We're marching to war, assuming we don't freeze to death in the mountains."

Pisakar folded his arms over his chest and shook his head. "I know you're in pain, Lucius, but don't go looking for a glorious way out. You have all the time in the world and more than a reputation. Here's something to think about. We've been camped out on the northern border, moving from the Rhenis to the Danuvius, fending off invasions from the fanged demons. Making friends with a tribe of Sarmatians wouldn't be a bad thing. You can hunt your enemy from this side of the border too. You've developed a reputation of trust with those the empire calls barbarians. Many of the people you've saved from a dark fate of serving the night demons weren't Romans."

Lucius nodded his head, staring off into the distance.

"I'll leave you to think it over, my friend." Pisakar patted Lucius on the shoulder and left their command tent.

WHEN MARPESIA and Lucius decided their forces were ready to move out, they broke camp. Lucius, on behalf of himself, his men, and his allies, sought the blessing of Mithras on their upcoming enterprise and paid homage to the legion's patron deity. Marpesia and her Roxolani Wolf Clan plunged their swords into the ground and called on their fire god and their war god to see them safely through the mountains and onto the glory of victory over their enemies. Prayers given, they set out.

Each day saw them delving deeper into the Montes Sarmatici, the air growing colder and thinner. Despite Lucius's deep melancholy, Marpesia and Pisakar did their best to lighten his mood, seeming to coordinate to ensure one or the other was nearby. Although, when Pisakar was not around, Lucius, either on foot or hoof, sought Marpesia's company under the guise of getting to know his allies better and to integrate himself into their workings so when the time came, they'd trust him and follow his orders.

They saw few people, most choosing to avoid the party of Roman Legionnaires and mounted Sarmatians. Occasionally, they'd spot a curious shepherd gathering their herds to move to lower country in advance of the coming winter, the season more imminent with each day.

A few days march in, Lucius woke to the sight of his breath steaming out of his mouth. Pulling his cloak around him, he stuck his head out of his tent to greet a skiff of snow on the ground with more falling from the sky.

He dressed and sought Marpesia. "You know these mountains better than I do. What do you make of the weather?"

"This isn't bad, and we're about to wind our way down to the lowlands. We'll be fine to march through this."

Lucius smiled at her. "Care to break your fast with me while everyone finishes tearing down the camp?"

"I'd love to. I could use a hot meal."

That became their pattern, Lucius becoming more creative in finding reasons to consult with the leader of his allies. For her part, she sought out Lucius as much as he did her. On the few occasions she accompanied her advance scouts, Lucius missed her, feeling like something was absent. His eyes roved restlessly, looking for her wild hair or brightly colored cloak or the golden Sogdian. On a few occasions, he'd turn and start to speak her name only to not see her and remember she was gone. Pisakar caught him at it a few times, chuckling and shaking his head at Lucius's inevitable scowl. His friend was entirely too observant.

When he couldn't find other distractions, he avoided thinking about his banishment by thinking about Marpesia, finally admitting to himself he was infatuated with the beautiful warrior. She possessed the qualities he found most attractive in a person. She was a competent leader, respected by her people, a skilled fighter, and highly intelligent. Her spirit, her untamed joy in living, made her unique in his eyes. When they took time to ride out together, finding some pretense of responsibility, she couldn't help but laugh joyously as the wind whipped through her hair while her Sogdian stretched out finding its speed.

Lucius was nearly as impressed with the beast as he was with its rider. The horse was fiercely loyal to Marpesia, elegant and efficient in its gate, and seemed tireless, deriving just as much joy from running as Marpesia. He never pushed his gelding to keep up, knowing the animal was good for what it had been raised to do but was no match for the stride and spirit of the Sogdian. He'd have to live vicariously through Marpesia's joy in her mount as he watched them dash about.

So far, their passage had gone smoothly. They'd been able to move through the growing cold weather and occasional snow with relative ease. The heavy food the troops had been feeding on for weeks prior had fattened them up nicely, giving them the insulation and reserves to handle the cold and the hard marching. As they worked their way through the mountain lowlands, doing their best to avoid any villages or do anything to prompt an attack, they drew ever closer to the part of the journey Lucius knew would be most difficult as they drove deeper into winter.

When their scouts linked up with the messengers coming through from Marpesia's advance position, Lucius breathed a sigh of relief that they were once again connected to their world. They still had a few weeks of hard marching in bad weather, assuming they didn't get snowed in or there weren't other delays, but knowing Marpesia's other forces and their supplies were in place took one worry off Lucius's shoulders.

It was about a week after their first contact with the messengers of their allies, and Lucius was about to fall asleep, when Marpesia stepped up her campaign to win his heart. He'd finished looking over the day's reports and was ready to slide under the furs and blankets on his camp bed. Stripped down, he practically flung himself into the bed to feel its warm embrace. He felt sleep approaching when a blast of freezing air ripped through the tent briefly only to be stopped with the closing of his tent's flap.

A woman cleared her throat to alert him to her presence. "I'm cold."

"Where's Aella?" Lucius asked groggily.

"She's found another bed to warm tonight."

"Isn't she your lover?"

"Yes, but just because we're lovers doesn't mean I own her. She's free to seek others out if she so desires."

"And now you're cold," Lucius replied.

"Yes."

Lucius, too tired to fight his attraction to Marpesia tonight, lifted his arm, raising the edge of the blankets. He shivered as a rush of cold air infiltrated his warm sanctuary. The rustle of clothes being shed and the sound of bare feet padding toward him were followed by a feminine body jumping into his bed. He rolled to his side and scooted over, making room for her as she turned her back to him and wiggled into his warmth. Her curly hair tickled his nose as he moved his head around to find a space where it wouldn't.

Leaning back into him, she rotated just enough to bring her face around. "Kiss me, Lucius."

He pushed himself up on his elbow and brushed his lips across hers.

"Nuh uh. More."

Lowering his head, he brought his lips into contact with hers and let go of himself for a moment, coaxing her mouth open with his tongue, and embraced his desire to be with her. When he finally pulled back, Marpesia made a contented sound and rolled back over, pushing her back into Lucius to snuggle in closer.

"Sleep well, Marpesia." He rested his hand on her bare waist, his thumb resting on the cloth of her chest binding.

"Mmm," was all Marpesia replied with as she fell into sleep.

ELEVEN

THE NEXT NIGHT AFTER THAT, Lucius found Marpesia in his bed before he fell asleep. Beyond the kiss he and Marpesia exchanged before sleep, nothing happened other than two warm bodies sharing heat and comfort. Lucius wasn't sure why she didn't press him further, although he was glad he didn't have to make a decision about taking their association to a deeper level. He was grateful for the exhaustion of each day's hard march rendering them ready for sleep.

After the first few nights, he waited, hoping she'd return for another. When she inevitably did, he heaved a silent sigh of relief. Lucius had grown to crave the contact of her skin against his, sleeping deeper than he had in ages with her lying next to him. He even looked forward to the tickle of her hair on his face, missing it when it wasn't there. In the morning, they'd rise to the first sounds of the waking camp, exchange another kiss, then dress, Marpesia slipping out on silent soft-soled boots. And each day, as the tent flap closed behind her, he'd smile sadly at her departure, wishing they weren't marching to a battle where they would be, in most probability, hugely outnumbered.

On the morning of their last day before meeting with Marpesia's other force, Lucius sat tying the heavy winter caligae after Marpesia left, when Pisakar announced himself and stepped in. "I see she finally took more direct measures?"

"What are you talking about?" Lucius replied, not looking up from his task.

"Marpesia. I just saw her sneaking out. So she finally bedded you, eh?"

Lucius sighed, shaking his head, and sat back in his camp chair. "No. Nothing is going on. She's just been cold. Aella has found another bed to warm, so Marpesia comes in here at night to share my blankets and body heat. That's it."

"Really? She's coming in here to just get warm? And you're under your blankets together and neither of you do anything about it?" Pisakar sounded incredulous. He looked like he wanted to say more, but when he saw the warning look on Lucius's face, he changed the subject. "Anyway, got a report back. Looks like the advanced forces have our fort ready. It'll be a hard day going straight through, but we can get to camp and bed down."

Lucius stood and made room for his valet to bring in his breakfast. "Any update on the disposition of the Tervingi?"

"Yes, they're gathering, but not in large numbers yet. They're being very cautious. They suspect something is in these mountains, but they don't know what. They've been sending out scouts, but so far, we've captured all or most of them. Our allies are very thorough and know the hills and mountains well."

"Excellent. Have our forces started on advance fortifications?"

"Yes. Our allies have shown them a good spot to build our wall. The Roxolani are screening their work from prying eyes. I've started our first units moving as the rest finish packing their tents and get some hot food in themselves for the march."

"Alright, I want you to go with that group to ensure everything is ready. I'll want a report as soon as I arrive."

Pisakar saluted and left the tent to carry out his orders. Lucius, now free to attend to his breakfast, shoveled the warm porridge into his mouth, savoring the richness of the added pork belly and dried fruit. It was a thick bowl designed to fuel them for the march and against the cold. As soon as he finished, he left the tent for his people to tear down while he saw to the rest of camp.

It had been a long, hard, cold march through the mountains, and barring a few small injuries, their preparations had seen them through. He just hoped when they got into camp tonight, they'd have a day or so to rest the men and their Roxolani allies before meeting the Tervingi in battle.

With the Goths now blocking the passes out onto the plains below and the storms building up the snow behind them, the only option was to win through their enemy's lines. As Lucius surveyed everything from the back of his nameless gelding, Martininius found him.

"Any final messages or reports that need to go out, Centurio?" Martininius asked.

"No. If there's something we missed, we'll deliver it in person tonight. You're dismissed to finish any preparations you need to make."

"Aye, Centurio." Martininius saluted and disappeared into the busy hive of activity.

Nodding to himself at the progress, he walked his horse toward the eastern gate, his lead cohort forming up for today's march. The sound of Marpesia's jingling tack alerted him to her presence as she pulled her tall Sogdian in next to him.

"I hope you slept well, Centurio," Marpesia said, looking straight ahead.

"Very well, thank you." When he found the Pilus Prior, he waved the man over. "Ready to move out?"

"Aye, Centurio."

"Good. You have your orders. The rest of the legion will be along shortly."

The Pilus Prior chuckled and nodded, giving Lucius a casual salute before turning and marching to the front of his cohort. He drew his whistle out and gave the order to march. As the cohort moved forward, Lucius turned his gelding and moved it so he was side by side with Marpesia and her mount.

Lucius, remembering the warm feel of her body, couldn't contain the smile from spreading across his face. "Are your Wolves ready to move out?"

"Of course. I sent a hundred of my best mounted archers with Pisakar to act as scouts. The rest are ready to respond to your orders." She let her eyelids grow heavy, sensually licking her lips.

Lucius lost his train of thought, imagining her lips on his, halting himself before he could imagine them kissing more than his lips. He cleared his throat and gave his head a little shake, his cheeks flushing pink. He hoped Aella wouldn't find her way back to Marpesia's bed tonight; the thought of sleeping alone nearly pushed aside the good mood caused by Marpesia's flirting. Seeing his reaction, she laughed, the sound a bright tinkling bell on the cold morning.

The sound returned the smile to Lucius's face. "I should make sure the rest of my people are ready to move out."

Marpesia, having routed Lucius yet another time, laughed some more. But as Lucius passed, she rolled the hand resting on her thigh over, extending it slightly. Without thinking, Lucius extended his hand, gripping hers briefly before letting his fingers drag over her palm as he rode out of range.

THE NEXT MORNING, Lucius woke in their fort with Marpesia curled up next to him. Upon getting into camp the previous night, he conferred with Pisakar, determining they had time and issued an order allowing his men a late morning to catch up on sleep. The advanced cohorts and the Roxolani could take care of their defenses for the day, and a horn blast would summon the loafers if they were needed.

Marpesia snored softly, deep in sleep. Lucius, snuggling in closer, decided to rejoin her in the land of his dreams. He rarely slept in, except on nights where he hunted the blood demons into the late hours, but those were rare. The hundreds of trained and skilled hunters among his legion could handle those tasks. Besides, if he could, he preferred finding their nests and attacking during the daylight hours deadly to the creatures of darkness. The world could wait today, at least for a little while. Lucius closed his eyes, the scent of Marpesia coaxing him back to sleep.

ALL PREPARATIONS HAD BEEN MADE and tomorrow Lucius would give the command to attack. Still maintaining the fiction of her separate tent, Marpesia joined Lucius for a private meal in his quarters, ostensibly as two commanders conferring, although all the decisions had been made for the day and new decisions hadn't presented their needs yet.

"Princeps Primus Centurio Lucius Silvanius Ferrata, I would ask a boon of you ere we go to war tomorrow."

Responding to her formal tone, he replied in kind, "And what boon would you have of me, Marpesia, Clan Chieftain of the Wolves?"

She smiled softly. "I would have you gird me for war tomorrow and allow me the honor of doing so for you."

He met her gaze with the intensity of his own. "Nothing would please me more."

When they finished their meal, Marpesia had her battle gear brought to Lucius's tent. Planning on rising early to be in place tomorrow, they made ready for bed, stripping down to the minimalist of coverings, Lucius in his waist cloth, Marpesia in a similar loin cloth and her chest wrappings. She hesitated for a moment before unwinding the chest wrappings.

Stopping just before the final unwind, she looked at Lucius. "I wish to sleep in comfort tonight."

Lucius nodded. When she was finished unwrapping the bindings, she walked up to Lucius, running her arms over his chest and winding them around his neck, pulling him into a kiss. Goose pimples rose on both their skins as the cold tried to rob them of the heat they were generating. When Marpesia pulled back, she rested her head on Lucius's shoulder. He felt shivers vibrating through their bodies, so he reluctantly let go of Marpesia and climbed into his bed, making room for her. She slid in after him, pulling the covers up and over them. Tonight, she faced Lucius, her hand on his cheek as she stared into his eyes in the dim light cast by the coals in the brazier.

She took a breath, her mouth opening, her eyes closing in a blink she held for a moment before opening her eyes again. "Lucius, I… I need to speak openly to you, while we have the opportunity, before…" She left it hanging, not needing to go into detail with battle looming on the horizon.

"As do I."

"I never thought to meet someone like you. Someone who could draw my eye to them so completely as you do. I hope tonight is not the last night we may have together."

Lucius leaned forward, brushing a kiss across her lips. He swept an errant curl that'd fallen across her face out of the way. Using the time to force the words he knew he felt to the surface so he could say them.

"These nights lying like this in your arms, my arms around you, have meant more to me than all the nights before them — before you." His words were true, but he knew they only scratched the surface of what he felt, even though he couldn't articulate it in the exact way he wanted. "Marpesia, I've never had feelings this strongly for a woman. I will make sure tonight won't be our last, even if I have to cut my way through every Goth to ensure it."

Marpesia leaned forward and kissed him before resting her forehead against his. "Sleep well, my centurio."

Their sleep was too short as they were woken several hours before sunup to make final preparations for their upcoming battle with the Goths. Lucius pulled on his warmest clothes — thick, black wool leggings and a tunic. The day had dawned bitter cold and promised to stay that way. After he'd pulled on a padded coat, he approached Marpesia likewise attired.

She wore her signature black trousers and tunic with their white zigzags going up the arms and down the legs. She'd tied her soft soled boots with their intricate embroidery over her trousers, then pulled a three-tailed padded coat over her tunic. He caressed her cheek, leaning in for a simple kiss that stretched long and intense as the emotions of the day settled in — fear of losing one another, fear of failing their troops, and their need to express their feelings one last time. For Lucius, it also included his growing acceptance that he cared deeply about this woman, but it was also laced with anger over his treatment by Constantius and the loss of his entire world.

Before enshrouding themselves in steel, they embraced, holding each other's bodies covered in thick wool and padding. Marpesia finally pushed a way, wiping at her cheek and kneeling in front of Lucius. She picked up his greaves, strapping them to his shins. Standing, she reached over and lifted his lorica off its stand and walked behind him, opening the heavy steel, allowing Lucius to put his right arm in first then his left. She settled it onto the focale wrapped around his neck which padded against chafing. Letting the armor rest on his shoulders, she cinched the straps holding his manica in place on his right arm, from shoulder to hand.

Taking a leather thong, she closed Lucius into his lorica shell, tying it firmly closed. She hung the baldric that held his gladius over his right shoulder and ensured the scabbard lay flat on his left hip. Over that, the cingulum militare with its long leather strips and brass ornaments dangled in front. She strapped his wooden rudis on the right hip of the cingulum. Last, she pulled a simple, heavy black cloak around his shoulders. Marpesia stepped back, looking him over from head to foot, nodding appreciatively.

Lucius took her scale mail coat and held it up as she shoved her arms down the sleeves. He settled it over her shoulders, adjusting the long tails that lay just below her knees. Next, he took her belt and gathered it around her waist, pulling the scale coat up so the belt could bear some of its weight. He added her sword belt over that, letting the sword hang off her left hip. With her help, he placed her pointed axe across her back.

Stepping back, he admired her ferocity in stunning steel, with bronze edging each scale. The colorful embroidery of her boots served as a bright counterpoint to the black of her woolens and steel of her armor. Although what drew him to her most was the laughter and kindness in her eyes, today there was an added a nervousness and sadness. He felt it too.

Before, the stakes for Lucius were known. High, but still known

—wounding, dismemberment, death, or even being brought into the undeath of his enemies. Meeting Marpesia and falling for her added new dimensions to consider, new stakes to lose, new ways to experience pain. Looking into her eyes, he reached up and placed his hand on her cheek before turning and picking up a small scabbard from his camp desk.

"I have a small gift for you." He pulled the wooden rudis from the scabbard, handing it to Marpesia. "It's light and should attach to your belt easily enough."

She turned it, letting the flickering light from the oil lamp glimmer off the intricate silver filigree worked up the blade from the hilt guard to the tip.

Lucius continued, "I give these special rudii to everyone in my legion who kills one of the blood drinkers. The wood and the silver will destroy them as soon as it penetrates the heart. It's dark out now, and might be again before we see each other again. Now that we're about to make contact with the Goths, I wanted you to have a way to properly protect yourself."

Marpesia attached it to her belt on the right side. "It's beautiful. I'll use it well."

He wanted to say more, even opening his mouth to speak, but couldn't do more than release a puff of air.

She leaned forward and kissed his cheek. "Tonight?"

"Tonight," Lucius replied, hoping he'd see her again.

Marpesia turned and strode out of his tent, picking up her helmet on the way. Lucius, grabbing his own helmet, followed her out just in time to see her leap into the saddle of her mare. The golden horse caught the light of the torches in the pre-dawn darkness and glittered like one of the stars. The horse, like her rider, was covered in scale mail from head to stomach with only the legs exposed. A long set of horns affixed to the horse's head piece curved forward before curling back and out, like the horns of a Sable Antelope he'd once seen in a menagerie.

Once Marpesia had her quiver and bow case situated on her left hip, she pulled back on the reins of her mare, causing the horse to rear up on her hind legs and paw the air with her front hooves.

Marpesia raised a hand to Lucius, then settled her mare and trotted toward the gate where her cadre of guards and war leaders awaited her. He watched her until she disappeared into the darkness.

A cleared throat behind him got his attention. His valet had the nameless gelding ready to go. An armor skirt covered the gelding's chest, front shoulders, and withers. The horse shook its head, uncomfortable with the transverse centurions crest affixed to its headpiece that marked it as his horse. Its crest was the standard style, sticking rigidly up several inches above the metal frame holding the hair.

In contrast, Lucius's crest was long and fell back and over the back of the helmet and down mid shoulder blade when it was on him. At one point, someone had suggested lengthening the crest on the horse's kit to match his, but he'd rejected that, not wanting the hair flying into his face. He sighed and took the reins to his horse, watching his men file out of the fort by the century to assemble outside their gate before heading toward the front to join the units already in place.

Pisakar rode up and waited until Lucius mounted up. "She leave already?"

Lucius nodded.

Pisakar reached over and patted Lucius's shoulder. "You'll see her again."

"I just hope it's alive and in this world."

TWELVE

LUCIUS STARED FORWARD, looking over the forming lines of the Goths. He and Pisakar had interspersed the best of the borrowed cohorts with his battle-tested legion, the remainder of the borrowed cohorts in the reserves. Dressed in their black winter gear, his heavy infantry effectively plugged the small pass their troops had captured. His three alae of cavalry, two light units and one of heavy kataphraktoi—both horse and rider covered in heavy armor—were hidden in the tree line to his right. Marpesia and her horse archers had been steadily harassing the Goths, trying to keep them from forming up cohesively while screening their own lines. The light lancers and the unit of heavy horse from her Wolf Clan joined with the other Roxolani to form Lucius's left wing and were led by an experienced warlord sent by Marpesia's cousin, the leader of all the Roxolani.

Marpesia, taking command of the horse archers, had divided her force in two. She led one while Aella led the other. Lucius admired the finesse of their attacks, flying in to unleash several volleys only to turn and retreat, firing back into any forces stupid enough to press into the space they'd vacated. The constant harassment was cutting wide swathes through the Goths, leaving piles of dead and injured in their wake.

He kept his eagle-eyed gaze peeled for the golden mare and its fierce rider, the woman he couldn't stop thinking about. They'd only shared kisses and warm embraces, but together, they'd shifted the lines of his thinking into strange and explored territories. He couldn't lose her after only just finding her.

"The Goths have passed the line. Send up the call to the artillery?" Pisakar asked, sitting next to Lucius.

Lucius nodded.

"Ballistae and Catapulta!" yelled Pisakar.

The cornicen put the curved brass horn to his lips and blew the call to loose. They'd placed the ballistae and onagers up on a series of ridges, elevating them and increasing their range. In answer to their call to action, they launched their ordnance skyward. At the blast of the horn, Marpesia's horse archers increased their distance, turning and firing further volleys as they retreated.

"Archers to the front," Pisakar called.

The cornicen blasted out the signal for the archers to advance through the line of legionnaires to the front. His fierce German long bowmen looked sharp as they marched forward, spreading out. And although he couldn't see them, he knew the unit of Syrians, with their heavy recurve bows, was getting into position, using the trees hiding them and his cavalry units as cover. At this point, his archery commanders would take over, knowing their business and the battle plan.

As he focused on the opposite side where Marpesia and her horse archers were working, a flight of arrows rose from the front of his cohorts, arcing into the sky before reaching their zenith and plummeting down in gravity's rainbow, felling droves of Goths. Yet, the Goths kept advancing in their ragged line. Next, Lucius's Syrian archers opened up, tearing apart the first rows of Goths nearest them.

Lucius wasn't sure how many Goths were arrayed in front of them. His scouts never could get a firm number of warriors, since they were mixed in with a seething mass of humanity of noncombatants. He hoped his better trained and coordinated forces would be able to counter the sheer weight of an entire people on the march. The thrum of the longbows in front of him alerted Lucius to the next volley rising skyward.

Despite his forces engaging and the Goths closing, Lucius's eyes drifted to the left, seeking Marpesia as she surged over the battlefield, leading her squadron of archers to deliver round after round of arrows. When he finally found her, she rode with her people back to their position. As they slowed, forming up into lines, the waiting light cavalry charged through the gaps Marpesia left. The light lancers had left their lances behind, pulling their bows from their cases. The heavy kataphraktoi remained in their rows, held in reserve for later when the shock troops would do their most damage.

All the Roxolani had bows, even the heavy kataphraktoi. He guessed Marpesia and her squad must have run through their first quiver and were making for the resupply wagons to get new arrows while using the time to give their horses a breather. The steppe ponies were still in good shape; they were renowned for their robustness and stamina.

Seeing Lucius's distraction, Pisakar issued the order for the cohorts to begin their advance. The cornicen barked out the order to advance which was taken up by each of the carnyx players, announcing to the battlefield that their cohort was marching to battle. Each carnyx had its own unique call that matched its shape, from natural animals to mythical beasts. The eerie sounds of carnyx floated over the battlefield. Legends of the wild Gauls marching to war under the battle calls of the carnyx before succumbing to Julius Caesar were still told around fires in Gallic villages. As the Romans subsumed the Gauls into the empire, the horns were nearly wiped from history until revived by Lucius for the Black Legion. For over two hundred years, the battle call of the carnyx horn warned the enemies of Roma that the Black Legion was on the field, affording them an opportunity to retreat and live.

When Lucius was able to pull his eyes back to the unfolding battle, his brows drew together in consternation. "Why are the Goths not forming up? Their reputation is formidable enough to scare a lot of the people along the border."

"I don't know. They really haven't even returned fire except for some sporadic shots," Pisakar replied.

"Send out some more scouts. See if we can get around this mass and find out if they're screening something in back."

Both their heads snapped forward when the sound of horns, probably from animal horns, vibrated through the air. As the archers moved into columns so the legionnaires could advance around them, the bowmen continued launching volleys into the air. Lucius, his breath coming shallow, waited to see what the horns meant. He wished the sun would burn off the cloud layer and occasional snow flurry obscuring their view into the distance.

For the first time, they were seeing some organization in the front lines as the seething masses formed into a rudimentary line, shields creating a more formidable frontage. Another call went up, and archers worked their way through the lines of the Tervingi to form in front of their shield walls. When the next call went up, they took aim and sent a flight of arrows into the sky.

Lucius, tipping his ear forward, sighed in relief when his centurions blew the call to tighten ranks and form a shield wall. The rear ranks raised their shields to form a roof over their forces as they continued their march. The tortoise like formation slowed the cohorts' advance but provided maximum protection from the missiles arching through the sky.

The screams of men washed over the field as arrows found gaps in the shields or punched through finding flesh beneath. Lucius flexed his left forearm, remembering when an arrow had pierced his own arm after puncturing his scutum.

From his left, Marpesia's call blasted out from their lines as they recalled their light cavalry so she and her archers could return to the field. She charged forward on the back of her glittering, steel-covered golden mare, her warriors following in her wake. As she got within distance, she poured arrow after arrow into the ranks of the Goths.

A series of horn calls from the Goths snapped Lucius's attention back to the front line of Goths. Their archers had dissolved back into the writing mass of foot soldiers as Lucius's legions opened their formation up and increased their trot to a charge, the first ranks unleashing their pila into the sky. The heavy javelins arced forward in deadly flight, plowing down huge swaths of the front lines. At the sound of their own horns, the Goths finally committed, sending their poorly organized infantry against the rigid lines of the best trained legionnaires in the empire.

Lucius's legionnaires met the Goths with shield and pila, stabbing an endless horde until their javelins broke or bent only to be replaced by gladius and spatha. The well-organized Roman lines flashed with steel, punching with shields as they slowly advanced, mowing down any Goth brave or stupid enough to come within range of their swords.

"Send the light cavalry!" Pisakar yelled, the cornicen taking up the signal. Pisakar turned to Lucius. "You ready to give that gelding a little taste of battle?"

Lucius, eyes still fixed forward, nodded, reaching down to pull his spatha clear of its scabbard. He raised it and pointed toward the gap in between cohorts he wanted to hit, seeing the two units slowed under the weight of the Goths. He walked his gelding forward, picking up speed as the got closer. As they accelerated, they curved around and into the gap. His cornicen sent up the call that the Centurio Immortalis was entering the field of battle.

The sound of thundering hooves followed him as Pisakar and the rest of his elite guards formed a wedge. His voice, rising into a yell, preceded him as his gelding bashed into the first Goth, leaving the man's shattered body to be churned under the hooves of the Roman war pony. Lucius's arm fell and rose, slashing and stabbing. Taking an axe on his shield, he spun the gelding, knocking his attacker into the waiting sword of one of his guards.

The ferocity of their incursion into the front lines shoved back the mass of Goths, inspiring his men to surge forward and the enemy to fall back in the face of Lucius's onslaught. He lost track of how long he was there, his arm felling enemies, his legs guiding his horse to meet new threats. Not until he heard the horn recalling his small unit did he pull up on his advance, letting his infantry overtake the line and push past. Once it was safe, Lucius spun his gelding and trotted back toward the rest of his commanders.

Chest heaving from his exertion, he scanned the battlefield. His legionnaires were still moving forward, regularly rotating their lines to ensure fresh fighters moved forward to relieve those at the front. On his wings, the light cavalry swept across the flanks of the Goths, darting in to slash at the edges and keep the superior numbers of the Goths from wrapping around the lines and outflanking his infantry.

At the newest call from the Goths, their front lines gave ground, retreating, at first orderly, then less so as they ran from the Romans. The Goths, with their mass of forces, shouldn't have given in so easily, still outnumbering the Romans and Roxolani significantly.

"Do we give the order to pursue?" Pisakar asked.

"No. Hold the line. Reform in order."

The cornicen barked out the orders. When the front line of his legionnaires cleared the last of the Goths still fighting, they stopped instead of breaking into a run to butcher the fleeing Goths. Both wings of cavalry, responding to the call, pulled back and formed up to the left and right of the wide line of legionnaires. They waited.

"Lucius!" Pisakar pointed to their right.

A man in Roman armor rode low across the neck of his pony, spurring his horse on. As he approached Lucius and his guards, he yelled out the pass code, riding through. He yanked back on the reins, the horse sliding to a halt.

"More Goths, sir. Heavily armed. Advancing. Cavalry on each wing." The man panted to catch his breath, drinking from a water skin someone had handed him.

As if on cue, a new set of horns broke the stillness. The sound of heavy boots and hundreds of hooves swept over them. On a shallow hill in the distance, a dark mass emerged, spreading across the narrow valley the Romans and Roxolani currently held.

"Fuck," Pisakar said.

"Archers, advance to forward position!" Lucius shouted orders. "Slow retreat all units! Send in medics and reserves while we can to pull any wounded from the field."

The cornicen sent out the orders, and Lucius waited for the return calls acknowledging receipt. His eyes drifted to the left, looking for the golden mare and its fiery rider. He held his breath as he scanned over the lines looking for her, worry filling his heart. When he saw a horse turn, light gleaming off its curved horns, he exhaled, holding his hand up to acknowledge the rider he couldn't be without. He wasn't sure if she saw, but it didn't matter.

LUCIUS'S LUNGS heaved as he worked to catch his breath after a rotation at the front, driving back the hordes of Goths. His presence had inspired his tired men to push forward, hoping to break the will of the numerically superior but under-armed foe. He blinked his eyes, looking toward the left of their lines. Marpesia, her arrows spent, was leading her Roxolani in a slashing attack on the flanks. Her heavy kataphraktoi were taking a breather, grabbing unbroken lances for those who needed them.

Her axe flashed down, carving arcs of reflected light as the Wolf Clan used their speed and skill to wear at the edges of the mass of Goths. Lucius's breath came in shallow gasps as he watched her, waiting for her to turn her forces and dash away to let the next wave of cavalry punch into the Goth's flank.

For only a moment, he closed his eyes to gather himself, but when he opened them, he couldn't find Marpesia. Adrenaline surged through his body as his eyes shot open wide. He frantically scanned over the Roxolani, looking for the bright warrior he'd come to care for deeply. When a glint of light flashed off the curved horns of Marpesia's golden mare, he heaved a sigh of relief, only to gasp in a surge of air when the mare turned to present its empty back.

"No..." His gelding, picking up on his body language, sidled to the left. "Marpesia..."

His stomach dropped, his eyes stinging as he tried to get his breathing under control.

"NO!" Lucius bellowed, kicking the tired gelding forward.

As he picked up speed, he ripped a lance from someone's hand, his eyes locked on where he'd last seen Marpesia. His vision tightened into a narrow tunnel. Behind him, the distorted call of a horn barked orders into the air. With the butt of the lance, he forced his pony into a full run as they charged toward the area where Roman and Roxolani struggled to hold the line against a seemingly endless tide of Gothic warriors.

Focused entirely on his goal, he didn't notice when the surrounding bodies changed from his allies to his enemies. As faces and hands grasped toward him with steel clawed swords and axes and spears, his hand, guided by his fury and desperation, darted out, his lance piercing anyone within its range, its steel point lashing out as fast as lightning and twice as brutal.

He shoved out with his hexagonal cavalry shield, catching faces and arms with its iron rim. Surrounded, he guided his gelding around as the animal bucked up, kicking out with his hooves, shattering bodies in his desperate drive to survive the hell his rider had forced him into.

When the shaft of his lance shattered, Lucius shoved the ragged end into the face of the nearest Goth, letting the lance pull out of his fingers as it stuck in the skull of one more vanquished foe. Reaching across his saddle, he yanked the long spatha from its scabbard and carved into anyone who drew within range, kicking his horse closer toward the mass of Roxolani horse warriors.

His fury and supernatural speed drove back the Goths who'd made the mistake of thinking Lucius entering their grasp was an opportunity. Lucius screamed, the ground rushing up at him as his horse fell forward. The world froze into an infinitesimal moment as Lucius tucked his arm and head. Crashing to the ground, he rolled over his shoulder onto his knees. Steel screeched across the armor protecting his back, missing where his head had been a moment before.

Lucius kicked out with his hob-nailed boot, the impact of the foe's knee bending backwards shivering up his leg. He swept the spatha wide, cutting deep into any shin foolish enough to be within his range. He sprang to his feet. He punched out with his shield, shattering a face against the dented boss at its center.

Seeing nothing but red, he let out a ragged bellow and ran ahead. Lucius's fury and speed wreaked havoc around him. Eyes narrowed in concentration soon widened in fear. Where his sword reached, only bodies and severed limbs remained in its wake.

"Marpesia!"

The weight of an axe sinking into the wood of his shield pulled him to his left. He ripped the shield around, yanking the weapon from its wielder's hands and following with a slash that took the head. Lifting the shield, he rammed its rim into the faceless body in his way. The weight of the axe was throwing him off balance. When he brought it around, he let the edge crack into someone's face, then let go of it.

His left hand free, he ripped the gladius from its scabbard at his left hip. With razor sharp steel in each hand, he unleashed his full rage, carving bodies into blood and corpses. Each swing was a step closer to his goal. Every Goth vanquished was one less person to harm his Marpesia.

"Marpesia!" he screamed.

"Lucius!"

He shifted toward the sound of his name, finding a new level to draw upon. The steel at the end of his hand struck over and over, biting deep. Instead of rushing to meet their outnumbered enemy, they quailed before him, unable to find an opening. Only death awaited those who stepped within his reach. Then he saw her.

Marpesia, her axe in her right hand and her sword in her left, cut a swath through the crowd around her, seeking Lucius. As they hacked toward each other, their opposition melted before them. They were nearly within reach of each other.

"No!" Lucius's eyes went wide as he lunged forward, an axe painting a silver streak through the air as it plunged toward Marpesia.

Lucius knocked into Marpesia with his shoulder, shoving her aside as he buried this spatha through the face of the axe-wielder. His lungs heaving, he ripped his arm back and kicked out, dislodging the Goth from his sword. Marpesia recovered her balance and continued her bloody work, protecting Lucius's back as he freed himself from her attacker.

Together, they carved a circle, heaping hewn bodies about them. The only sounds in his ears were their rough gasps of breath and the butchery of their weapons carving through bone and sinew and armor. His shoulders burned from the constant effort. He could only imagine the fatigue fighting to overcome Marpesia's body and its non-supernatural abilities to heal and push beyond normal endurance.

Each parry slower. Each slash more ragged. Each thrust sloppier. He could hear voices crying in languages he knew—Greek, Latin, and the various tongues spoken throughout the empire as they met and mingled with the calls of the Sarmatian dialect coming from the other side. Marpesia grunted, staggering back into Lucius. Only a little longer… They only had to keep going for a little more…

Her warriors had made their way to her, flanking out on each side of her in a wedge. When the sea of his legionnaires swept past him, meeting with the brutal tide of the Roxolani, his arms fell, his hands shaking. His lungs heaving like bellows, he staggered around in time to see Marpesia collapse to her knees. His swords fell from his hands as he dropped too, catching her before she could fall into the pile of corpses surrounding them.

"Marpesia…" Lucius's hands trembled as he tried to stroke her cheek, only to be blocked by the steel cheek guards of her helm.

"Lucius… You came for me." Marpesia was having trouble keeping her eyes open.

"I'll always come for you."

She weakly squeezed his hand. "Are you hurt?"

"I don't think so. I don't think anything serious. You?"

"I don't know." Her armor rose and fell heavily as her body tried to get air.

"Lucius!" called a deep masculine voice. "Lucius?"

"Here…" Lucius coughed, clearing his throat. "Pisakar. Over here."

A horse's head came into view, followed by the giant figure of the Kushite. "Do you need a medic? You're covered in blood."

"I don't think so. I don't think it's mine. Do you have a horse I can borrow? I need to get Marpesia away from here."

Pisakar extended his arm. Lucius carefully laid Marpesia's head on the ground before taking Pisakar's offered hand. On his feet, his knees trembled. He took a deep breath and let it out slowly, trying to get control of his body.

"Help me get her up." Lucius's eyes begged his friend.

Between them, they got her standing and onto the back of Pisakar's pony. Making sure she was stable, he noticed something wrong with the leg of her trousers. The white zigzags of her leggings were stained. Lifting the skirt of her armor, Lucius found a deep gash across the front of her thigh leaking blood.

"Pisakar, I've got to get her to the medics." Lucius started to lead her back toward their lines when Pisakar stopped him with a hand on his shoulder.

"You, legionnaire, your mount," Pisakar barked at a Roman milling about.

"Sir!" The man dismounted and handed the reins to Pisakar.

Pisakar helped Lucius onto the back of the horse, handing him the reins of both horses. Once they cleared the mass of bodies, wounded and dead, he squeezed his legs, getting a trot from the pony. When he got back to their initial lines, he turned Marpesia over to a medic.

"She gets highest priority. Treat her as if you're treating me or Pisakar," Lucius ordered.

"Yes, sir!" The medic saluted and transferred Marpesia to a stretcher.

Marpesia reached up and grabbed Lucius's hand. "Lucius, tell Aella you're in charge." She let go and pulled a golden bracelet from her wrist. "Give this to her. It's our sign. She'll listen to you and relay your orders to the rest of the Roxolani."

Lucius bent over, brushing some hair from her face. "The medics will take care of you. I have the best surgeons in the empire." He bent over and kissed her forehead. "I'll see you soon."

She nodded weakly, her eyelids dipping closed. He tilted his face toward the sun, offering a quick prayer to Mithras, Sol Invictus, and Selene for her recovery and to watch over her.

Lucius turned the tired pony around and found Pisakar directing the reserves into battle.

"Report, Pisakar."

"I think your crazy charge broke their back, Centurio. We're seeing heavy surrenders or other groups and bands retreating southeast. Do we pursue?"

"Hmmm, mercy to all who surrender. Send runners to our cavalry alae and the Roxolani. Tell them to encourage the retreat but no heavy engagement. I don't want to give them a reason to turn and fight. Let Constantius deal with them. We're not here to win the war for him. We have other tasks. Oh, let the Roxolani know Marpesia is alive and with the medics."

While Pisakar rounded up messengers to execute Lucius's orders, Lucius watched as the lines of his legions advanced slowly, rotating their lines to keep the men at the front from getting overly tired. He knew they had to be exhausted, but their conditioning ensured they were still going strong. As he examined some of the bodies laying about or those rounded up and contained, he guessed the Goths had to be nearly done in. Most looked emaciated with too little meat on their bones, their eyes haunted and dim as if they expected death no matter what.

THIRTEEN

LUCIUS'S LEGIONNAIRES rounded up the Goths throwing down their arms and asking for mercy. The cavalry, both Roman and Roxolani, spent the rest of the day harrying their retreating foes, returning at sunset. As he directed his men, he longed to check on Marpesia and then collapse into his bed. Normally an efficient warrior who conserved his energy, the furious charge to save her had spent his reserves. He knew his actions were foolish and unbecoming of the leader of a legion, but he didn't care. Normally, if a soldier went down like Marpesia, they were on their own.

Just the thought of leaving Marpesia to the mercies of the Goths without her horse or her warriors beside her carved out a deep hole in the pit of his being. Thankfully, he'd gotten to her in time, and they were able to stand long enough until their lines caught up with him. He knew he was in for an ass chewing from Pisakar, but Marpesia was alive. Exhaustion, and yelling from his best friend and second-in-command, were small prices to pay.

"Lucius!"

He sighed and thought, *What now?* He turned and saw Aella trotting toward him. Raising his hand, he waved. "Aella!"

She stopped in front of him, sweat streaking the blood and dirt on her face. "I found Marpesia's mare. I had her taken back to paddocks to make sure she's uninjured."

Luke exhaled in relief. "That's good. Marpesia would be devastated if her Day Star were hurt. How are you doing?"

"Exhausted. You?"

"Same. Do you want to join me? I'm going to see how she's doing."

Nodding, Aella mounted and waited for Lucius to climb onto his horse. Together, they rode back to the camp, handing off their reins when they approached the hospital tents. Aella fell in beside him without saying a word as he went to the triage center. When the head surgeon saw him, he walked over briskly.

"Centurio. I'll be quick; I still have a lot of work. Your friend took a long slash to her thigh. It wasn't too deep, so we stitched her up. She's pretty groggy from the mandragora and corn poppy. She's probably ready to be moved out, and frankly, we need the room."

Lucius nodded. "Move her to my tent."

The surgeon flagged down a couple of orderlies with a stretcher and issued the orders. Aella followed the orderlies as they removed Marpesia from the tent.

Lucius watched until she was no longer visible. "Thank you, Marcus. I'll let you get back to work. If you need more bodies to help, let me or Pisakar know."

"Thanks, Centurio."

Lucius patted the surgeon on the shoulder, then turned around. Marcus put a hand on Lucius's shoulder, stopping him from lowering his arm.

"Sir, I think you need to get stitched up yourself," Marcus said.

Lucius sighed, reaching over to his left shoulder. He found a hole ripped in the arm of his wool shirt and drew back bloody fingers from his bicep and triceps. Marcus flagged down one of his assistants and directed him to take care of the centurio's arm. While the assistant surgeon prepped, Lucius stripped out of his armor and tunic to give the surgeon easier access.

"Do you want something for the pain?" the assistant asked.

"Just put something on the cut."

"OK, sir, I'll put some henbane around the slash."

Lucius hissed as the assistant cleaned the wound site then applied the henbane.

"I'll let that take effect. I'll be back shortly."

Lucius nodded. While he sat, his valet showed up to take care of his gear. Getting back to Lucius, the assistant stitched him up and sent him on his way. Lucius pulled his tunic on and walked out, running into Pisakar.

"Hey, Lucius. You look dead on your feet. Go get some rest. I can handle things," Pisakar said.

Lucius opened his mouth to object, then decided not to argue, and nodded. "Alright, wake me if I'm needed."

He forced one foot in front of the other until he found his tent. His valet was waiting outside.

"I have food and hot water prepared for you, sir. I've set up a second bed as well."

Lucius nodded, yawning. "Thank you."

"Is there anything else tonight, sir?"

"No, get some rest."

"Thank you, sir."

Lucius pushed through the door of his tent. They had laid Marpesia in his bed and draped a blanket across her. The second bed was set up against the wall. At the noise of his entrance, she stirred. Aella knelt on the floor alongside her mistress, holding her hand.

"Lucius?" she said groggily.

Aella looked up, smiling softly, and stood. She patted Lucius on the shoulder as she left the tent. Weariness dragging him down, he grabbed a camp chair and set it by Marpesia's head.

He gathered some hair from her face and moved it aside. "How do you feel?"

"I feel weird."

"It's what they gave you for the pain. It'll clear up after a while." He lifted the blanket, checking out her wound. The slash extended over several inches and was tightly stitched up. "That's a good slash. You'll have a grand scar."

"I'll add it to my collection."

"Are you hungry? The surgeon said you lost a lot of blood."

"Mhm."

"OK, I'll help you sit up." Lucius flipped the blankets off her legs.

Careful of her wound, he helped her sit and slide into his backed camp chair. He draped the blanket across her legs. They must have removed her wool trousers to clean and stitch her wound. Seeing her hands were too shaky from the blood loss and the pain killers they'd given her, he pulled up a second chair and slowly spooned the broth into her mouth.

When she finished her soup, he grabbed a rag, pulled the steaming water from the brazier, and mixed it with some colder water to temper it. Dipping the rag in the warm water, he gently wiped the dirt and blood from her face and neck before uncovering her unwounded leg and cleaning it. When he finished, he set the blanket across her lap.

Marpesia lifted her arms, trying to pull her tunic over her head. "Help."

She'd gotten her arm and head stuck in her tunic, the herbs affecting her coordination. He reached over and helped her guide the shirt and tunic over her head. There were several rips. He tossed them aside. Pouring more hot water to heat the bowl, he wiped her arms, cleaning a few shallow cuts and scratches. When he found a new one, she'd hiss and jerk. Judging by the discoloration rising under her skin, she'd have several large bruises.

Marpesia pointed to the chest wrapping. "You can remove it. It's soaked in sweat," Marpesia said, words slurring.

He unwound it from her chest, and cleaned her chest, stomach and back. Setting the bowl aside, he wrapped another blanket over her shoulders. He arranged the two camp beds, so they were next to each other but allowed her space on the side if she needed it. Satisfied with his arrangements, he helped Marpesia into her bed and covered her with blankets and fur. Bending over, he kissed her forehead. Bowl in hand, he tossed the water and poured himself a fresh bowl to bathe himself. Clean, he ate the now cool bowl of porridge filled with chunks of meat and dried fruit, then crawled into his bed, missing the heat of Marpesia's body pressed against his.

He felt Marpesia's hand trying to find its way under his blankets. He guided it into his hand, squeezing it before passing out.

THE NEXT DAY, he woke late and sore. Pisakar had issued orders he wasn't to be disturbed. After Lucius relieved himself, his valet fetched his breakfast and broth for Marpesia, per the surgeon's orders. He also brought back one of the junior surgeons, who checked on Marpesia's stitches. Satisfied, he cleaned the stitches and applied the herbs to keep the wound from suppurating and to keep the pain down. The surgeon checked Lucius's wound and declared himself happy with both patients.

The inspections and work of the surgeon roused Marpesia from her medication-induced slumber. Lucius helped her up and out of the tent so she could take care of her needs. When she finished, he guided her back to the tent where they broke their fast together.

He looked fondly at Marpesia, a half-smile on his face. "How are you feeling now that you have a little something warm in your belly?"

"I hurt everywhere except my thigh. It's numb."

"That'll be the herbs they put on it to help the pain and keep the wound clean."

He thought she looked nervous, beyond any residual effects from the surgical medications, as if something important was weighing on her mind.

"Lucius… Day Star?"

"She's fine. Aella found her last night and coaxed her back in. She's resting. No injuries that I saw."

Marpesia sighed, relaxing. "I feared the worst…"

He lowered his eyes, fixing them on his clenched hands together. "I feared the worst when I saw her go down and didn't see you come up with her."

"Did you charge across the field by yourself and cut your way to me?"

Lucius nodded. She didn't reply, looking astonished. She reached across the table and squeezed his hand.

"I'll check on Day Star and make sure she's uninjured," Lucius said.

"Thank you, Lucius. I think I'm going to lie down some more." Her eyes drifted half shut as she struggled to keep awake.

He helped her back into bed, then left his tent. He checked on Pisakar but was told he was seeing to the surrendered Goths. He went to find the horsemaster next.

"She's a spirited mare, sir, but she appears no worse for wear other than a few minor cuts. Your gelding, though, that's another story."

"Bad?"

"He won't be carrying you for a long while—he may never carry another rider again. Only time will tell. I'll select another mount for you, Centurio."

"Thank you. In the meantime, I'll need a mount to use today. Have one sent to the western gate. See that the gelding gets some extra oats. He fought well." He hoped the animal would recover fully.

"I will."

He returned to his tent and quietly put his armor on before seeking Pisakar. As the Centurio Immortalis marched through camp, legionnaires saluted their commander as he passed. When he approached the western gate, his mount was waiting. He leapt into the saddle and trotted out the gate toward the stockade they'd built in anticipation of needing a place to keep prisoners. He found Pisakar with a troop of legionnaires outside the stockade, sitting with a Gothic man.

"Ah, Centurio. Good timing. I sent someone to rouse you out of your bed. This man has useful information," Pisakar said.

"We must have missed each other," Lucius replied.

When Lucius emerged through the crowd of armored men, the prisoner stood and bowed deeply. Pisakar had been sharing food and drink with the man. One of the legionnaires set another folding stool down for Lucius. He sat, still tired and sore, and gestured for everyone else to sit.

"Pisakar. What's the word?"

"Beremund, here, is the chieftain of one of the smaller Gothic clans. Evoric,"—Pisakar pointed to another man—"speaks the language of the Roxolani. We've exhausted ours, so we've sent for Aella. Once she's here, he promises to tell us what we need to know."

"Why?" Lucius asked.

"They're starving."

Lucius and Pisakar chatted while they waited for Aella, keeping to unimportant topics in case someone understood more Greek or Latin than they were letting on. When Aella finally joined them, they got down to business. Beremund would speak, then Evoric would translate it to the Roxolani dialect for Aella to render Beremund's words into Greek.

"He says he leads a smaller clan of the Goths. They were sent ahead of the full tribe to clear the way of any opposition. They were not expecting our force to be here."

"Why are they coming south?" Lucius asked.

"They're starving, and they're being driven south. He says everything has gone terribly since the night lords gained influence."

"The who?" Pisakar rubbed his chin.

"Tell him to start from the beginning," Lucius instructed.

"He wants to know how much you know of the ones called the 'Visigoths?'" Aella translated.

"Not much, other than what I've heard from the Sarmatians and Germans along the border."

Beremund nodded, then making eye contact with Lucius, began speaking, Aella translating. "There are many Gothic peoples. The two main divisions are the western tribes known as the Visigoths and eastern tribes known as the Ostrogoths. It started a few years ago when one of the larger Visigoth clans, the Tervingi, began growing more powerful. Their neighbors would start losing territory, and their people would disappear, thinning the defenders. Then Tervingi would move in, offering the choice to join them in a subservient role or face total annihilation. When it started happening near us, we sent warriors to help. Most of them disappeared at night, and we've never seen them again. By then, we, along with many others, swore fealty before we started losing our people.

"But even then, at night, the dark lords would visit our people. Folk would wake up next to dried husks of bodies or to no one at all. We have lived in fear constantly, never knowing who would be next."

Lucius interrupted to ask a question, "What kind of people were being killed? Who was disappearing?"

"It was mostly men, the strong men who disappeared. As far as the dead? It could be anyone—children, women, the elderly, the young. It is without pattern."

Pisakar and Lucius exchanged a look. To expert hunters of di inferi like them, they knew the patterns weren't random. Strong men became new monsters, everyone else was cattle.

"Why are the Goths coming south?" Lucius asked.

"We've had too many crop failures and not enough people to bring in what does grow. We are allowed little for ourselves, the best taken by the Tervingi."

Lucius inspected the Goths more carefully. Their clothes hung off them. Their faces looked thin, their skin slack against their bones. Most of the Goths they'd initially faced had looked similar when they sorted the bodies and prisoners. The second wave, however, looked far more fit.

"I'm guessing those we fought, those who fled the battle, are the well-fed Tervingi? Why were you sent in the vanguard?"

Beremund laughed bitterly. "We were sent to kill, then die to protect the warriors of the Tervingi. They thought we'd break the lines of our enemies so they could sweep up and take out the rest, but they bit off more than they could chew with you." He looked around. "At least as your prisoners, we are allowed the dignity of being human."

Lucius nodded and stood up, gesturing at Pisakar with his head to follow him. When they were out of ear shot, Lucius stopped. "How are we looking on our supplies?"

"Solid. The Roxolani have been generous with their herds, and we availed ourselves heavily of Constantius's stores."

"OK. Don't hamstring us, but see that the prisoners are fed."

Pisakar nodded. "Of course. Even what we'll be able to offer will probably be a feast based on their ribs poking out."

"I want you to separate out Beremund and Evoric and ensure they're given extra rations. I want them in better health. We're going to need guides." Lucius spared a look back at the two Goths.

"Do you trust them?" Pisakar asked.

"I think so. I feel no deception from him. He is a man stripped of his honor who keenly feels the indignities of not being able to care for his people. He'll do what's right."

"What do you have in mind?"

Lucius walked back to where everyone sat. "Beremund, do you know who I am?"

Once the question went through the translators, Beremund replied, "You are the Centurio Immortalis. Even in the far north you are known."

Lucius nodded. "What rumors are known in the north?"

Beremund sat up straight. "You are a man of unrelenting integrity who doesn't violate his word. You are undefeated in battle. Fair to your enemies in victory. You slay the monsters who prey upon humans. You are the enemy of the dark lords, the drinkers of blood, the allies of the Tervingi."

"Beremund, will you guide me to the ones who prey upon your people? Will you help me destroy the night demons?" Lucius fixed his gaze upon the Goth, not letting him turn his eyes with the intensity of his stare.

Beremund sat perfectly still for several heartbeats, finally agreeing with a single nod.

Lucius nodded in acknowledgement. "Thank you." He looked toward Pisakar. "See that the prisoners' rations are increased and make sure these two men are fattened up some before we move out so they can keep up."

When the words were translated through to Beremund, he stood and bowed. "Thank you, on behalf of my people."

"We'll speak more later," Lucius said, turning and walking away. He stopped, looking toward Pisakar. "When you're finished making the arrangements, come see me in my tent."

LUCIUS TOOK his time preparing for the next stage of their mission, finding reasons to delay as Marpesia's wound healed. Consulting with the head surgeon, Lucius got the clearance he was waiting for. The surgeon would send one of his assistants with Lucius when they departed camp.

"Does your surgeon say I'm free to resume my life?" Marpesia asked, once Lucius stepped into the tent. She sat with Aella.

"You're cleared. We'll be bringing one of his assistants with us so they'll be able to remove your stitches and manage any wounds we pick up along the way."

Marpesia smiled and gestured with her head that Aella should depart. Standing up, Marpesia walked over to Lucius, a limp still evident in her stride. She wrapped her arms around him and pulled him in for a kiss.

"Good, I'm tired of lying around. When are we departing?" She ran her hand through his shaggy hair. It had been months since it had been cut.

"Soon. I think we're ready. Our guides look a bit healthier."

A few minutes after Aella left, she poked her head back into the tent. "It's ready, Marpesia."

Marpesia nodded and turned back to Lucius, smiling. "I have something for you. A thank you gift for saving me."

"I don't need anything. It was my duty to aid my ally."

"Duty?" She raised an eyebrow. She took his hand and led him outside.

Aella held the reins of the most beautiful horse Lucius had ever seen. It was a Sogdian, like Marpesia's; its coat threw off a metallic sheen. Unlike Marpesia's gold, this mare was a silver-black point, her body and neck a metallic silvery blue-gray with black legs up to her elbow and stifle. Her mane and tail were black. The silver-gray of her neck blended into black on her head, save for a white diamond on her forehead. She had a few black dapples across her rump and onto her back and sides.

Marpesia took the reins from Aella and handed them to Lucius. "She is yours."

"She is a princely gift."

Aella moved around and handed Lucius a dried apple. He stepped forward, apple held before him as the horse took a step to inspect and sniff the offering. The horse lipped the apple into her mouth, lips and whiskers tickling Lucius's palm. He reached out, whispering soothing sounds, and placed his palm on her cheek. She snuffled his face and hair and stepped closer, bumping him with her head.

"He's got a way with horses," Aella said to Marpesia.

She nodded, rubbing the silver's neck. "He does. She is called Moonlight Dancing."

"Moonlight Dancing," Lucius repeated. "I'll have to get a saddle fitted for her."

"I have one mostly done. Our saddle maker just needs some measurements from you."

"A Sarmatian saddle?" he asked.

"She's a gift from a Sarmatian. It's only fitting she comes with a saddle."

"Will it be ready in time?"

Marpesia nodded. "I'll make sure of it. You set the departure, and my people will be ready."

Lucius ran the back of his fingers over Marpesia's cheek, pushing hair away from her face. His thumb traced a line along her cheekbone. He smiled softly. "We leave the day after tomorrow."

FOURTEEN

LUCIUS AND MARPESIA ROSE EARLY, helping each other to don their armor and eating the last full, hot meal they'd have that wasn't quickly prepared marching rations. When they emerged from Lucius's tent, the camp buzzed with activity as Pisakar prepared the legion and their Roxolani allies to provide a distraction for Lucius and his vexillation. Day Star and Moonlight Dancing were waiting for them when they stepped out of their tent. Lucius helped Marpesia mount, per the surgeon's request to keep unneeded strain off the leg until it was fully healed.

Together, they trotted out the gate to find Pisakar. The legions were forming in their battle line, once again plugging the valley claimed as their temporary sanctuary.

"Ho, Pisakar!" Lucius yelled.

"Centurio!" Pisakar turned his pony and trotted toward Lucius and Marpesia.

For once, Lucius sat taller than Pisakar, the Sogdian a few hands higher than the typical Roman war pony.

"What news, my friend?" Lucius absentmindedly stroked the neck of Moonlight Dancing.

"We're seeing larger bands passing, including some more warlike elements. They've noticed us and are milling about. I'm guessing they're waiting until someone with authority shows up to tell them what to do."

"Good. As soon as you begin your push, we'll wait until you give the call that we're clear to move out."

"Right. Luck, Lucius. May Mithras guide and watch over you."

Lucius walked his new horse over to Pisakar until their knees touched. He clasped Pisakar's hand. "Thanks. Luck to you to, Pisakar. I leave the legion fully in your hands. You're the commander until I return. Hopefully, we'll see you soon."

Pisakar nodded, let go of Lucius's hand, and trotted back to the cluster of officers he'd been coordinating with.

Lucius and Marpesia stood and watched, a matched pair on beautiful horses mirroring their riders' demeanors. Marpesia—joyous, bright laughter, and untamed spirit. Lucius—serious and moody with sparks of flashing brilliance. Each of them clad in their armor, they stood sentinel, war gods waiting for their tribute to be offered. A light wind picked up, tugging the long black hairs of Lucius's helmet crest out behind him.

The loud call to advance shattered the silence as a delicate snow pattered down across the field. The line of black-clad legionnaires stepped forward, their cohorts spread in an open formation, lines shallow but wide to put as much frontage on the field as possible. The poor visibility would mask the numbers of the Romans arrayed on the field. On each wing, Roxolani and Roman cavalry units flanked the infantry, contributing to the width and intimidation factor. Pisakar didn't want a full scale assault, only wishing to create a frightening distraction for Lucius to use.

Lucius's two centuries of mounted legionnaires, along with Marpesia's two hundred handpicked horse warriors, made for a fast force that could fight hard if it had to. Their pack train of horses and mules had already started, weaving its way along the backs of nearby hills and through the trees.

He admired the precision and professionalism of his troops as they marched in sync, keeping their rows aligned. When the call

Lucius awaited drifted back on the breeze, he reached out and clasped Marpesia's hand through the thick gloves they wore.

"It's time," he said.

She nodded, and together, they turned to the north and nudged their mounts into a trot as they rode out to hunt the ones the Goths called "dark lords."

They rode for seven days, the going slow as they evaded roving bands of Goths while navigating the snowy, hilly landscape along the foothills of the Montes Sarmatici. On the fourth day, the surgeon removed Marpesia's stitches after their day in the saddle. On the morning of the eighth day, the clouds blowing in from the north grew dark and hostile, threatening more than the occasional dusting of snow slowly piling up as they rode.

"This doesn't look good," Lucius commented.

"It's not. I've seen these kinds of clouds rolling out of the north. We need to find shelter. If we're caught in this blizzard, we'll die." Marpesia looked at the landscape and pulled one of her maps from her bag. "I think I know about where we are. There's a place I know that'll be perfect for riding this out."

She looked at Lucius, a smile on her face. The look made Lucius nervous. There was some mischief in her eyes he couldn't place, equal parts assessing and plotting.

He pulled his bearskin cloak tighter around him. "Tell me about this place."

"It's a small ravine. It's a narrow opening that'll be easy to defend with a wider space after, perfect for a small camp. The way the ravine opens, it'll be hard to see, although I doubt many Goths will be out in this, not once it really starts coming down."

"Alright, I trust you. Let's make for your ravine."

Marpesia's smile broadened as her eyes grew even more danger-ously playful. Lucius felt his heart thump hard in his chest. Seeing his nervousness, she laughed, the sound sending a bright light of warmth dancing through him. She turned and flagged down Aella.

"Aella, we're going to make for the Heart Ravine. Take a hundred riders and clear the space for the camp. We'll be along. I want to make sure no one follows us."

Lucius called over to one of his centurions, sending them with Aella to start laying the defenses. Once the two hundred departed, Lucius and Marpesia sent scouts out wide to ensure they made it to their hiding place undetected.

THEY'D SET up camp at the mouth of the small ravine, erecting earthworks and a picket line. It was still early, but with the threat of weather coming on, Lucius took Marpesia's advice. Her knowledge of the territory beyond the border of Roma, and these mountains in particular, meant he yielded to her.

While he checked with his men, ensuring they were on top of their tasks, he found Marpesia loading up three horses, including his new Sogdian. "I'm surprised my groom let you take her back out after being put to bed."

"Don't worry, we won't be going far."

"Are you sure this ravine doesn't empty on the other end?"

She raised and lowered her eyebrows quickly, winking at him. "Trust me. I'll show you, if it'll make you feel better."

"Should I organize a troop to escort us?"

"We won't need them. Leave them here to enjoy the fire and some drink. Go tell Tinkomaros he's in charge for a couple days. We won't be far. The ravine dead ends about a mile up. It's sheer walls on all three sides."

Lucius's eyebrows shot up. "A couple days?"

Marpesia waved her hand through the falling snowflakes. "This isn't stopping anytime soon. We'll check back in a couple days. We could be snowed in for a week. We have shelter and a safe place. No one else will be out in this mess." She stepped forward and looked into his eyes, brushing his left hand with hers before deciding to take it. "You're beyond the border now, Lucius. Who is to discipline you for choosing to go with me?"

He suspected she knew there was no going back to Roma, not as the same man he was when he left—prisoner or conqueror were the only two ways he could return to the empire. His jaw clenched lightly, the muscles in his cheeks flexing as he stared into her stormy gray eyes. There was a deep vulnerability he'd never seen there before. His right hand drifted up, floating near her cheek. They stood there for a moment surrounded by the hustle of their small camp, ignored by the Sarmatians and Romans more worried about setting up their camp so they could escape the snow.

He let his hand touch her cheek, rubbing his thumb along her cheekbone to wipe aside a melting snowflake. His jaw relaxing, he licked his lips lightly and nodded slightly. "OK."

Marpesia smiled softly, a look of triumph in her eyes that made Lucius nervous. "Good. I have everything we'll need. Go find your Primus Pilus."

He nodded and turned, looking for Tinkomaros. A legionnaire directed him to the centurion's tent.

The grizzled old veteran raised his hand as Lucius approached. "Ho, Centurio."

"Tinkomaros, got everything in hand here?"

"Yeah. The boys know their work and the Sarmatians are pitching in nicely. Everyone wants to get next to fire and tuck into a skin of drink." The Gaul stroked his long mustache absentmindedly.

"Marpesia says we could see a lot more snow. She knows this range. Says we could be here for maybe a week. Let's make it secure and snug."

"Aye, Centurio, we always do. None'll be out in this storm, I reckon."

"No, I don't expect we'll see anyone for a bit. You're in charge for a few days. Keep an eye on our Gothic guides. I don't want them to start feeling homesick."

"I doubt they'll want to drift to far from the food, not in this mess. Wait, you're going somewhere?"

"Marpesia wants to show me something."

A smirk spread across his face, disappearing into this gray-shot beard. "I bet she does."

Lucius narrowed his eyes as the centurion forced the smirk off his face. "And I want to make sure there's not a way into the back of this ravine."

"Aye, sir. We can manage. I'll send someone up that way if you're needed."

"Thank you, Tinkomaros. I'll check back in a couple days, sooner if the weather breaks. She says it's only a mile or so back to the end."

"Aye, sir. I'll make sure we're all still here when you get back."

Lucius nodded and walked back toward his tent to let his valet know. That done, he went in search of Marpesia, butterflies suddenly filling his stomach as he tried to keep his pace respectable so he didn't look the fool to his men, running through camp. He found her under the bow of a tall pine, the three horses tied in a line. When he broke away from the camp light turning him into a dark shadow, and the retreating sunlight caught his face, she smiled, stepping out to meet him.

"Ready?" she asked.

"I think so."

She turned and pulled on the lead of her golden Sogdian. "We'll walk. I don't feel like knocking into every snow covered branch on the way up."

Lucius accelerated to catch up, patting the blue-gray Sogdian she'd given him on the way by. A few yards out of camp, a handful of Sarmatians passed by them, heading back into camp, their leader nodding at Marpesia and telling her everything was ready. She waved as they passed, saying nothing to Lucius in the way of explanation.

"I take it you weren't waiting for me to agree to see whatever it is you want me to see?"

"I had few doubts of the outcome."

Lucius laughed, not sure how else to reply. As they turned a bend in the ravine, the sound of the camp behind them disappeared, replaced with the silence of snowfall. Their feet crunching through the thin layer on the ground was the only sound disturbing the scene. Pines sheltered the ravine, some finding purchase on narrow ledges above them. After a few minutes of silence, Marpesia reached out and took Lucius's hand in hers.

Her hand, like his, was callused from the tools of their common trade. His mouth went dry, his body tensing at the prolonged contact.

"Relax, Centurio. There's no one to command up here," Marpesia whispered, looking over to him, a content smile on her face.

Taking a breath in through his nose and releasing it through his mouth, he took her advice, letting the tension slide away.

"It's not much further. We'll be there with plenty of light to spare." She squeezed his hand, swinging it lightly forward and back as they walked.

The warmth of her hand and the silent beauty around him soaked into his being, the burden stooping his back slightly lifting, as if they were entering a secret place where the outside world couldn't find them. His armor felt unaccountably heavy. Usually he felt naked without its weight on his shoulders. Now, it fought against his desire to be free, if only for a brief moment in time.

They turned another bend, and Lucius saw their destination. The ravine opened into a wider space surrounded by pines. A sizable tent had been set up along one side of the rock wall—that's what her Sarmatians had been doing up this way. Against the back of the ravine, a large pool steamed merrily in the frigid air, a rivulet trickling away from it to disappear into a crack along the southern rock wall.

"Why do you call this Heart Ravine?" Lucius asked, breaking the silence.

"The pool is heart shaped. I can't wait to get into that water," Marpesia replied.

Lucius sniffed the air, picking up faint notes of sulphur from the hot spring. The thought of immersing himself in the hot water after the cold of the last several weeks and today's storm felt glorious, almost enough to warm him before his toes touched water. No matter how much wool he had between him and his lorica, it was still a metal cage around him, carrying the cold through to his bones. "Me too."

They stopped as he looked around their camp site. Aella stepped out of the tent and when she laid eyes on Lucius, smirked and chuckled to herself. Marpesia dropped Lucius's hand and walked over to her friend. Aella said something too quietly for Lucius to pick up. His Sarmatian was getting better, but still wasn't good enough to pick up on a mumbled comment. Her eyes kept shifting back and forth between Lucius and her mistress. They periodically laughed. When they were finished, Marpesia gave Aella a lingering kiss on the lips. As Aella turned, Marpesia ran her finger along Aella's jawline before she stepped out of arm's reach. Aella looked at Lucius and said, "Enjoy the spring," with a mischievous look on her face before she disappeared back down the ravine.

Marpesia turned, a knowing smile on her face. "Come help me unload the horses so I can slide my body into that hot water."

"I'm already in hot water..." Lucius thought. They'd been flirting for weeks now, sharing each other's body heat at night, along with the occasional kiss. Now, they were alone in a peaceful sanctuary with no legionnaires to command or enemies to slay.

Between them, they stripped down the horses and made ready their camp. Inside the tent, Lucius discovered what Aella had been doing—tending a brazier in the center of the tent with a pot hanging from a tripod. The smell of stew and burning hard wood wafted toward Lucius as he inhaled deeply. Marpesia walked over and looked into the pot.

Above the fire, a small hole opened to the twilight sky, letting the smoke drift up and out. Along the back side of the tent was a pile of blankets and furs. A couple armor stands were set up along another wall. Nodding to himself, he looked about approvingly. The felt mat covering the earth would make for a cozy time away from the cold outside.

"Where am I sleeping?" Lucius asked. Nervous, he breathed shallowly as his stomach twisting in knots.

Marpesia, crumbling some herbs into the pot and stirring, pointed to the pile of bedding along the wall.

"And you?"

She pointed, Lucius's eyes following in the direction to the same pile. He didn't know why he'd asked. They'd been sharing the same bed for a while now, even if they'd done little other than kiss.

Lucius's mouth went dry. The sound of her armor clacking as she stood drew his eyes to her.

"Come here."

It sounded soft and courteous, but Lucius, growing used to her tones, could feel the steel of the order she'd directed at him. He obeyed.

"Help me remove my armor." She raised her arm, turning the laces toward Lucius.

He silently stepped into range and unbuckled the straps holding the mail together. When he let out the last buckle, he helped Marpesia pull it over her head. When it reemerged, her normally wild curls jutted out in all directions after being mussed by the armor. He draped it over one of the armor stands.

"My padding?"

Lucius reached for the tie near her neck but had trouble catching the tails of the bow. Looking at his fingers, they trembled lightly. He scowled at himself, steeling his nerves. The tails in hand, he pulled, one after the other until the lowest one was left untied, leaving the padded coat only held together with the tension of the ties still crossed. Starting from the bottom, he slid his finger under the ties and broke the tenuous grasp one side of the padding had on the other.

When he pulled them apart, Marpesia took a deep breath, sighing happily. He helped her slide it off, setting it aside. When he turned around, she'd already stripped off the long-sleeved black wool tunic and long-sleeved undershirt covered in white stars. She folded it, standing there in the wool pants that matched the tunic with only her binding around her chest. She walked slowly toward Lucius, swaying her hips as she closed the distance.

She unclasped Lucius's black bear skin cloak and draped it carefully over her armor. While she was behind him, she unbuckled his cingulum, letting one side drop and sending a clatter of brass to blend with the crackling of the logs. She draped it across the unoccupied armor stand and stepped in front of him. She held Lucius's gaze as she untied the knot in the leather strip holding his armor together before removing it from the lacing loops. She stepped behind him and helped him shrug it off, setting it on the empty armor stand.

Next, she removed his focale and his padding, sending them to the pile with her own padding. His beltus and black tunic followed it. He pulled the tunic she'd given him over his head, admiring the black wool with its white stripes running up and down the arms and legs.

Goosebumps rose over his nude chest and arms and sent shivers through his body, although he wasn't sure if his trembling was caused by Marpesia's sultry gaze, admiring his broad chest with its moderately sparse hair, or the cool air. The high calorie rations he'd been on steadily for the winter campaign left him with a little cushion around his stomach and waist. No doubt he'd burn it away in the coming weeks on short rations as they penetrated deep into frigid northern landscape.

Stepping closer to Lucius, she reached up, placing her hand on his chest over his heart and looked into his eyes. She rose on her tiptoes and kissed him on the cheek then matched it on the other cheek. Lucius's breath came in short shaky bursts. His hands hovered over her waist; he brought his skin into contact with hers, her soft skin over ropy muscles searing his fingers. Like him, the heavy rations had added a bit of padding.

He felt the faint wisp of her breath against his face as she kissed the corner of his mouth, moving to the other side. His heart thundered, feeling faint. She looked at him through her eyelashes, vulnerability coloring her gray eyes. The corner of her lips tipped up into a gentle smile.

"Your hands are shaking, Centurio. Do I frighten you so?"

He shook his head slowly. "You do, Chieftain."

"Good."

Marpesia's eyes, triumph blending with vulnerability, drifted shut as she leaned forward, her lips meeting Lucius's. At first, he froze as she halted, before his lips pushed into hers, kissing back. He didn't understand why he'd frozen. They'd kissed many times before, but somehow this time felt different. Her other hand ran up his arm and shoulder, cupping the back of his neck. She pulled him in tighter, the dam bursting as she coaxed his mouth open with her tongue.

When their lips broke a part, Lucius rested his forehead against hers, his breathing deep but shaky. He removed a hand from her waist, bringing it up to caress her cheek. He stepped back, taking a deep breath, and turned away from Marpesia, moving closer to the fire. He stared into the dancing flames, letting the crackle of the burning logs punctuate the tension with occasional pops washing over him.

The warmth of a hand on his shoulder alerted him to Marpesia's presence behind him. "Why do you fight yourself still? We've been on the cusp of this for too long."

A slight tremble in her voice caused him to turn. She ran her hand up his shoulder and brought it to rest on his cheek. He placed his hand over hers, gripping it and pulling it away from his cheek. He turned his head and kissed the palm of her hand, but didn't let go of it.

"Lucius, would you participate in a ritual with me?"

He couldn't pull his eyes away from hers. He nodded. "Yes."

She gave him a closed-mouth smile and dragged her finger along his jaw as she walked away. Rustling through her pack, she pulled out a pouch and a small bronze cauldron and brought them to the fire, setting them on the felt floor next to the brazier. She took her woolen stockings off, throwing them into the pile of cloth wares, and knelt in front of the brazier. With a set of tongs, she pulled out eight small rocks. Lucius pulled his stockings off and tossed them before kneeling next to Marpesia, facing the fire.

"What are we doing?" he asked.

"I wish to commune with the gods and thank them for the safe journey so far, and entreat them to watch over us as we continue."

"I don't pray to Sarmatian gods."

"Do you think Roman gods are so different from Sarmatian gods? I've heard rumor on the winds to whom you owe your allegiance, who is the font of your power. Mithra wanders the steppes as well as the forests of Belgica. He looks after Roxolani and Nervii both as they fight those who stalk the darkness."

He nodded, taking her offered hand.

"I'm going to burn our sacred herb in the cauldron. Normally we'd set up a small lodge tent, but,"—she gestured around—"we're short on baggage space and this will do. Waft the smoke to your face and inhale deeply."

She oriented herself so she was over the cauldron. Lucius joined her. She grabbed a nugget of dried green herb from her pouch and crumpled it in her hand, breaking it into smaller pieces before sprinkling it over the cauldron. The dry herb quickly caught on the hot rocks and started smoking. Surveying the smoke, she pulled another nugget out and added its crumpled pieces to the cauldron.

Marpesia gathered the rising smoking in her hand and pulled it toward her face, breathing deeply. The first handful in his face pushed his head back on his neck at the pungent smell of pine, spice, and something musty. He inhaled, tickling a small cough from his throat. Gathering more, he breathed deeper, now prepared for the strong smoke.

To his side, Marpesia said, "That's probably enough for you to start with if you've never experienced kannabis before."

"I haven't."

She gathered another scoop of smoke to her face with her left hand, placing her hand over her heart. Lucius repeated her motions. He gave thanks to Mithras for the low losses they'd suffered so far fighting the Goths, at the speed they'd made before getting snowed in. He implored his master to extend his good will to those he and Marpesia led on their mission. He was sure to include Sol Invictus, thankful for their victory at the pass. Last, he gave his thanks and affection to Selene in appreciation for her continued blessings.

His praises given, he felt small bursts of light in his head. Marpesia's hand tugged his attention away from everything else. Opening his eyes, he focused on their hands clasped together, her strong hand and long, delicate fingers. He watched as Marpesia lifted their hands, bringing his fingers to her lips. Her eyes pulled his up, locking under the intensity of her gaze. She leaned forward, her lips drawing Lucius closer to her as they kissed above the hot cauldron, tendrils of smoke rising and snaking over their bodies and heads before escaping to the ceiling and out the hole at the top.

Marpesia pulled away from Lucius's lips, sitting back on her heels before standing, his hand still in her hers. She urged him to join her on her feet. "Let's go slide into the water." Raising her arms, she looked down at the cloth wrapped around her chest. "Help me with my bindings."

Lucius's heart stuttered before banging into a gallop. He found the tail tucked into her side just under her armpit, lifting it free from the cloth covering. He walked around her, unwinding it until the other tail fell free from her skin, pooling on the ground in a small pile.

"Thank you," she said, bending over and pushing her wool pants to the ground and removing the cloth around her waist.

Before he could take in her nude form in its entirety, she ran out the tent. As soon as her feet hit the snow outside, she squealed and laughed, the sound quieting as she ran to the pool.

FIFTEEN

LUCIUS HESITATED for a moment before pushing his wool pants to the ground along with his loin cloth. He tried to be more dignified as he stepped into the snow in his bare feet, but he ended up hopping and laughing as he ran toward the edge of the pool. The warmth rising from the water kept the shore snow-free for the moment.

Marpesia had already sunk to her neck and was floating in the middle. A contented smile spread across her face as she stared up into the snowing sky, occasionally opening her mouth to try to catch a flake on her tongue. He stood at the shore watching her float lazily, turning slowly.

"It's much warmer in here, but if it amuses you to stand there and shiver, don't let me get in the way," Marpesia called to the shore.

Lucius stepped forward, dipping his toes in, the warmth immediately warring with the cold of his foot. A flat space found to place his foot, he brought the other leg in, carefully advancing until he was immersed up to his waist. The hot water melted away the cold. Although cooler than the warmest part of a Roman bath, the pool was perfect for a good, long soak.

Sighing, he drew up his feet, letting the water take him. Treading water, he rolled onto his back, slowly moving his way toward Marpesia. A faint pink tinged the edge of the western mountains looming above them, leaving the grotto in darkness only lit by the light of the brazier glowing within their cozy tent. Relaxing, the water carried him, keeping him afloat with no effort.

Marpesia's fingers brushed at his until she found his full hand and held on. The snowflakes glittered like crystals as they entered the dim light rising to meet them. Waves of tingling passed over his scalp as he stared dreamily up into the falling flakes. If he concentrated on one of the big flakes, it felt like he could slow time to capture it in its moment.

"Lucius?"

"Yes, Marpesia?"

"Do you think I'm pretty?"

He smiled before opening his mouth, trying to catch a fat snowflake on his tongue. He couldn't hide the fact he'd often found himself looking at her. Admiring the eagle-eyed squint of her eyes and the raptor like bend of her aquiline nose. Entranced by the dimples in her cheeks as she laughed, the wind of a galloping horse tugging her messy curls behind. The flash of her axe flying about her, as enemies shrank from her fury.

"You are beautiful, Marpesia."

"Do you like kissing me?"

Her questions in another would have felt insecure, but maybe the answers weren't meant to reinforce *her* confidence. "Every time our lips have met, it's been more wonderful than the previous. I wonder if the next will continue the pattern…"

She tugged his arm, pulling him toward her until she floated over his legs and into his lap. She let go of his hand and wrapped both her arms around his neck. "I see through your strategy, but I'll allow it."

She tipped her head and closed her eyes, leaning into Lucius's lips. They kissed deeply, Lucius wrapping his arms around Marpesia's waist, running his hands up her back. She teased his mouth open, seeking his tongue; it sent thrills through him when they met. Marpesia, her hands sliding into Lucius's hair, pulled him in tighter, her kiss growing hungrier.

By the time they emerged from their kiss, the last of the sun had disappeared entirely, leaving them covered in a black blanket of clouds only lit by the cheery flicker of the fire in their tent. Marpesia turned her back to Lucius, pulling his hand around her to drape his arms across her upper chest. She floated back into him, letting him bear her weight as they leaned back in the water, watching the snow drift from the sky. Lucius, resting his chin on her shoulder, periodically leaned forward to kiss her ear or cheek.

"Thank you for sharing this with me," he whispered, not wanting to disturb the silence of their hidden corner of the world.

"I wasn't sure you'd be willing to…" she whispered back.

"I couldn't resist you." He paused, thinking about the time he'd known her. "I've not been able to take my eyes off you since the first time I saw you sitting in the sunlight in Constantius's antechamber. If you're not around, my eyes are always seeking you out. Each night laying against your body has been torture as I resisted seeking more…"

"Do you miss me when I'm not near?"

"Yes." It was as much an admission to himself as it was to her. "When you asked me to join you with your horse packed and ready, the thought of you gone for several days…felt wrong."

They floated in silence, looking up into the snowy night. Lucius could feel her strong heart beat under his hand. She reached up and slid her fingers around his hand, grasping it. As he gazed into the black nothingness above him and floated in the warm pool, he felt as if his head drifted in the ether.

He'd heard about the intoxicating smoke of the Sarmatians, assuming it was wild speculation, but had never been invited to share it until now. Whether it was the warm water, the gentle company, or the ritual he'd participated in with Marpesia, the cares burdening him receded, allowing him to relax for the first time in who knew how long.

"Lucius, I wish to return the kindness you gave me after my wounding. May I bath you?"

"I didn't bring any oil or my strigil to do a proper bath." He hadn't thought to see what all was packed. His valet might have included his bathing effects, but when Marpesia asked him to leave with her, his only thought had been going, not checking his packs.

"We'll do it in the manner of my people."

"OK."

Marpesia pushed away from Lucius, swimming toward the small stream that exited the pool. "It's set up over here where the stream can carry everything away."

He swam after her, stopping when he reached her. Reaching out, he put his hands on her hips, bringing her in for a kiss. After their kiss, she reached to the shore and pulled out a large leather pouch and opened it, holding it under Lucius's nose. It smelled of herbs, evergreens, and spice. It had been mixed into a thick paste.

"Is there enough for two?" he asked.

Marpesia, a smile splitting her lips, nodded. "More than enough."

She rose out of the water and beckoned him over. Standing in front of her, the water coming only to their knees, he couldn't help but look over her body, the soft light from the tent casting shadows from her curves and teasing the shape of her numerous tattoos and scars.

"Do you like what you see?"

He nodded, reaching out and running his hand over her arm.

"Turn around. I'll start with your back."

He turned. The cool feel of grit scrubbing onto the skin of his shoulders alerted him that they'd started. He inhaled deeply, taking in the scent of the paste. Excitement coursed through his veins. It was her scent, the one that had tantalized him, distracting him as he tried to identify it every time he was close enough to her for it to tease his senses. Every night it haunted him as they lay in each other's arms. He felt himself stirring, trying to maintain his calm, but losing the battle as she scrubbed the paste over his chest and stomach. When she touched him, he inhaled sharply, stiffening as she worked paste over his midsection.

"I was beginning to think you didn't actually hold me in much regard," Marpesia said, scrubbing from his upper legs to his knees as if nothing at all had happened.

Setting the pouch back on the shore, she lifted a large flat rock from the pool and set it in the dirt next to the water. "Sit here. The rock will keep you warm."

He sat on the rock as she knelt down on one knee in front of him, picking up his calf and setting the foot down on her other knee. With a handful of the paste, she scrubbed it over one calf and foot, working between his toes before setting it back in the water, then turning to the other one.

Finished, Marpesia sat in the water, seeking the warmth of its liquid caress, her elbows on her knees and her chin resting on her clasped fingers. She stared into Lucius's eyes as he sat on the flat stone, his elbows resting on his knees. He couldn't figure out what was passing through her eyes or her mind, her face a guarded mask.

"May I bathe you, now?" Lucius asked, cringing internally at how timid his voice sounded.

He held his breath as he waited for her answer, the seconds stretching into eternities. When she nodded, a tender smile coloring her lips, he exhaled and stood, offering his hand to the beautiful warrior he longed to touch. Despite the lengthening exposure to the cold air, he felt hot, his breath shallow and expectant as he tried to control his nerves. Taking his hand, she stood, the grace of the movement nearly robbing Lucius of his breath again.

Lucius reached down, scooping a handful of the paste, and stepped close to her, looking down into her gray eyes. Her brows furrowed slightly as she gazed back at Lucius. He'd seen hints of vulnerability in her eyes off and on since she'd invited him to this oasis, but this was the first time she was laid emotionally bare before him. He swallowed, licking his lips to moisten them, and caressed her cheek with his other hand. He tipped his head down and kissed her forehead, then the tip of her nose, before brushing his lips against hers. The bathing paste forgotten in his hand for the moment, he rested his forehead against hers, sharing each other's steaming breaths.

"Don't take too long, Centurio. It's getting cold," Marpesia whispered, chiding him for forgetting his duty.

He nodded, stepping back, and began working the paste over her shoulders, using the same circular motions she'd used on him. He covered her back, sides, and arms before moving to her front. As he approached her breasts, the light brown of her nipples puckering under the attention of the cool air and Lucius's hot gaze, challenge filled her eyes, curious if he'd continue now that he could go no further without looking like he was intentionally avoiding touching her intimate areas.

Taking some more paste from the pouch, he let his hand circle clinically over her breasts and the tight buds at the end before moving to their underside and down over her stomach. She chuckled at his efforts. As he warred with his desire to touch her, to kiss every part of her body, to become one with her, he continued presenting a placid exterior as he worked the paste over her soft, round butt, and down over strong, muscular legs. When he reached her knees and the water, he stood and pulled the flat rock back out of the water, setting it down for Marpesia to sit on. Offering her his hand, she walked to the rock and sat, letting him finish with her feet and lower legs.

They'd both been out of the warm embrace of the hot spring for a while, and he could feel genuine shivers starting to spread through his body. He thought he saw her shivering too. Even if she lived in this climate, she had to be freezing as she sat in the frigid night air.

"Come closer, Lucius. This is a finer paste. Keep your eyes and mouth closed. I'll work it through your hair and over your face and neck. Then submerge yourself in the deeper water, but not too far away. Let the current carry it away. I'll apply it to my face, then join you. I'd let you come back and reciprocate, but I'm getting too cold."

When she finished, he worked his way to a deeper part of the pool and sank over his head, rubbing water through his hair and over his face. He emerged, sputtering, Marpesia's nude, paste-covered body walking toward him. He treaded back to make room for her to submerge herself in the pool. She sank, letting the water cover her. Her face clean, she shoved her thick hair so it fell behind her, clearing her face of any runoff. Her curls were still thick with the paste. Floating toward Lucius, she turned her back to him.

"Help me clean it all from my hair please."

He massaged water through her curls as she floated on her back, her breasts bobbing just above her in the water. The intimacy of bathing her and the sight of her body teased him. He kept his waist away to keep from embarrassing himself with his lack of control.

"I think your hair is clean now," he said quietly.

She let her body sink into the water, turning to face him. "Can you ensure the rest of my body is clean?" He opened his mouth to object, but she covered his lips with her finger. "I want you to."

Swallowing, he nodded and ran his hands over her body, ensuring all the paste was gone. As he worked, she continually bumped into him, teasing him. When he finished, she swam behind him and worked water through his hair to make sure it was clean before running her hands over his skin to rub the last of the paste away. As he floated on his back, she worked water over his legs and feet.

He sank back into the water so only his head was above the surface as he let the gentle movement of his arms keep him in place. He startled as hands ran over his sides, under his arms and settled over his chest. Marpesia pressed her body into his back.

"Your heart races so fast, Centurio…" She practically purred into his ear, kissing around edge of his earlobe.

He let out a small groan.

"Are you cold?" Marpesia whispered.

"No."

"Then why does your body tremble?" Her was voice tinged with knowing humor.

"It…it has been a long time since I've been this intimate with anyone."

"I know; I can tell. Do you want me to stop?" She kissed his jaw just under his ear, trailing little kisses up his cheek.

He turned his head. She kissed the corner of his mouth.

"No, I don't," he replied, barely audible.

"I've wanted you since the first time I saw you, standing in the sun with your finery over your battle armor. My desire has only grown since I've gotten to know the man you are." There was a small hitch in her voice, an air of vulnerability seeping in. "Do…do you want me?"

He took a deep breath, letting it out as a sigh. "Yes, I want you."

"Good. Tonight, we can have each other."

Lost in the haze of events moving faster than he could keep up with, he remained silent, basking in her warmth and touch as they floated in the black pool of warm water, the snow falling steadily, stacking thicker on the ground of their little slice of peace, his head floating from the smoke they'd shared.

AFTER THEIR EXERTIONS, Lucius stepped out to relieve himself, returning quickly to the warm embrace of the brazier and the tent. Marpesia, sweat glistening on her skin and her wild hair scattered about her head, lay on her stomach watching him add more charcoal to the brazier—only her calves were covered in a blanket. Satisfied with the fuel situation, Lucius lay down next to her, propping himself up on his elbow so he could look over her back and its mix of tattoos and scars.

He traced his finger along a long, curved scar, silver with age, along her left shoulder blade. Along the concave side, a stag curled around the lines of the scar in its elegant out of proportion style he was coming to learn was the preferred style of his Roxolani allies. On the convex side, a griffin, in the same style, dove toward the stag. He leaned down and kissed the scar.

"Who gave you this one?"

She let out a short harsh laugh. "Some Alan princeling trying to make a name for himself objected to my wolves riding across the patch of grass he claimed for his clan. He thought defeating my warriors would earn him much renown with the surrounding clans of Alans. Like many before him, he doubted a clan lead by a woman would be able to stand against his prowess. I sent his skull to his heir and offered to make it into a pair of goblets for my kumis if he decided to stand in my way or press for revenge.

"He was a more reasonable man to negotiate with. He wasn't fond of his elder brother. He's sure to give me a wide berth when I choose to ride through his lands." She reached up to touch a round, puckered scar along Lucius's left forearm. "That looks like an arrow."

"Aye. Took a Parthian arrow. Punched through my scutum and kept going. I snapped it off and shoved it through." He rotated his arm around to show her the matching scar on the other side.

She tipped her head to the side, blowing an errant strand of hair out of her eyes. "Parthians? My father used to tell tales of his grandfather's father raiding the Parthians when they'd grown weak, their empire crumbling around them."

Lucius nodded. "I took this about a hundred years before that during Traianus's Parthian War."

Her eyebrows tipped up. He wasn't sure if she was skeptical, even after their earlier discussion of his age, or if the evidence and story shocked but confirmed the stories about him and his age. Instead of asking for elaboration, she shifted slightly and pulled her nearest calf out from under the blanket and rolled onto her side, pointing to a similar scar about halfway up her calf.

"An Alan arrow. I caught it before it could pierce the side of my mare. I didn't get to repay whoever did it. When I called my warriors to order and let loose our wolf cries, they decided they'd shot at the wrong band of travelers and fled. If I ever find them though, I'll repay the kindness they paid me."

Lucius chuckled, kissing his fore and middle fingers before laying them across her arrow scar. "Different clan of Alans?"

"I think so."

"You seem to have a problem with the Alans."

She made a sound of profound disgust. "Those pointy-headed bastards are greedy. There are plenty of steppes for us all. I don't want to do much besides ride to the other side of the hill to find new things to trade for. But the Alans feel if they have eyes they can put on land, it should belong to them. Always pushing us west, further west."

Lucius was still coming to know the more complex expressions of her beautiful face, but he thought she looked troubled about the Alans' territoriality. Not knowing what to say, he leaned over and kissed her cheek. "Why do you call them pointy-headed?"

She made another disgusted sound. "They bind the heads of their babies to elongate their skulls. Unfortunately, they breed like maggots on a dead deer and raise their pointy-headed babies to be just as greedy as them, seeking new lands to raise more pointy-headed babies on. The Alans are a hungry beast trying to swallow all before them. I just hope they choke on something before they come to gobble my people up too."

Marpesia's forehead creased in worry, the muscles in her cheeks flexing. She sighed, giving her head a little shake that reverberated out through her wild curls. "No more troubling talk for this evening. This place is for peace and relaxation. And you seem to have lips that are eager to kiss my skin and I could use more of that right now."

She rolled onto her back, angling her chest toward him. When his eyes drifted to her breasts, she smirked, victory shining in her eyes. Lucius shook his head at himself and leaned down, kissing the silver scar across the bridge of her nose.

"Took a glancing blow to my helmet. The edge cut a gash in my nose." She pointed to her lips. "You can't see it well, but there's a scar here too."

The corners of Lucius's lips tipped up as he fought to contain a grin. "A Lugii spear?"

"No, I bit it."

"Dueling a horde of Gothic raiders?"

"I tripped."

Lucius could no longer contain the grin as his lips parted, about to make another joke.

"If you won't shut your mouth and kiss me, I'll have to shut it myself." She pulled him onto her, stopping his words with her lips against his.

SIXTEEN

THEY SPENT NEARLY a week tucked in the back of the ravine while the snow came and over-stayed its welcome. Lucius had checked in a couple times, sticking to the snow shadows to avoid the deepest drifts. Occasionally one of his sentries would report hearing sounds in the far distance if the circumstances were right, but with the angle of the ravine's mouth and the snow piled over their defensive works, they just looked like one more piece of the landscape.

Lucius couldn't remember a more wonderful week in his long life. His responsibility to his men discharged for the time, he spent every moment he could in Marpesia's arms. Sometimes lying on the floor of the tent under their pile of furs and blankets exchanging stories about their lives and adventures. Sometimes—most of the time—under the same blankets exploring each other's bodies, aided by Lucius's supernatural stamina and Marpesia's desire. When they needed a break, they'd slip into the pool of hot water and soak, letting the beauty of their little oasis seep into their souls, storing it for the hard ride and what lay ahead. He tried not thinking about it, wishing he could pause time and never leave this moment.

On the day they were to return to the camp and move out, they woke early to share each other's bodies one last time in their peaceful sanctuary, then bathe in the warmth of the pool. Together, they packed their camp until some of Marpesia's Wolf Clan showed up to finish the task, letting Marpesia and Lucius return to the main camp to oversee the final tear down and prepare the camp for moving out. The day promised to be a hard slog through the snow until they could make camp again.

THEY WERE another week north of the ravine in pursuit of the monsters driving the Goths south. Beremund and Evoric, in solid shape after several weeks of heavy rations, ranged out with Lucius and Marpesia's scouts, retracing the route the Goths traveled weeks ago before attacking Lucius and his allies. Each day, they ended their march early, seeking defensible, sheltered places to make camp while they had the safety of the light during the shorter winter days.

After the week snowed in and their blissful time at the sanctuary of the hot spring, Lucius and Marpesia no longer maintained the fiction of separate tents, not that anyone looked surprised after their previous poorly maintained attempts at subterfuge. Lucius's men seemed to find the situation amusing, their vaunted leader taking up with a woman in the middle of a campaign. Although, he never saw anyone sneering or casting judgmental eyes at him. Most seemed happy to see the old man acting like a regular human. It was a new side of Lucius to see, even for himself.

In the evenings, after camp was set, Lucius and his men ran training sessions with the Sarmatians. Few, if any, of the Roxolani had knowingly encountered a night lord, as the Goths called them. While silver weapons were non-existent save for the rudii Lucius's vampire slayers were armed with, the tools the Sarmatians had would suffice. Although an arrow head wouldn't kill one of the monsters if it pierced a heart, the wooden shaft it was attached to would. Each of the Sarmatians was also armed with the spike-backed axes some of them preferred as their primary melee weapons. If an arrow couldn't pierce an armor-covered heart, an axe to the neck would go a long way toward neutralizing the blood-drinking monsters.

The one piece Lucius had added to each of the Sarmatians' kits was a half-dozen steel-tipped wooden stakes per warrior. The steel tip would help penetrate most scale—either metal or bone and hoof—and chain mail, allowing the wood to do its work. Lucius hoped they wouldn't need them though. He wanted to strike after the night lords were bedded down for the daylight.

Their scouts, ranging far into the distance, found traces of the previous Gothic bands—discarded equipment, wagons, and far too many bodies left where they fell. Beremund and Evoric had proved themselves invaluable at keeping them on the right path while avoiding discovery. When the scouts finally made contact with the main body of the Gothic horde, Lucius and Marpesia set their plan in motion.

Three nights before their planned raid, they left a half century of Lucius's men to hold their small fort while the rest ranged ahead, camping quietly in a copse of trees his scouts had found and designated as a potentially safe waypoint for their strike. Under heavy sentry, they turned in early, planning to rise several hours before daylight broke so they could be in position.

Thus far, they'd relied on stealth, their two Gothic guides, and Marpesia's knowledge of the lands her people had roamed for generations to avoid the hordes of Goths moving south in trickles and waves. But tomorrow would see a direct incursion into the heart of the most powerful portion of the Gothic horde. Tomorrow, stealth would turn to speed and surprise.

While Lucius was always nervous before battles or raids against the di inferi, tomorrow felt different. Nothing before held stakes like tomorrow. Before, he'd only risked his own life and the men he led, each of whom had signed up for the legions before being recruited into the Black Legion. Tomorrow, Lucius would battle his ancient enemy beside a woman he had growing feelings for. If he was being honest with himself, his feelings had advanced beyond "growing."

The first time they'd fought alongside each other, they'd just met, although he'd felt his attraction for Marpesia developing even then.

The second time, he'd been nervous, but he knew she was an experienced war leader, capable of leading her own troops. When she and her horse had gone down, Lucius had reacted instantaneously, charging in to rescue her.

Tomorrow though, things could go sideways quickly. They were vastly outnumbered headed into the heart of the Gothic power structure—the best trained and fed warriors and their evil, blood-drinking, mind-controlling masters. If their surprise and dash away failed, they'd be lucky to escape alive. But there were worse fates than death when it came to the undead denizens of the night.

The greatest evil of the ones the Goths called "night lords" was their ability to turn life into undeath—to take living flesh with a soul and turn it into an immortal parasite devoid of the spark that made it human. The creature that rose into undeath did not love nor care, but only hungered to exploit and consume.

When Lucius slid into his bed, he found Marpesia waiting for him, naked. Without preamble, she kissed him, her tongue seeking his, her hands playing over his body. She had an agenda, her nervous energy finding its partner in Lucius.

Lucius was able to set his fears aside while he and Marpesia disappeared into each other's bodies for the first time since leaving their ravine and its sanctuary. This might be their last night to have this connection, one or both of them falling and never seeing the sunset again. There was a certain franticness to their coupling as they tried to express all their feelings in the one act before seeking battle in the morning.

After they'd spent themselves, Marpesia rolled off Lucius and fell into a deep slumber. Sleep failed to find Lucius easily, and when it did it was filled with unwholesome dreams. Marpesia dead in the snow, her blood staining the frozen whiteness red as her life steamed from her wounds. Marpesia, the telltale bite marks in her neck, rising from the dead, staring at Lucius with lust and hatred, needle-sharp fangs gleaming in the moonlight. He jolted awake when the nightmare monster he'd loved tore into his flesh, seeking his life. He shivered in the cold air, sweat trickling down his forehead and back as he sat up.

Beside him, Marpesia slept deeply, his startled wakefulness failing to disturb her. He hoped her dreams were more peaceful than what assaulted him. He sat upright, staring at her for a while until he felt sleep tugging him back down. He leaned over and gave her a kiss on the cheek before succumbing to the lure of sleep.

LUCIUS HAD RISEN sandy eyed and unrested from the nightmares. He didn't know which had been worse. The ones where she tore him to pieces, spilling his lifeblood, or the ones where he was forced to shove his rudis into her heart. As Marpesia stirred, he tried to school his expression so she wouldn't see the haunted look in his eyes.

When she rolled over, her eyes opening, a smile tilted the corners of her mouth up before her brow furrowed after seeing his face. "What bothers you, my Centurio?" She sat up and kissed him.

He inhaled a deep breath and sighed. "I…had bad dreams."

Marpesia smiled softly at him, caressing his check. "They're just dreams. We're awake now." She kissed his forehead.

"I know." He suddenly pulled her into him, hugging her fiercely. "Do be careful today, please?"

"There are bold deeds to do today, Lucius. Careful will get us dead." She kissed his cheek and rose.

She threw on a tunic and coat along with her boots as she ran out to relieve herself. Lucius followed her example. When they both returned to Lucius's tent, they helped each other dress and arm themselves, breaking their fast with a warm bowl of porridge loaded with dried meat and fruit.

While the servants broke down the camp, Lucius and Marpesia prepared their troops to move out. Before they departed, they checked with the men crewing the two ballistae broken down into pieces in sleds pulled by mule teams. Lucius had wanted to build onagers, but they were too heavy to move in the deep snow and too noisy to build on-site when relying on stealth. The large catapults could throw large pots of flammable substances. But in the end, they'd decided to go with the ballistae. The added range and accuracy coupled with their transportability made them the better choice, even if their payload wasn't as large.

When were finished readying themselves, they moved out under the dark cover of night, a few hours from the first hints of morning. They needed to be in place and set up. The location selected was close to the Goths' route, and they didn't want to risk being seen before they could set up their artillery. Though at night they risked vampires, Lucius could feel their approach if they got too close. He hoped they'd be more interested in bedding down before sunrise than finding last-minute prey, especially when they had their pick of Goths to snack on. In the game of risks, Lucius and Marpesia judged the risk of moving at night the better choice.

The servants were nearly finished with their duties and, with a dozen guards to escort them, would return to the fort to help defend it and prepare for what Lucius hoped was their victorious return. They took off, their breath steaming into the dark.

Their scouts led them through until they reached a small series of hills they could hide behind until it was time to attack. The ballistae crews, using the first light of the twilight period before sunrise, spent the remaining time assembling their artillery pieces on the hill, then camouflaging them behind banks of snow. While the ballistae crews worked, Lucius and Marpesia's scouts ranged wide in mixed teams in case they ran across Goths or blood demons, though the latter was less likely with each minute closer to sunrise. The rest of their people father in small groups, sharing the heat of their animals and each other.

As the first rays of the morning sun crept over the eastern horizon, Lucius and Marpesia, huddling together to share warmth, pushed apart, Marpesia following Lucius as he made the climb up the hill to the artillery embankment. When they reached the top, they were careful to stay behind the banked snow topped with pine boughs and other evergreen branches.

The optio in charge of the ballistae saluted Lucius. "Centurio. Chieftain."

Lucius nodded his acknowledgment and stepped into the small

view port cleared for observation. Marpesia squeezed in next to him. He could see little but shadows and snowdrifts. As Sol Invictus climbed higher into the sky on his sun chariot, the morning grew brighter. When the breeze picked up, he hoped it stayed reasonable so his ballistae could keep their accuracy.

A flash of color in the field below drew his eye. The breeze tugged at a scrap of fabric uncovered by the passing wind. As the wind pushed the top layers of snow around, it revealed more of the cloth and the body it clothed. Other little flicks of color attested to more than just the one body buried in the snow. They'd seen plenty of evidence of the death march the Tervingi and their night lords had forced on the rest of the Gothic tribes. The only ones who wouldn't be on short rations would be the blood drinkers. The parasites would drain the whole tribe and disperse and find new peoples to feed on and new ways to create mayhem.

"So many dead…" Marpesia whispered, gripping Lucius's hand tightly under their cloaks.

Lucius grunted affirmatively. "They left death in the north and found nothing better along the way. Driven by monsters who create and embrace death…"

"Will they find mercy in the south?"

"I fear not. The Tervingi have a mind for conquest and are driving the rest of their people before them. They'll be slaughtered by Constantius and his legions. The few left will become vassals to the empire along one side of the border or another, sending their sons to fight in Roma's armies."

She sighed heavily, expelling a heavy cloud of steam. "To squeeze my people into an ever tighter circle of Alans to the east, Germans to the west, and Romans everywhere to the south."

"I'm sorry, Marpesia." Lucius squeezed her hand through their thick gloves.

"You did not make the ways of the world. You and I just live in it and deal with the consequences."

"Centurio, mind taking a look at this?" the optio asked.

Lucius moved to the northernmost observation post, the optio moving aside so Lucius could look north by northeast through the small window they'd built into their snow embankment. Off in the distance, they saw the first sign of life as dark figures trudged through the snow, some on beasts.

"Good. I'd hate to think we'd missed them," Lucius said.

"Centurio?" a voice called quietly from behind.

"He's up here," the optio whispered hoarsely back.

One of his scouts finished the last bit of the climb and stood behind the ballistae, waiting to report. Lucius stepped away from the observation port and joined the scout so they wouldn't have to raise their voices.

"Report."

"The main group is approaching."

Lucius pulled his cloak around himself more tightly. "I can see the leading edge from here. Are the wagons we're looking for in this group?"

"Aye, Centurio. They're clustered fairly tightly in the middle."

Marpesia slid in next to Lucius to hear the report, the optio and his crew forming a circle around the scout and the two leaders of the vexillation.

The scout wiped a flat section of snow clear and drew the general shape of the horde of Goths. "Most of those in front, at least the very leading edge, look like family groups—women, children, a few men. Behind them appears to be a loose formation of horse soldiers moving in small to medium-sized bands. Next, arrayed out in a large hollow wedge, are more organized heavy cavalry and infantry, probably some archers as well. Here, in the center is the cluster of wagons you're looking for."

"What's behind them?" Marpesia asked.

"Not much of note. Smaller clusters of people," the scout replied.

"No one guarding the rear?" Lucius asked.

"Not that we've seen. Their forces are all arrayed to the forward."

The optio pointed a thumb over his shoulder. "Is there any chance they'll spread out below?"

The scout shook his head. "No. They'll run right through the center of this shallow valley. The ground on the other side is too rough to get the wagons through easily."

"Good, good," the optio said.

Lucius looked at the optio. "In range?"

The optio grinned wickedly. "Aye, Centurio. And if they're clustered up, we should be able to do a lot more damage with what we've got here."

A smirk spread across Marpesia's face. "I think I have an idea how to use this information."

Luke made eye contact with Marpesia and exchanged a moment. "Excellent." He turned back to the optio. "We have a little bit of time, Optio. Join us down below so we can listen to Marpesia's idea."

The scout and the optio followed Lucius and Marpesia down the hill as they grabbed the various officers and huddled together. Marpesia lined out their new strategy and ensured everyone was on board, including Beremund and Evoric, who'd they'd be trusting with a key piece of the plan. As Marpesia explained their role, he kept a tight gaze on them, ensuring they were comfortable with their parts.

When everyone was ready, Lucius had them strip anything overtly Roman or Sarmatian from their outward appearances. Marpesia grumbled as she removed the headpiece from her mare's kit. Lucius even pulled the crest from his helmet. When they were ready, they distributed some of the equipment he'd stripped from the Goths they'd defeated at the pass a couple weeks earlier. He looked over his motley band, nodding. It would have to do.

SEVENTEEN

LUCIUS and his mixed band of Roxolani and Romans waited in a thicket of pine trees as the horde of Goths meandered by their position. Movement caught his eye, and he turned his head. The Roxolani had their bow cases open and were stringing their bows in preparation. He watched admiringly as Marpesia strung her bow gracefully from the back of her mare and slid it back into her wide bow case.

He'd never seen Marpesia in close action with her bow. He'd watched her shoot at target practice and from a distance during the battle, but never next to her in her element on the back of her fierce mare. At the battle of the pass, she'd been too far away to really watch, even if he wasn't too busy to do more than catch quick glances.

He smiled at Marpesia then turned to Beremund and Evoric. "Are you ready to go?"

Beremund nodded confidently, Evoric less so.

"Alright, lead on," Lucius ordered.

Beremund and Evoric nudged their ponies forward, working their way through the thick copse into the sparser trees at the edges. Lucius and Marpesia followed along with the rest of their people.

They out into a disorderly cluster of riders and made for the end of the line of civilians bringing up the ragged end of the south-bound Gothic horde.

Lucius's eyes darted everywhere, trying to find any potential dangers before they spotted him and his people. As they got closer, no one seemed interested other than a briefly raised head to see what the noise was before looking down to follow the footsteps of those who'd tamped down the snow before them. Occasionally their eyes would halt momentarily on one of the long, shallow snowdrifts with bits of cloth peeking out. The brief glimpses of their possible future inspired them to pick up their pace for a bit only to descend back into their miserable trudging pace when their malnourished energy flagged. He didn't hate the Goths, only what their leaders and the monsters he'd dedicated his life to hunting had done to the poor bastards.

If Lucius and his people did their jobs well, the Goths would at least have one problem removed from their lives, leaving them to deal with only the winter and other mortals. Apparently, Beremund didn't see anyone he knew personally, although he delivered the occasional head nod of acknowledgment as he passed someone who gave him more than just a passing glance. Every now and then, he'd call out a greeting.

The rest of those he led remained stoic, staring ahead. They wanted to look unapproachable—the intimidating Gothic warriors with a purpose. They shouldn't have worried. The people trailing behind the wagons and warriors were, to a person, dispirited and uninterested in anything other than the promise of warmth in the south, placing one foot in front of the other because they had no other choices. Lucius felt for them. No one deserved to starve and die like this. But better a death taken by the cold than one ripped violently apart by the predatory monsters of the night. At least the snow let their souls pass on to whatever afterlife the Goths believed in.

As they advanced from the rear of the horde toward the middle, Lucius kept his eyes roving. Checking the nearing hills to his right, he gave the signal to slow their pace. The wagons were only a couple hundred yards in front of them. He trusted his ballistae crews, but those kinds of mistakes couldn't be undone. He forced his jaw open, trying to relieve the tension in the muscles clamping them shut. Around him, the heads of his people kept turning toward the hill before quickly returning to stare forward.

He thought he heard the twang of the twisted ropes unleashing their tension. A dark speck arced from the top of the hill, reaching its apex before succumbing to the grasp of the earth's grip. A second twang and another speck flying skyward…

The first bolt bashed into the wood of one of the wagons, punching a small hole through its wall. A few seconds later, another wagon sprung a leak. If the holes had been east facing, the morning sun would be trickling in. As it was, the calmer westerly light still inspired furious, fear-filled shrieks. Their range found, the ballistae threw their real payloads into the heavens. As one, Lucius and his comrades watched the specially engineered fire bolts soar through the air. His breath held, Lucius let it out explosively when the first bolt shattered against the top of one of the wagons, spilling its flammable liquid and a small coal. Within a few moments, the fire caught and started to spread.

"Come on…" he muttered.

A second bolt exploded, spraying flames that splattered over several wagons, including the one the first bolt had struck. Flames erupted as more fire bolts filled with pitch and bitumen rose through the cold morning air. His crews were working as fast as possible while safely handling flames and the potent mix of flammable substances.

Lucius quietly slipped his spatha from its scabbard and nudged Moonlight Dancing forward. Marpesia, pushing her mare to match Lucius's speed, had her bow in her left hand, a handful of arrows in the grip of the same hand. She kept her bow to her side. Around them, swords, axes, and bows were readied as they closed the distance to the wagons.

Shouts Lucius didn't understand drew his attention to the front of their group. Evoric kicked his horse forward as he shouted, waving his arms in the air, pointing behind him—pointing to the intruders.

"Shit. Evoric is betraying us. Marpesia, do you have a shot?"

"No!"

Beremund kicked his horse after Evoric, raising his sword as he closed the distance. Evoric turned in time to see the blade sweep toward his neck, as Beremund decapitated the traitor. The crowds of civilians stared at the bloodshed, then screamed, fleeing in every direction as Beremund rode toward them yelling, raising his sword ominously to scare them away. Seeing the readied weapons of Lucius and his force, the fleeing civilians parted around them and cleared the way between Lucius and his people and the wagons.

Lucius raised his sword and pointed toward the wagons. His soldiers with melee weapons formed a protective barrier around their riders carrying large satchels. When they reached the first wagon, the nearest rider pulled a small clay pot from the satchel and hurled it against the wagon. Another rider rode by with a lit torch, igniting the dripping pitch and oil.

As they worked their way through the rear wagons, Lucius's ballistae crews flung more bolts at the front of the line of wagons, torching them and grinding the procession to a halt.

"Lucius! Goths incoming!" Marpesia shouted as she flew by on her golden mare.

"Damn it!" He'd hoped they'd have more time before the Goths reacted.

He halted, letting his men flow around him to continue their torch work. Marpesia let loose with her arrows, reaching forward with her right hand and plucking one by the nock from the handful she held in her left. With one smooth motion, she seated the arrow, drew it back, and let it fly, repeating the motion. When she ran out of arrows, she reached down with her bow hand to grab another handful from her quiver to start over. Where her arrows landed, Goths fell. He watched in awe as she rained death from the back of her golden mare.

Lucius shook his head and charged forward to protect his fire team. The ballistae on the hill fell silent as Lucius and his people moved deeper into the mass of wagons. After they ignited one wagon, the door in the back shattered open as one of the demons busted through, only to start smoking as the rays of the sun kissed his skin. Between the flames or the sun, he chose the sun, running in search of any shade. One of Lucius's legionnaires rode him down and took his head, letting the sun finish its work.

A horn blasted three short blasts and three long blasts, repeating the call. Lucius swept forward as the fire teams quickly hurled their remaining clay pots at whatever they could, unloading their weight and the danger before joining the rest of their compatriots as they gathered on the west side of the caravan. When Lucius cleared the wagons, a running skirmish greeted him as Marpesia and her archers charged forward, pouring arrows into the first signs of resistance from the Tervingi. As they got closer, they'd spin around and fire more shots as they fled back toward their allies. The Sarmatians who'd been assisting with the fire teams sheathed swords and slung their axes aside, pulling their bows to reinforce Marpesia's archers.

Lucius spun around on his mare trying to see if any more of his people were tangled in the maze of burning wagons. He didn't see anyone else. The Roxolani with the ox horn rode up to Lucius, waiting for his order.

"Now!" Lucius yelled.

The Roxolani put the ox horn to his lips and blew a series of long notes. Lucius nudged his horse into a trot as they cleared the last few wagons, urging Moonlight Dancing faster as he led his forces away. Everyone with a bow drifted to the back of the fleeing mob of Romans and Sarmatians to screen their retreat. As the trees grew closer, but still not safely so, Lucius kept his gaze on the hill where his ballistae were positioned. He couldn't hear the telltale twang of the torsion bars, but he waited to see if his crews would respond after going silent earlier.

He heaved a sigh of relief when two more of the fire bolts soared from behind their hidden snowbanks. Pulling to the side, Lucius turned his mare and stopped as they fell among the leading edge of the pursuing Goths. The bolts exploded, spraying fiery oil in their wake and creating chaos as animals screamed and riders fell.

Another set of bolts rose to follow the first. When they landed further back, panic took hold. Lucius knew they had to be running short on fire bolts by now, but his optio was using them to the best of his ability, lobbing them at random into the horde of Goths trying to form up for pursuit.

When the last of Marpesia's Wolf Clan rode past, Lucius spun his mare and joined them. Taking one last glance over his shoulder, he didn't see anyone pursuing them. They kept up their gallop as they wound their way through the hills, only slowing when the trees grew too thick. Lucius called a halt when they reached the bottom of the hill where his ballistae were stationed.

He leapt off his horse, tossing the reins to someone, and dashed up the hill. When he reached the top, he was breathing heavily after the mad flight and run up the snowy hill. He slid to a halt at the one of the observation ports.

"How many bolts do you have left?" Lucius called behind him.

"Three, Centurio," replied the optio.

"Shoot them all wherever you want. Then get down the hill. We need to get lost while we still can."

"Don't we want to burn the ballistae?"

"No. Let's not give away our position exactly. Take a couple axes and bust them up as best you can."

"Aye, Centurio." The optio turned to his crews. "You heard the man! Let's get a move on it unless you're waiting for a personal invitation from the Tervingi."

Lucius, moving more carefully on the slick descent, grabbed his water skin and took a deep pull. The Sarmatians were sharing the cache of arrows left behind. Some of his men were readying the ponies the ballistae crews would ride. They unhooked the mule teams from the sled wagons and shifted some baggage to the freed mules. With the weight shared and no wagons, they'd be able to move faster through rougher territory and hopefully lose any tails. After firing off the last three bolts, the crews took axes to the ballistae, cutting ropes and busting up the finer mechanisms that kept the artillery pieces together and made them work. When the blow of axe against wood fell silent, the crews scrambled down the hill, running to their ponies.

Lucius mounted up. "Mount up. Let's get a move on it."

At Lucius's orders, the scouts moved out, sweeping west and deeper into the forests and hills. Lucius fell into the middle of the line riding out. At the end of the line, Marpesia ordered a handful of her Wolf Clan to take off, pulling pine boughs behind them to disguise their trail. Satisfied with the results, she trotted forward to join Lucius.

"It's not perfect, but if we get some wind to blow around the snow, it'll be better than a raw trail into the woods." Marpesia's finger played over the end of her bow in its case as she rode next to him.

"You were wonderful. I've never seen anyone shoot like that before."

"My people shoot just as well as I do; you're just not trying to flirt with them," Marpesia replied, smiling.

Lucius laughed and reached over, patting her knee as she rode within reach. "Well, let's hope you won't need to put on another display any time soon."

EIGHTEEN

THEY RODE DEEP into the foothills of the Montes Sarmatici, trying to throw off any pursuit the Goths might mount after their raid. Lucius considered it a success, taking out most of the wagons Beremund said were the safe daytime transportation of the night lords. Without the wagons, they'd have to travel at night and find places to hide during the day—those few who had survived the assault. Without surveying the results, he guessed most of the creatures had died when forced from their dark havens. The sun was a pitiless enemy.

They couldn't tell if the wagons burned constituted the majority of the blood drinking demons, but Lucius hoped it would weaken the power of their human allies, the Tervingi tribe, and allow the rest of the Goths to break free from their domination, assuming they lived that long.

They rode west for three days, finding what shelter they could to set up quick camps, relying on stealth and the experience of Lucius's elite monster slayers to keep watch during the long cold nights, then wiping evidence of their night's stay away the next day. After the third night, they started south, sending scouts east to make sure the Goths hadn't found them. They still had a long trip in the cold north, but they hoped for a night or two in the small fort they'd set up before the final leg north for their attack. The only saving grace was Marpesia's warm body by his side each night as they fell asleep together, exhausted after a cold day working through the forests and hills on their way to their fort.

"To arms! Invaders! Demons! To Arms!"

Lucius bolted upright, his eyes shooting wide as his heart pounded in his chest. As the feel of his age-old enemies nearby filtered through his groggy brain, he snapped alert. Marpesia wiped the sleep out of her eyes and forced her feet onto the ground, yanking her boots on. Lucius pulled his caligae on and helped Marpesia into her scale coat. She aided him with his lorica. He didn't bother with anything else beyond pulling his helmet on. Marpesia checked the rudis Lucius had given her to ensure it was in place. He yanked his gladius and rudis from their scabbards and ran outside.

Following the sound of fighting toward the edge of their camp, he slowed, stabbing out with the rudis in his left hand. He struck, drawing a painful hiss from the monster trying to sneak up on him. Lucius buried the gladius into the heart of the creature, turning it to a dust that joined the powder of the snow.

After the first one fell to his blades, they came fast and thick from the darkness. Some carried weapons, others relied on their fangs and claws, their bodies the only weapons they needed. Lucius's enhanced night vision allowed him to meet the creatures blow for blow, blocking weapons and disarming them, sometimes literally. The snow around Lucius grew thick and dark from the sludge remaining from the corpses of the younger demons stupid enough to come within range of the Centurio Immortalis's deadly blades.

"Horse! Protect the horses!" yelled a voice from the dark.

"Shit," Lucius mumbled, and started working his way toward where the horses were picketed.

As an arrow whistled near his head, he instinctively ducked, looking for its source. Marpesia, on one knee, fired arrow after arrow, grabbing another handful as she tried to take down the monsters flooding into their camp.

"Marpesia! Behind you!" Lucius yelled.

Eyebrows furrowed in concentration, she either didn't hear him or didn't process it as a shadow moved up behind her. Lucius broke into a sprint just as two demons tackled her to ground. His heart screamed in agony as he poured everything into closing the distance. When his toe caught on a fallen limb, he crashed to the ground. Scrambling, he snatched up his weapons and staggered forward.

One of the monsters was struggling to climb on top of Marpesia as she thrashed, the creature trying to get his teeth to her neck. The other, dodging flailing legs, attempted to get Marpesia's lower half under control. Lucius, bordering on panic, couldn't run fast enough, couldn't close the distance in time. The sounds of clashing around him disappeared until all he could hear were Marpesia's screams. Despite his need for breath, his chest wouldn't expand as his growing desperation took hold.

Marpesia's dead face, pale and bloodless flashed across his mind. The image of her body covered in her own blood burned in his eyes as he tried to force the tears from them. Closer. He was finally getting closer. He raised his gladius, letting loose a bellow of rage and fear. The furious scream distracted the monsters for a brief a second. Marpesia's hand, scrabbling for anything, fell on the rudis spilling from its scabbard. Lucius swept his rudis through the neck of the creature holding Marpesia's legs, then skidded to a halt, turning. Her legs freed, Marpesia jolted the other demon back, allowing her to plunge the rudis into its chest and penetrate its heart.

The monster puffed into dust, a breeze pushing its remains away as Marpesia scrambled backwards on her hands, scuttling like a crab. Lucius finished the second monster, sending it oozing into the snow.

He slid onto his knees next to her. Tears streamed down her face, mixing with a smear of wet blood that covered her jaw and neck.

"Are you OK?" Lucius asked frantically.

Marpesia, her eyes wide, gasped in and out, too shocked to answer. Lucius dropped his weapons and looked for the wound causing the blood. The demon had gotten close, nicking her neck. It didn't look deep despite the blood.

"You're OK… It's not deep," Lucius said, almost as much to reassure himself as to calm Marpesia.

She nodded back jerkily. He looked around, making sure nothing was sneaking up on them. He didn't feel any of the demons that close, but better cautious… He stood up, and Marpesia grabbed his wrist.

"No, don't go…" she said, fear thick in her throat.

"I'm not going anywhere. I'm gathering your bow and arrows." He picked up his gladius and rudis and wiped them clean. Next, he gathered everything he could see and handed them to Marpesia so she could stash them in her bow case. "We've got to get moving. Are you OK to stand?"

"I think so."

Still holding her bow, he moved it to the hand with his gladius and offered to help her up. Once she was standing, he gave her bow back.

"We've got to get to the horses." Lucius gestured with his head.

She nodded. Lucius started at a crouching walk to see if Marpesia was steady enough on her legs to keep up. Once he was sure, he picked up the pace, the sound of fighting growing louder. Keeping close to Lucius, Marpesia stowed her bow in its case on her left hip and unslung the pointed axe.

When they found the source of the noise, they hung back and worked their way around the edge of the clearing. Lucius's men and Marpesia's Wolves surrounded the horses, doing their best to keep the monsters from breaking their line and getting to the animals. Without their horses, they'd be stranded in the north surrounded by deadly enemies and a deadlier winter. Everyone knew it and fought like fiends to protect the animals.

Once Lucius and Marpesia had worked their way through the darkness, they picked the section with the weakest presence of the di inferi and charged in. Lucius tried to put down the demons as fast as he could, making every thrust count. Missing a heart shot, he aimed for their necks. Between them, Lucius and Marpesia broke through, freeing up those pinned down in that section. The freed people surged to the sides, adding their weight to that of their comrades.

Lucius's lungs heaved like bellows as he thrust and slashed with both swords, brutally exterminating his enemy without mercy. His arms burned from swinging his sword, but he couldn't slow down, digging deep to pull on every reserve his gods provided and sucking energy from the demons. Finally, they turned the tide.

The near taste of victory drove the humans against the fanged monsters. They had attempted to massacre their horses so they could pick them apart at their leisure. Instead, the tide turned, the demons fleeing, running with supernatural speed into the darkness of night. Lucius helped his people take down the last few, then went through the dismembered demons and sent them onto a true death with a quick stab through the heart. He took a moment to drain a couple for himself. Kneeling by a body, he shoved the rudis into the demon's heart, placing his forehead onto the pommel of his sword. He spoke the incantation that activated the rudis and waited for the white light to move down the blade into the monster and make its return trip.

After the first one, his heart slowed, and the burn in his muscles lessened. After the second one, he felt fresh and alive. Once they'd cleaned up the bodies left by the dark lords, he sent teams through the camp to make sure there weren't any more of the creatures lurking about. While they swept the camp, Lucius had teams gather their wounded and their dead so they could be organized and dealt with.

When the bodies were sorted, they'd lost about seventeen horses and forty-seven souls—twenty-one Romans and twenty-six Sarmatians. Surprisingly, the cantankerous mules held their own, breaking the bodies of several fanged attackers. Many of the people had suffered wounds, although most were light. Heavier wounds had led to death as they bled out on the forest floor. When he found Marpesia, a medic was seeing to her neck. He'd cleaned the wound and was putting in a few stitches. Marpesia looked exhausted, the adrenaline dump of being awoken then attacked finally draining from her body.

Seeing that Marpesia was being attended to, Lucius went to collect the signaculum tags from the dead so their names could be entered into the records as killed in action and their survivors paid out their benefits. He sent out details to gather wood so they could burn their dead. As he waited for updates and for his orders to be carried out, his eyes drifted toward Marpesia, the image of her struggling on the ground indelibly burned into his mind as it mingled with the nightmares fueling his terror at the possible future Marpesia would have with him.

He shook his head, tears burning the corners of his eyes. He couldn't be responsible for her death. He cared about her too much, loved her too deeply to selfishly bring her into his world. She was too fierce to play it safe when his life was on the line. He couldn't lose her to the teeth of the monsters he'd dedicated his life to eradicating. They'd already taken too much from him; he wouldn't give them Marpesia.

The camp stayed awake, completing the tasks they needed to accomplish to honor the dead and send their bodies to the next world and the various other tasks, including butchering a few of the fallen horses for fresh meat. Also, especially for the Sarmatians who'd never withstood an attack by the monsters they'd joined Lucius to hunt, no one really wanted to tuck back into their tents to sleep for the remaining hours of darkness. Everyone remained on high alert. Deciding it would be better to move on, he ordered camp to be broken and everything to be packed to move out as soon as they sent their comrades' souls to the afterlife.

Once Lucius and Marpesia led their people through the death rites they observed, they set torch to the funeral pyre. They maintained their silent vigil as the sun rose over the eastern horizon, the first tendrils of smoke rising to the heavens. Lucius had his artillery men mix up a small batch of the oil mixture they'd lobbed at the Goths and their demon transportation wagons to aid the fires in the green wood. As they stood there, Marpesia reached out, winding her fingers through his.

Her touch sought reassurance, a feeling he wish he could find as well. He craved the warmth of her skin against his, yet he felt hollow inside, knowing he couldn't keep this going if he wanted to keep Marpesia safe. But why couldn't he keep her? Didn't he deserve some happiness after dedicating two centuries of his life to protecting humanity from monsters they didn't even know were preying on them?

Give him a battlefield, and he could make the snap decisions that balanced life against death and come out victorious. But this decision rendered him confused and anxious. What was best for Marpesia and what was best for him? And why was figuring out which was which so difficult? As he stood there with her, he couldn't figure out a way to make both possibilities true. Could he stay with Marpesia and keep her safe from his life?

With a sigh, he let go of her hand and cleared his throat. "Mount up. It's time to move out."

NINETEEN

AS THEY RETREATED from the site of the attack, Lucius sent their scouts wide to locate the Goths. When they returned with no report of any in the vicinity, he decided to angle out of the thick forests toward more open country. There, they could take advantage of the speed of their horses while providing less opportunity for the demons to sneak up through the darkness of the forest.

They stopped early, setting up a basic earthwork and stake picket, risking fire for the night watch. When he fell into his blankets and furs. Marpesia joined him; they were exhausted from a short night and the brutal fight. Marpesia quickly lost her battle with slumber. Despite his own need for sleep, he had trouble finding it, visions of Marpesia's near death haunting him. Each time he'd look down at Marpesia to reassure himself, the shallow cut in her neck with its dark stitches reminded him how close she'd come to death in that moment. A tiny bit deeper and it would have cut her jugular, and she'd have bled out even if one of the blood drinkers hadn't been there to sup off her.

Every time he'd calm down and doze, his eyes would flutter open and fall on those stitches staring back at him. When exhaustion finally claimed him, nightmares replaced his waking fears until screaming tore him from his dreams back to the world of the waking.

It was Marpesia's screams. He shook her awake. Sitting up, she panted heavily trying to catch her breath. When she turned to face Lucius, tears streaked down her face as her chest and shoulders heaved. She flung herself at him, wracking sobs shaking her body as she clung to him desperately.

When someone poked their head into Lucius's tent, he waved them away while holding Marpesia. After a while, the tears slowed to a trickle then stopped as she calmed in his arms. He hated that the vampires had gotten so close to killing her, that the encounter had caused her more than physical harm. This was one of the reasons he'd kept his distance from romantic entanglements. His world was brutal and dangerous—far more so than people who only dwelt in the mortal realm.

As Marpesia's breathing steadied, she kissed Lucius's cheek then laid down, pulling Lucius into her arms. She rolled over onto her side, pushing her back into Lucius so he formed to her back. Pulling his arm over her, she used Lucius as a protective barrier as she attempted to fall back asleep. Lucius gently stroked her hair, the stitches on her neck drawing his attention constantly no matter how hard he tried to look away. When she finally fell asleep, he joined her, his dreams once again troubled with visions of all the ways she could die or be hurt.

They made it through the night without further disturbances, either from the demons hunting them or night terrors. They made quick work of their camp, eating fresh horse steaks and porridge before mounting up for another day of cold riding.

Lucius, riding up and down the column, took special note of the faces of the Sarmatians. They'd never fought an enemy like that before—one that looked at them as food. Troubled expressions and signs of poor sleep were nearly universal. On the other hand, his legionnaires held the hardened expressions of jaded warriors who'd fought too many of the monsters, each of them had slain one of the demons, most many. Lucius had selected the men who were the most experienced hunters. Each of them bore the white fangs on their shields that marked them as someone who'd killed a di inferi. The only man in his vexillation who hadn't, Martininius, could no longer claim that distinction. When they returned to their fort, he'd earn a pay bump and have his shield decorated with the four thin triangles that represented fangs, the points aimed toward the center as if the shield were the dark maw of one of the creatures.

When he'd pull his horse in line with Marpesia, she'd smile at him sadly, her eyes tired and vulnerable. She needed him, and he couldn't bear the weight of it. He'd look at her pretty face and her soulful gray eyes, and he'd picture it covered in blood, her eyes life-less. He'd return a perfunctory smile and head off to check in with his officers about some matter that didn't actually need his attention.

That night, they camped in a valley surrounded by hills sepa-rating them on one side from the plain the Goths had been using as a road south. The scouts reported no one of consequence for miles. They'd made camp early so they could keep their cooking fires concealed under the light of day, the wind scattering their smoke before it could give their location away. Then they turned in early, wanting to be moving at first light so they could make the small fort before nightfall.

As he and Marpesia laid down to sleep, she turned to him, laying her hand on his cheek. "What troubles you, Lucius?"

He sighed, hoping his avoidance of her hadn't been so obvious. "We're a long way from the majority of our people, fleeing through territory occupied by thousands of Goths and the monsters that drive them. The monsters found us. That attack could have gone a lot worse. We were fortunate not to lose more…" He trailed off, afraid to make it about his fear of losing her. "I'm tired, Marpesia."

"Isn't this what you do, though? Slay the monsters?" She leaned forward and kissed the tip of his nose. "Protect us from the things that make people huddle closer to their fires at night?"

He nodded. "I nearly lost… We nearly lost more people."

"We're all soldiers. You and I are leaders. Risk is the nature of our lives."

"I know, it's just…" He sighed, closing his eyes. "Sometimes the weight is heavier than others."

He felt like a coward. He couldn't bring himself to say the words that screamed in his head. He'd nearly lost her. Just the thought of that loss felt like the weight Atlas bore on his back, crushing him. He'd consigned his life to this mission when he accepted his position as Mithras's weapon against the creatures of the night. Marpesia hadn't.

She'd known what he was when she'd requested his assistance from Constantius, but now she'd seen the hard truth of his life. He doubted she'd had any idea she'd become romantically involved with the leader of the monster-hunting legion.

Marpesia ran her hand through his hair. "I know. I see my people's lands being eaten up by Alans to the east and now the Goths from the north. There's no place for us to go. Now our souls aren't even safe from the darkness. It's a harsh world, and harsher for those of us in a position of leadership. We can share that burden, make the lifting lighter."

"I wish…" He didn't finish his thought, unable to put voice to his desires. "I've been bearing this load for a long time and have buried so many friends in that time, losing them to time and to the creatures who dominate my existence. It's dangerous to be close to me."

"Shh." Marpesia placed her fingers over his lips. "It's warm under our blankets in each other's arms. This is a problem to examine in the light of day after a night of sleep." She gently nudged him onto his back so she could rest her head on his chest and drape her arm and leg over him. "Just hold me, Lucius, and let us just be here tonight. Tomorrow, we can share a bed behind stout walls and get a proper sleep."

"OK." He reached out to stroke her hair.

Soon, she fell asleep while he stared at the ceiling, occasionally tipping his head to kiss the top of hers. His eyes burned with exhaustion, but he couldn't put his worries to bed. He couldn't reconcile his desires against the safety of Marpesia. Her people needed her thoughtful leadership. It would be selfish to put his needs over theirs when a life with him was death. He hated the decisions his logic was forcing on him. When Marpesia rolled over, he wanted to fold against her back, but the stitches stared back at him. It would be better for her…

It was late in the night when troubled sleep finally claimed him.

WHEN THE FORT first appeared in the distance, the mood lightened as the destination they'd yearned for become a tangible reality. For Lucius, it meant the end of something he could barely think of being without. He had to end whatever this was with Marpesia—for her own good. It would be easier for him not to be in constant fear of her violent death.

Why'd it take so much courage to make a cowardly decision? He tried to tell himself that his decision was for the good of her people and the good of her future health, but the dark part of his mind knew it was at least partly so he didn't have to feel the pain of losing her, feel the guilt of causing it.

When they crossed the threshold into the camp, he dismissed everyone to tear down their packs and get some rest. The men who'd been holding the fort could continue its stewardship for another night. Despite the addition of fresh meat, they'd been running mostly on cold trail rations and thin meals for a while. Tonight was the first thing resembling a feast they'd had since leaving the fort in the pass.

While Marpesia made sure her people were taken care of for the evening, Lucius sat in his tent, sitting in his chair, leaning forward with his elbows resting on his knees. He stared at the ground, his stomach a pit of emptiness. He hoped she would hurry up so he could get this over with while simultaneously not wanting her to step through that door because it would mean that much longer he could hold on to the idea of her.

When she walked into the tent, he sagged in on himself, his heart dropping even further. "Marpesia. We need to talk."

She looked at him, her brow furrowing as her head tipped to the side. "What is it, Lucius? What's going on?"

"I don't think we can keep being together." Lucius's voice shook.

"What?" She looked confused. "Why?" A flood of emotions flashed over her face, joining the confusion.

"I just don't think it's a good idea to be involved with me."

At the moment, her face settled on anger. "Is it because I'm a *barbarian*?" she sneered the word.

"No. That has nothing to do with it."

"Why, Lucius? Do you not care for me?" She sat on a stool, facing Lucius.

Lucius wouldn't look up to make eye contact. "I care deeply for you."

"Then why? If you care for me, why can't we be together? It can't be because of your duty to an empire that doesn't want you... You're not going to cross the border, are you?" Concern and a note of panic tinged her voice.

"No. There's nothing for me south of the Danuvius."

"But there's something for you here. Come with me, be with me. My people will welcome you. I want you to..."

"I can't."

"Why? Why are you doing this?" Her jaw flexed.

"I can't lose you." He spoke barely above a whisper.

"But you're pushing me away? I don't get..." She reached up and touched the stitches. "Oh, I get it."

He looked up into her eyes. "I can't get the image out of my head. Your death haunts my nightmares. My life is endlessly tied up with the monsters that nearly killed you. I can't subject you to that. I can't have your death on my conscious."

"The responsibility for my life and my death are my own. They always have been."

"I know."

Her eyes narrowed and her spine stiffened. "Do you, though? You're trying to take them on as if they were yours. I am not one of your subordinates. Their lives are your responsibility. I am my own woman."

He avoided making eye contact with her, knowing the steel and fire she held in her eyes. "But I won't be able to protect you. Without a legion of trained—"

Marpesia interrupted. "I don't need you to protect me. Or a Roman legion. I'm one of the finest warriors on the steppes. I have an entire clan of fine warriors to fight by my side. I can call on my cousin and muster all the Roxolani. I've been far closer to death than this little nick on my neck. I don't want your protection. I want your love."

"You have it and that's why I can't. I can't watch you die because of my burden. I can't witness your life stolen. I can't…"

Marpesia's eyes hardened. "You can't what? You can't let me make my own decisions about my own life? Do not infantilize me, Roman. I am a grown woman. I know what danger is and how to deal with it. I know what I want for my life. You cannot steal that away from me." Her voice landed whip hard.

"But—"

"No! You cannot take that power from me." She inhaled deeply then exhaled sharply. "We are done with this conversation for now. We are both tired and could use a night of rest. I'm going to stay with Aella tonight, so use this time to get your priorities straight. But, when next I see you, the first words out of your mouth had better be an apology." She turned and shoved her way out of his tent.

He stared after her as the tent flap swayed and settled, only turning his eyes away when he felt his neck stiffen uncomfortably from disuse. For the rest of the evening, he stared at the ground, not saying a word to anyone, just stewing in Marpesia's hard words until he gave up trying to piece together his thoughts.

TWENTY

IT FELT like he'd only dozed off when he heard a commotion and the sounds of violence. He leapt from his bed and threw on his armor and weapons. He'd done this repeatedly over two centuries, and when he tapped into the extra reserve after slaying and consuming his enemy, he could be fully ready in moments.

He sprinted out his tent into the dark night, his blade naked. He expected to see Goths or maybe some blood demons they missed. It took a moment to adjust to the sight of people in the equipment and garb of Constantius's legions. The fighting was coming to an end as more Romans surrounded their camp, subduing his men and their Roxolani allies. He couldn't believe his eyes as he looked for someone to fight.

His feet carried him toward the sound of a raging woman. When he found the noise, he stopped, stunned. Marpesia thrashed in the arms of a couple legionnaires, her screams of rage only matched by the fury of her body as she tried to kick and yank herself free. Finally, someone wearing the armor and crests of an officer walked up and placed his blade against her neck.

"No!" Lucius screamed, charging forward.

"If you come any closer, I'll spill her blood into the snow, Centurio," the officer called out.

Lucius slid to a halt in the snow.

"Drop your gladius."

When Lucius hesitated, the man grabbed Marpesia's hair and pulled her head back, pressing the blade to her throat. He could see where the blade pushed into her skin. He thought he saw a glint of blood along a spot where the blade might have broken skin. Lucius's heart thundered in his chest, his mind grinding to a halt while simultaneously running around in his skull looking for a solution. He let the sword tumble from his hands.

"No…" Marpesia whispered, afraid speaking any louder might push her own throat into the blade.

"If you harm her, sword or no, I will rip you to pieces limb from limb." Lucius's voice was low and deadly serious. "You don't have enough men to prevent that from happening. They may eventually bring me down, but it will do you little good as you bleed out into the snow."

The man took Lucius seriously, his eyes widening. He cleared his throat. "Well, we can work together on that." He pulled his blade away from Marpesia's neck but kept it held up and close.

Lucius looked around him. His men had been disarmed, some forced to their knees. A few bodies lay motionless in the snow. Their captors were waiting for something as they stood static, holding Lucius's forces immobile. The sound of armored men on armored horses grew from the darkness until it materialized into a troop of heavily armored warriors on horses wearing scale mail, flying the Chi Rho banner of Constantius.

When the men dismounted, they formed around a figure shorter than most of his escort. He was too small of stature to be the Dominus, nor did he have the limp. He pulled his helmet off, handing it to one of his men and turned. It was the little shit that had insulted Marpesia, the Dominus's eldest son, Flavius Claudius Constantius.

Flavius walked up, nodding to the man who'd been holding a blade against Marpesia's neck. "Excellent work, you have indeed earned your promotion."

The man bowed. "Thank you, Caesar."

Constantius turned and stepped toward Lucius, a couple of his guards moving forward so they could intercept him if needed. "The infamous Centurio Immortalis. You were captured far easier than I thought. All alone in the wilderness with only a few hundred men. Where's the vaunted Black Legion?"

"It's not far away. Perhaps if you turn around, you can stay ahead of them."

Constantius laughed. "Bold even in captivity. I know where they are precisely. My scouts report them still holed up in that pass."

A man ran up, bowing deeply, and addressed the boy general. "The camp is secure, Caesar. There's no more resistance."

"Excellent."

Lucius stood impotent, his chest heaving with rage. He calculated whether he could reach the son of the emperor. Tapping into everything he had, he might be able to. The two guards picked up on the calculation in Lucius's eyes, their hands drifting to their spatha. Deciding not to risk it against a man with as towering a reputation as Lucius, they pulled their swords, stepping into ready positions, their shields braced and ready.

Flavius laughed, although Lucius thought he heard a bit of fear in its tones. "If the Centurio moves, kill everyone, starting with the Sarmatian bitch."

Lucius clenched his jaw. He could no longer restrain the look of pure hatred he directed at the boy who one day would be dominus. His eyes drifted to Marpesia against his will. She practically quivered with rage, her eyes burning into the back of the boy who was playing at power. Flavius's words burned into Lucius's head. Marpesia would die first. Fear slithered down his spine and into his eyes as they drifted back to the Caesar.

Constantius saw the shift in Lucius's eyes, a knowing smirk spreading across his face. He raised his hand into the air. In response, the sword was pressed back against Marpesia's neck. Lucius's eyes darted around the camp, seeing blade after blade pressed against the necks of his men or to Marpesia's Wolf Clan.

Short, shallow breaths forced their way into Lucius's lungs as his body clenched in anguish and rage.

"Let them go," Lucius said, barely above a whisper.

"What?" Flavius turned his ear to Lucius condescendingly, a knowing smirk on his face.

A little louder. "I'll surrender, but let them go. I'll go with you willingly."

"That's better," Flavius said, lowering his arm.

Lucius checked around him; swords lowered but still at the ready. He sought everyone he could until he could see no more as the darkness curtained the rest of his people from view. When there was nowhere else to look, Lucius took a deep breath and let his eyes fall on Marpesia. The look of sadness in her eyes nearly buckled his knees, breaking him.

Her voice drifted to Lucius's ears. "No..." Her whole body moved as she breathed heavy and fast, her jaw clenching, the fury building in her chest. "NO!" She yanked at her captors, pulling them a step forward until they got her reined in somewhat. She fought like a wildcat, trying to get free, her eyes boring into Lucius. "You little bastard!"

"Shut her up!" Constantius called.

Someone stepped forward and rammed a fist into her gut. Her air wheezed from her lips as she slumped for a moment before renewing her efforts, an incoherent roar ripping from her lips as she tugged forward.

"I said... Shut. Her. Up."

Lucius, motion slowing around him, watched a punch pound into Marpesia's stomach, even harder than the last, doubling her over before another punch took her in the face, rendering her a limp mess held up by the two legionnaires tasked with controlling her. Lucius surged forward.

"You little shit!" He wanted to rip Flavius apart with his bare hands. He didn't care if the swords held at the ready would pierce him; he still would have enough strength to make Flavius pay. He made it half way until his foot landed on a rock under the snow, and his ankle twisted as he tumbled forward, landing on his hands and knees in the snow. He tried to get up but slipped in the muddy, snowy slurry churned up by too many feet, falling onto his face.

Flavius laughed.

Lucius felt hands on his arms, yanking him from the snow. Cold iron kissed his wrists as they quickly fixed manacles into place. Hot tears streamed down his cheeks as his chin quivered and jaw clenched.

Flavius walked up and patted Lucius on the cheek. The two men who had Lucius's arms in their grasp tensed, pulling him slightly back. They weren't anticipating his power and anger though, and he lurched forward, pulling them with him. Flavius stumbled back, fear shooting across his eyes. Lucius's captors lifted up, robbing Lucius of his traction and putting painful pressure on his shoulders. His spleen vented, he slumped, his captors strengthening their grip and bracing their legs against further lunges.

Enjoying the impotent rage of Lucius's breath sizzling in and out of his mouth, Flavius laughed again, notes of relief tinging his false bravado. "I'm feeling generous, Centurio. I'll grant you the freedom of your men and the Sarmatians. I'm only here for you. You'll make an excellent prize to present to my father."

Off in the distance, Lucius heard the angry cries of a horse. He turned in time to see someone drag Moonlight Dancing into the darkness on a long lead. The horse kept rearing, raking her front hooves through the air. As Flavius stepped forward, Lucius was dragged backwards while the boy general bent over and plucked Lucius's gladius from the snow.

"Ah, the vaunted sword of the Centurio Immortalis." Flavius looked at the fine engraving, flipping it to look at the other side of the blade. He gripped and swung it about, feeling the balance. He looked to a man behind him. "Be sure to get all his personal effects."

"Yes, Caesar!" The legionnaire jogged off, signaling a couple men to follow him.

Pulling his eyes away from Flavius, Lucius looked at the slumped figure of Marpesia still held aloft in the hands of her captors. He thought he heard a faint groan from her, her head rolling on her neck of its own accord. She'd have a blinding headache when she came to and a burning inferno of rage that would quell the effects of the headache — his fierce Marpesia.

A man ran up and saluted. "Caesar, we have everything."

"Good. Let's go before anyone tries anything stupid," Flavius replied, turning away.

"Caesar, what about this one?" said one of the men holding Marpesia.

"Leave her, she's more trouble as a captive than she's worth. We can't offend our *allies*," the boy Caesar sneered.

They dumped her in the snow. As they dragged Lucius away, he thought he could see more signs of her stirring before he could no longer turn to look. As much as he wanted to resist, he knew it meant the life of his men and Marpesia. He couldn't stand the thought of her dead because of his actions. He wouldn't sacrifice her life on the altar of his pride. As much as he wanted to yell, to tell her what she meant to him, he'd pushed her away out of his own fear of being hurt. And now, he might never see her again.

Lucius's eyes drifted down, watching the ground absentmindedly. As they neared the gate, Lucius identified the drifts in the snow as bodies, some wearing the black of his legion, some the woolens and scale of the Roxolani, and some the purple of Flavius's guards. As his eyes phased to blurriness, the faces of his men flashed into his mind as he passed their corpses, trying to avoid recognizing his dead but failing. When they walked past the young face of his secretary, the night sky turning the blood-stained snow gray, Lucius closed his eyes, caring not if he tripped or if the two men half-dragging, half-escorting were inconvenienced.

Martininius had just earned his fangs, just become fully one of the elite of the legion who could claim such an honor, and now he was dead. Not at the hands of the nightmares they hunted in the name of protecting humanity, but at the command of a duplicitous, power-hungry boy with more legions than sense. So much promise…wasted.

He quit caring, merely going through the motions as they forced him onto a pony, tying his legs together with a rope slung under the horse's belly. They bound his hands in front of him, his captors holding the reins as he became one more piece of baggage on their march to meet what Lucius guessed were the several legions the boy Caesar commanded. He'd not have penetrated this deep into the lands of the empire's barbarian enemies and dubious allies without a sizable force to protect him.

Lucius fell into a numb stupor as they rode into the night. He'd won the battles he'd been ordered to fight, but had lost the war he'd never wished to be a part of. After two hundred and forty-six years of life and survival, he'd been captured by an ambitious boy.

TWENTY-ONE

FLAVIUS DIDN'T APPEAR to be in a hurry after his small detachment rejoined the several legions he'd brought. He took time every day to interrogate Lucius, usually with the aid of a burly guardsman or three.

Spitting blood, Lucius lifted his head, fixing a murderous stare through the one eye not swollen shut. Fortunately, they seemed to like working his body to keep his mind from becoming too hazy from the punches. It hurt when he breathed too deeply. He probably had a cracked rib or two.

"So tell me, *Centurio Immortalis,* is the sword what makes you immortal? It's a beautiful weapon, but it's been two hundred years since this style was really used. Why else would you carry it when you can get a more modern weapon?" Flavius paced back and forth in front of Lucius while two of his goons held Lucius upright and a third waited for his signal to punch Lucius some more.

"It's a sword. Its only special power is to deliver a true death to di inferi, but a sharpened branch can also do that," Lucius replied.

"More children's tales of pagan monsters… I think you're lying."

"Of the two of us, I'm the only one who hasn't broken his pledge—"

The muscle-bound goon didn't even wait for a command, punching down into Lucius's cheekbone. Lucius hung, dazed, in the grip of the two men holding him upright, hot, sticky blood dripping from his cheek and falling onto the ground. When most of the fog cleared from Lucius's head, he tried to straighten some until his two captors decided to aid him by yanking him back to vertical. Lucius felt lucky they hadn't yet dislocated his shoulder with their delicate assistance.

The boy Caesar continued his pacing. "After serving in the legions for two hundred years, I'd figure you'd have learned to respect your superiors."

"An accident of birth no more makes you superior than it earns you respect."

The puncher drew back for another blow, only halting when Flavius raised his hand to stop him.

"Let's keep him conscious. He won't be able to feel pain if you knock him out again." He stopped pacing. "Is it the armor? I can read the engraving all over the bands of this antiquated lorica, but I don't know what they mean."

"It's just armor. It protects me from the enemies of Roma, human and non-human."

It was the same answer he'd given already. The answers were nearly verbatim at this point. Flavius asked the questions over and over, hoping to catch Lucius up and draw the answer he wanted instead of the answers Lucius had. He spoke truth in the answers. The weapons and armor did all the things he said. The only one he was cagey about was the rudis. For that, he gave the half-truth that the wood and silver were inimical to the demons of the night. The only edits Lucius had made during his interrogation was mentioning the font of their enchantments — Mithras.

The young followers of Christ, as they called themselves, refused to acknowledge a divine power separate from their new god. He couldn't tell if the boy was a true devotee or just more enthusiastic about courting the potential power the Christians were flexing now that they'd been brought into the light. Flavius's father's devotion felt more transactional, at least from Lucius's observations as Constantius rose in power, but perhaps the wily emperor's beliefs were becoming truer as he aged, and he bought into the newer religion as the font of his power and the salvation the Christians promised for their adherents in the next life. Lucius's curiosity about the boy's religious exuberance would have to stay speculative. He didn't feel like taking beatings fueled by the boy's rage; he'd settle for merely annoyed.

Each day at the end of their ride south, the boy Caesar took the time to ask the questions again. The hunger in his eyes when he talked about Lucius's gear spoke of a desire to steal Lucius's equipment, seeking to gain some advantage in case there was a struggle to replace his aging father.

His gear was superior to any made by a human, but only the rudis had anything to do with Lucius's immortality, so Lucius kept that information to himself. Nor did he tell the boy that it would only work for Lucius. If the equipment was useless to the boy beyond their value as weapons and armor, Lucius would cease to hold value and would probably cease to hold his head on his neck. As long as he could keep the boy interested in the information he desired, Lucius could keep breathing for another day and find a way to escape.

Several days into their daily sessions, a scout interrupted their interrogation to report that a small band was trailing them, keeping their distance.

"Who are they?" Constantius asked.

"We don't know, Caesar. They always disappear when we try to track them down. Without going too far out of range, they melt into the snow, then show up later. All we can tell is that they're armored. We can see the glint of metal."

Flavius turned to Lucius. "Is it your pitiful little party hoping to find a way to free you?"

Lucius shrugged, grimacing as sore, bruised muscles ground against his bones. "I have no idea. It could be the di inferi driving the Goths for all I know. We didn't get them all."

"You're going to stick to that story?" Flavius raised a skeptical eyebrow.

"That's why your father sent me here."

"He sent you with the barbarian witch to get you out of the empire. It was expediency, no more. He should have just executed you." The boy returned to his nervous pacing.

The scout cleared his throat to get the young Caesar's attention.

"Anything else to report?"

"No, Caesar."

Flavius gestured toward the exit of the tent, shooing the scout out of his way. Lucius caught the rolled eyes of the scout as he turned, ensuring his face was fully turned from the boy's field of vision. He repressed the urge to laugh. The small gesture wasn't worth another punch from whichever fist of the day Constantius had brought with him. A spark of hope ignited in Lucius at the scout's report. It could only mean Marpesia and his troops were in pursuit. He just prayed they'd made contact with Pisakar and the rest of their forces.

The brief glimpses he'd seen of Flavius's forces told him the boy hadn't brought all the legions his father had mustered to block the Goth's incursion, but he'd brought a significant force that outnumbered Lucius's single legion, even with the added cohorts he'd absconded with before crossing the border. Marpesia's Wolves would no doubt add to Pisakar's forces, but the elite cavalry units the boy had with his infantry would more than counter the number of the Roxolani unless Marpesia could come up with troops from her cousin.

At the moment, there was little he could do but trust the woman he loved—but had pushed away—and the man he'd left in charge of his legion. Pisakar was a brilliant strategist and brutal foe. That was the reason Lucius had recruited the young pit fighter when he'd stumbled across him Anatolia. If anyone besides Lucius could figure out how to counter Flavius's elite infantry and cavalry units and superior numbers, Pisakar could.

A punch to the gut knocked the air from Lucius, doubling him over as he fought to breathe. When he recovered and straightened up, the boy Caesar smirked at his own cruelty. Lucius must have let his hope show on his face.

"Do you think your tiny bandy of legionnaires and a pack of

barbarians will be able to free you? Even with your full legion, they don't stand a chance against my men. They're the elite of my father's forces. What do you have? Antiquated armor and weapons wielded by soldiers using antiquated tactics. We'd grind them beneath our caligae."

Maybe it was wishful thinking, but the boy didn't sound as confident as his words indicated. Flavius stood in the shadow of a giant, and even though Lucius didn't care for his father's treatment of the Black Legion, Lucius still respected his military prowess and the semblance of stability he'd brought to the people within the borders of the empire. The boy, however, had yet to disprove the initial poor impression he made on Lucius when he first met him months ago in Constantinopolis.

"Feeling quiet today?" Constantius asked when Lucius didn't rise to the bait. The boy shook his head. "Get him out of here. Maybe tomorrow he'll feel more loquacious."

When they tossed Lucius back into the box wagon they used as his prison, they loosened his bonds to allow him the limited movement the wooden jail allowed. He rubbed life back into his wrists and rotated his sore shoulders before sitting and inspecting his ankles. If he had to do this much longer, infection from the sores the ropes were causing would be more serious than the punches of the boy's enforcers. Either that, or he'd freeze to death like the Goths who'd been left for dead on their forced march.

Trying to find a place he could hide from the wind cutting through the wagon, he pulled the tattered blanket they'd left him around his shoulders and tried to pull his limbs in close. He wished he were with Marpesia so they could share warmth under his blankets. The weeks of being pressed up against her body had been some of the most content moments of his life. He missed her.

The thought of Marpesia should have provided at least some warmth, but he'd ruined that with his own stupid decisions. He sighed, rubbing his arms to create friction. No matter how much he tried, he couldn't banish the cold. He eventually crawled under the bench, hoping the bit of wood above him would hold some heat in as he shivered into the night, eventually falling into a fitful sleep, his dreams haunted by the face of the woman he'd left behind.

OVER THE NEXT SEVERAL DAYS, the Caesar kept Lucius cooling in the wagon as the legions marched through the snowy landscape in the shadow of the Montes Sarmatici. Lucius thought he recognized a piece of landscape here, a formation of rock and trees there from their ride north. He guessed they were now south of the ravine where he and Marpesia had first shared their bodies with each other.

Lucius missed the questioning sessions. At least getting beaten by the boy's thugs warmed his blood and allowed him proximity to a roaring brazier. Thoughts of the hot spring and Marpesia's warm body couldn't even stop the near constant shivering. Eventually, someone tossed in another blanket, this one more solid. Either they'd taken pity on him, or the Caesar had decided to keep his prize alive for a while longer. Despite the slow movement of Flavius's legions through the wintery plains and foothills, each day drew Lucius closer to the valley his men held and beyond that, an ever dwindling chance of escape or rescue.

As the wagon gently rocked, Lucius lost himself in his mind, unable to escape his thoughts of Marpesia—the feel of his hand on her cheek or the touch of their lips igniting a fire in his belly. The Roxolani woman had waged a steady campaign to win Lucius's heart, and through it all, Lucius felt more alive than at any time in recent memory. Now he sat in a frigid box waiting for a sixteen-year-old boy to decide his fate. He'd die sooner or later, either beheaded and dumped in the snow for carrion animals to find or presented to the boy's father where he'd be executed in style. The Dominus wouldn't free Lucius a second time, not if it meant reversing his son's actions and weakening the future heir's authority with the legions. The Dominus might apologize elegantly, but Lucius would be just as dead at the end of the day.

It was midmorning on the fourth or fifth day south of where

Lucius estimated they passed the hot spring ravine when horn calls went up and down the lines and the legions scrambled from a marching column into battle lines. Lucius tried to spot what lay ahead but couldn't see much through the tiny windows of the wagon. All he saw was a long, wide valley and forests obstructed by Flavius's cavalry moving about.

Lucius had just settled back into the sheltered spot he'd selected when the door to the wagon opened, and he was dragged out by a platoon of the Caesar's personal guards. They marched him up to the small rise where the Caesar consulted with his legati.

"What do you make of it?" Flavius asked.

"Well, Caesar. The earth is freshly turned from under the snow. The defenses are newly built within the last three days tops, since that was the last snowfall we've had," an old man in a fine cloak and armor replied.

"But where are the defenders?"

As if to answer, a cornicen blew the signal the Black Legion used to advance. The call stiffened Lucius's back as he looked up toward the earthworks and picket line of sharpened stakes. If it was indeed Pisakar and the Black Legion, he'd selected their ground well. The hill where they'd set up their defense works blocked the exit from the valley. Unless Constantius wanted to reverse course and find another way, they'd have to go through the Black Legion. Even if they did decide to go around, Pisakar could easily attack them in the rear or flank them from the hills.

Out of the trees, a century's worth of his legionnaires advanced in their battle line, carrying the legionary banner. A moment later, a similarly sized troop of Roxolani bearing Marpesia's wolf banner joined them. Between them rose a banner of truce.

"Well, they offer a truce. Shall we offer a banner of truce and see what they want?" asked a gray-haired legatus with a neatly trimmed beard.

"Yes. In the meantime, finish ordering my battle line so we can encourage them to pay their respects to their Caesar," Flavius replied, a glint of blood lust in his eyes.

"Very well, Caesar." The legatus saluted and set off to carry out his orders as the other legati murmured quietly among themselves. Flavius stared out over the valley floor separating his legions from the two centuries' worth of warriors.

After Flavius's banner of truce was raised, they waited for the response. A single rider trotted down the hill toward them, carrying the truce banner with him. After he made it to the Caesar's lines, he dismounted and was escorted through to the Caesar and his legati.

"Hail, Caesar." The messenger bowed perfunctorily.

"Do you bring a message for Caesar?" the gray haired Legatus asked.

"Aye, Legatus. Legatus Legionis Pisakar wishes to treat with Flavius Claudius Constantius Caesar in order to secure the release of the Centurio Immortalis. If you accept his offer of truce, please erect a canopy fifty meters in front of your lines so both parties may negotiate a peaceful resolution to this impasse."

"And should I choose not to speak with traitors?" Flavius asked.

"Legatus Pisakar says that when he is finished with you, he'll send condolences to your father and congratulations to your brothers. Your bones will lie where they fall."

Lucius thought the messenger may have given him a slight wink, the corner of his mouth quirking up. Flavius fumed at the threat. The legati, on the other hand, looked concerned, giving furtive glances up toward the well-built defensive works of the Black Legion. They also had to be wondering where the Black Legion actually was. The only troops visible were eighty men and a similar troop of Sarmatian cavalry. Every man in the legions knew the reputation and the history of the Black Legion. The legati didn't look as confident as the boy leading them. Finally, the gray beard acknowledged the messenger's terms and agreed to the meeting.

The messenger bowed and returned to his pony. The legatus ordered a canopy to be erected in the requested spot. When it was finished, Lucius was dragged out to the tent to wait with the Caesar and a handful of his commanders.

TWENTY-TWO

LUCIUS STOOD under the large canopy Flavius Claudius Constantius had set up in the field in front of his legions arrayed in their battle line. Shivering, Lucius wore his black tunic and the black wool with white diamond bands circling up and down the arms and legs of the shirt and leggings Marpesia had given to him. The cold wind whipped through his shaggy, curly hair. He'd not cut it since before he left the borders of the empire on his final mission for Roma and its imperator.

The boy general hadn't even allowed him to keep his bearskin cloak. Flavius had claimed it as his prize, wanting to own something from Marcus Aurelius, who'd gifted it to Lucius over a century ago. He tried to keep from shivering, but the cutting wind bit through the thick wool of his leggings and tunic. The iron manacles at his wrist didn't help, forming two iron bands that relayed the cold directly to his skin. Despite all that, Lucius kept his back straight, his demeanor relaxed with an edge of arrogance to it.

He knew, just beyond the hill in front of them, his legion and Marpesia's Sarmatians waited. Marpesia had made good time, swinging wide around Constantius's numerically superior force, getting in front of them to alert Pisakar of Lucius's capture. Together, they'd selected a prime battlefield and secured the high ground to block Constantius's advance.

And even though Flavius outnumbered Lucius's legion and Marpesia's Sarmatian horse archers at least three to one, no one with a lick of sense would attack the Black Legion uphill when the Black had established fortifications. Even if Flavius appeared not to have much sense, someone on his staff did. They'd halted their line of advance and readied for battle in case they couldn't negotiate with Lucius's second-in-command and closest friend.

Ignoring the discussion happening around him, Lucius kept his eyes on the thick line of sharpened stakes lined up near the top of the hill. So far, no one was visible on the line except for a century holding the main banner of the Black Legion and a matching number of Sarmatian horse archers holding Marpesia's wolf banner. A third banner of truce rose slightly higher between the two other banners.

Pisakar had a flair for the dramatic. He knew that theatricality could go a long way to even the odds, especially with the reputation and legends surrounding the empire's most elite of legions. There wasn't a legionnaire in the empire who didn't know the stories of the Black Legion, been weaned on them, stood in awe of them, hoping to be selected to join them.

A smile quirked the corners of Lucius's mouth at the sound of the wolf calls coming from the distance. A double line of cavalry road up the hill, between the banners, and split left and right along the picket line. When they reached their predetermined full line, the lines filled a second, third, fourth and fifth rows, leaving a large gap in the middle. He admired the precision of Marpesia's men and women. Flavius's legati turned and joined Lucius in watching the action unfolding ahead of them.

When the wail of the first carnyx split the silence, Lucius's heartbeat picked up.

"The Dragon cohort," he said, breaking the silence and pointing out the mournful call his first cohort used to call his men to attention and to warn the legion's enemies who they were about to fight.

Lucius could feel the stares of Flavius's commanding officers.

Behind them, he heard the nervous jangling of the Flavius's legions as the situation changed after their long wait.

When a horn approximating the screeching of an eagle broke the silence left by the Dragon call, Lucius quietly added, "Eagle cohort." Lucius called out the cohort after each call. "Bull cohort. Boar cohort. The Horses, the Capricorns, the Elephants, the Harpies, the Gorgons."

In the silence after the ninth horn call, every ear strained toward the hill. As one, every foot in lock step, all ten cohorts of the Black Legion appeared on top of the hill, the cohorts they'd formed out of the borrowed men from the border forts fleshing out their ranks and standing in reserve. The thunder of caligae stomping in precise order washed over everyone until they gave a quick double stomp as they halted between the wings of the Sarmatian cavalry. The last carnyx filled the sudden silence, giving its best imitation of the eerie call of the wolf.

"And Wolf cohort."

The Sarmatians joined the wolf call. Lucius took a moment to check Flavius's legions. They shuffled side to side in place, looking nervously at their neighbors in the line. None of them wanted to charge uphill into the fortified Black Legion with a horde of armored Sarmatian horse archers to pepper their flanks. Flavius ground his teeth, his jaw muscles flexing, anger pouring from his young eyes. They knew as well as Lucius how the warriors of the steppes were just as deadly with their lances, swords, and axes as they were with their bows. Lucius wondered where his three wings of cavalry were though, not seeing them mixed in with the Sarmatians. He knew Pisakar was up to something and had them doing something useful.

From the front line of Lucius's troops, a banner of truce was raised several times. Next to him, a similar banner was raised by Flavius's men. Getting the response that Flavius was ready to speak, two groups split off—one from the command line at the center of the Black Legion just behind its arrayed cohorts and a small group of Sarmatians, pulling out of the front of their right wing. Along with the banner of truce, Pisakar advanced under Lucius's personal banner. Marpesia—he recognized her steel and bronze scale armor along with her golden Sogdian mare—and her Sarmatians moved forward under her wolf banner with its hollow tail catching the wind. Both groups met up and joined into one mass, halting a bit from the canopy. Pisakar and Marpesia dismounted, as did the three banner bearers and Aella.

Pisakar looked at Lucius. "I trust you're doing well, Lucius."

"Tolerably, Pisakar."

Pisakar nodded. Marpesia yanked her helmet off and tossed it to the attendant accompanying her. The bruises left by Flavius's men had turned to a nasty yellow and purple and covered her left eye and part of her cheek. Glaring at Flavius's, she stalked toward Lucius, pulling her cloak off and spreading it across Lucius's shoulders.

"Thank you, Marpesia," Lucius whispered in Sarmatian just loud enough for her to hear.

She nodded, staring at his swollen and bruised face, and leaned in, whispering in Greek loud enough for everyone to hear. "If they've harmed you, I'll revisit each hurt they've done to you upon the boy's body." She turned, giving Flavius a withering glare. At five feet eight inches, she had a couple inches on the boy general who'd just turned sixteen.

She smirked slightly as he winced, unable to control his reaction to her naked hostility.

"Have…" Flavius's voice cracked as he addressed Pisakar. "Have you come to surrender to your Dominus and join us as we march home in victory?"

The tall Black man, towering over everyone under the canopy, pulled his helmet off, tucking it under his left arm, and looked at Lucius. "What say you, Princeps Primus Centurio? Do you feel like surrendering to this snot-nosed little shit today?" Pisakar let his deep, resonate voice carry so the nearest of Flavius's legionnaires could hear it and carry his words to their comrades.

Lucius kept his face steady, fighting to keep from smiling at his audacious friend. Lucius looked Flavius up and down, letting his contempt finally show as the boy fumed at the insult.

"You know, Pisakar, I don't think I do." Lucius turned to Flavius.

"I hope you're sure of your men's loyalty and fighting ability, because from where I stand, they don't seem too long on either."

"I don't negotiate with prisoners," Flavius spat out. "I've defeated the entire Gothic people. Your one legion won't stand against my forces.

His eyes betrayed his own lack of confidence, although he tried to bristle and posture to cover it up.

"The winter and hunger defeated the Goths. You just butchered the weak." Lucius snorted. "I may be the one in manacles, but you're not the one in control." Lucius turned so he could easily look between both armies while keeping an eye on Flavius and his officers. "In all the years I've commanded the Black Legion, we've never once drawn gladius against a legion of Roma. But since your father has seen fit to expel us from its borders, and you've betrayed his word to me about the safety of myself and my men, I guess today will be the day."

Lucius nodded to the man who carried Lucius's personal banner, Pertinax, who nodded back. Pertinax lifted the banner up then tipped it to his right. Keeping his stare firmly on the Imperator's son, Lucius had no idea what Pisakar had planned but knew his second had something up his sleeve.

Out of the corner of his eye over the top of the hill and his legion, Lucius caught a speck arcing into the sky, leveling out, then completing its arc gracefully as it fell to earth, plunging into the turf about ten yards from the tent. Flavius winced at the closeness of the ballista bolt still quivering in the ground.

When the bolt landed, the Black Legion started banging their pila against their shields in rhythm, letting a loud, deep wordless chant of, "hah-room" punctuate each hit of the shield. Out of the corner of his other eye, Flavius's legionnaires took a small step backwards, looking uncomfortably left and right to check the mettle of their comrades. The several wings of horses on each end of the infantry line danced nervously, picking up on the tension in their riders.

Lucius stared lazily at Flavius, a wry smirk on his face. "I think your men are questioning their own mortality as they stare uphill at the best trained and most feared legion in the empire."

With his legion on his right and Flavius's legions on his left, Lucius had a perfect view of the situation, including a copse of trees where the right wing of the Sarmatians had ended their line. "Ah, so that's what you did with my cavalry, Pisakar."

Flavius and his officers whipped around as the three cavalry alae formed up a line on the other side of the trees, putting them in position to easily flank the left of Flavius's line. His men took another step backwards, their centurions and optios bellowing to keep control of their men. Lucius admired the precision of his cavalry as the two light wings spread wide with the ala of heavy kataphraktoi jangling forward, the sun glinting off the full armor of horse and rider. When they halted, the cornicens barked out their presence over the potential battlefield.

"Get my men under control, kill any cowards who flee!" Flavius yelled at his officers, his voice squeaking under the strain. He turned to Lucius. "If your men make another move, I'll have you killed."

Flavius couldn't see his officers shocked looks and the loaded glances they shared among themselves, but Lucius could.

Marpesia stroked the side of the blade of her axe with her thumb. "If you give that order, it'll be the last thing you ever do, boy."

The blood drained from Flavius's face at the venomous hatred in her eyes and the proximity of her hand to the deadly weapon she could put against his neck before anyone could respond. He staggered back, his face flushing from white to red as fear and rage warred for dominance.

Lucius nodded at Marpesia before returning his gaze to Flavius. "I think you're starting to understand the situation, boy. I'm going to give you two options. You can withdraw your legions from the field and return home the victorious son of a proud father. Or, I will let the Roxolani emissary gift me your head. Then I'll take your head back across the border into the empire with your legions at my back where I shall return your rotting skull to your father in a box just before I take the empire from him. The choice on how you return is entirely."

"My men will never follow you." Flavius didn't sound as sure as his words.

Marpesia had been staring at the hills behind Flavius's lines for a while when a vicious smile spread across her lips. Lucius checked to see what she was looking at. Sunshine glinted off row after row of heavily armed and armored Sarmatians, far more than their combined forces at the pass. He didn't have time to count them, but guessed they numbered well over two thousand. Focused on Lucius, Marpesia, and Pisakar, Flavius and his officers hadn't noticed the newest change in their circumstances. She tipped her head to the right. Her banner bearer took his banner and walked out of the shade of the canopy.

"Pisakar, please fetch me my new legions." Lucius smiled condescendingly at the furious teen boy in front of him.

Pisakar walked behind Lucius, stopping at the edge of the canopy where the lines of Constantius's legions could see him. After the chaos of the previous hundred years of legion turning on legion, the chaos that had led to the new Domini and Constantius, Lucius and Pisakar wanted to put the fear of the boy's own family history to work against him.

"Tirones! Attention!" Pisakar commanded.

As one they snapped to attention, halting their creep backwards and straightening their lines. Every legionnaire had been called a tiro when they entered the legions until they graduated training. When a legionnaire was selected to join the Black Legion, they returned to tiro status until they proved their ability. To be called a tiro by Lucius or Pisakar was a high honor. By calling them all trainees of the Black Legion, Pisakar had just claimed them all, extending to them the glory associated with the Black.

Lucius held Flavius's gaze. "You were saying?"

Selecting the perfect timing, Marpesia's banner lifted high into the air, signaling the lines of Sarmatian heavy cavalry lined up behind Lucius's newest legions. Down the line, horn calls sounded across the valley, bouncing off armored warriors and hills. Flavius's head snapped to hills. His eyes went wide as fear won over rage, the blood draining entirely from his face as his knees shook.

One of his officers, an older man with mostly gray hair who'd been issuing most of the orders, placed his hand on Flavius's shoulder. "Caesar, we must accept his terms. We're surrounded. And your men would rather join him than face a better positioned enemy surrounding them on three sides."

Lucius noticed his careful wording designed to carry the point home while providing some cover for the ego of the empire's heir.

"No!" Flavius yelled. "I will not surrender to this Gallic peasant!"

"My Lord, Constantius Caesar, you have the chance to preserve your father's empire and your future throne." He paused before hissing, "Take it before all is lost."

The boy looked like he wanted to refuse, but mastered himself before grinding out between clenched teeth, "Fine." He stalked away from the officer, leaving the legatus standing alone between the other officers and Lucius.

The man stepped forward and bowed deeply to Lucius. "Princeps Primus Centurio Ferrata, Caesar has elected to quit the field and return home."

"Very good, Legatus…" Lucius paused, looking for a name.

"Cornelius, Centurio Ferrata. Tiberius Cornelius," the gray beard replied.

"I believe you have some orders to issue to your men, Legatus Cornelius."

"Um, I'd feel more comfortable if you were to inform your men and your allies of our decision to take the peaceful option. Not that I'm questioning your honor—"

Lucius interrupted him. "Nor should you. Between your Caesar and myself, only one of us has never violated his word to imperator and empire."

"Pardon me, Princeps Primus Centurio. I spoke poorly. I only meant I wish to ensure no bloodshed or mistakes on anyone's part. I will keep our men still until you've had a chance to let everyone know we mean no harm and only wish to depart."

Lucius nodded curtly, turning to Pisakar. "Legatus Pisakar. Stand down my men. There will be no fight today. Legatus Cornelius has elected the path of wisdom."

"Aye, Centurio." Pisakar saluted, strode back to the cluster of riders waiting out of range of the tent, and issued Lucius's orders, sending a pair of riders back toward their lines.

"Legatus Cornelius, I'd appreciate the return of my equipment and the fine horse that was gifted to me by the Roxolani's emissary."

Cornelius turned and issued some orders to one of the legionnaires who stood guard, waiting to be of use. He ran off toward his lines and through them to retrieve Lucius's effects from where they'd been stashed.

Marpesia walked up to Cornelius, scowling at him. "Take his manacles off."

Cornelius nodded, eyeing the powerful woman who intimidated the Roman officers gathered under the canopy. Her anger at the empire's betrayal and how she and Lucius had been treated radiated from every glare and action. They feared her axe and that a woman should wield it so well. Cornelius whispered something to Flavius, who took the key out and threw it to the ground. Cornelius bent over and picked it up, approaching Lucius.

Marpesia snatched the key from him. "Keep your distance, Roman."

She walked to Lucius. He gave her a crooked smile and extended his manacled hands in front of him. She smiled softly at him, gently removing the manacles and scowling at the damage they'd done to his wrists.

"Don't worry about it, Marpesia," he said. "They'll heal."

She nodded. He reached out but hesitated before touching her, finally letting his hand collapse by his side without feeling the warmth of skin. A brief moment of hurt flashed through her eyes. He opened his mouth to speak but was interrupted.

"Sir, we have your equipment." The legionnaire had returned, along with several people carrying Lucius's effects.

Lucius nodded at him.

"Allow me," Marpesia said, sweeping her cloak off Lucius's back and around her own shoulders.

She took Lucius's lorica from the legionnaire who held it and gently settled it around Lucius's shoulders, tying it shut for him.

Next, she took the baldric attached to his gladius and rudis and slid it over his head, laying it along his left hip. His belt followed. She knelt and strapped his greaves on. Last, she took Lucius's bearskin cloak and placed it over his shoulders, clasping it in front. The last legionnaire in line held Lucius's helmet respectfully, offering it up to Lucius, who took it, holding it under his left arm.

He had no idea what they'd done with his armor padding or his scarf, but he'd be fine until he got back to their camp and dug out his spares.

"My horse?"

"The groom is bringing him."

Lucius thought he understood. Moonlight Dancing had bonded with Lucius and had kicked at and bit most everyone except for a young groom who finally calmed her enough to be handled. Flavius had thought to take the beautiful silvery blue-gray black point Sogdian as a prize. The horse, taking his measure, had refused to let the boy Caesar near.

In the distance, where his cavalry lined up, a small cluster of riders galloped from their lines. Once they rode closer, he could make out their Sarmatian banners and armor. He looked at Marpesia, who'd noticed them as well, a wicked smile spreading across her face.

"Friends of yours?" he asked in Sarmatian.

She nodded. Seeing Marpesia's banner, the new Sarmatians headed toward the small cluster. A giant of a man dismounted from his short steppes pony. Long red braids hung out the back and sides of his helmet. His beard was likewise braided. As he stalked toward Marpesia, he pulled off his helmet, a feral grin splitting his beard and mustache.

He called out in Sarmatian, "Cousin! Why are you standing around talking? Shouldn't we be killing Romans?"

"They have decided to tuck tail and run, Siauakos."

The giant folded her in a rib cracking hug that she returned, patting his back hard. When they broke apart, Marpesia turned to face Lucius.

"So, cousin, is this the man you've raised all this trouble for?

He'd better be worth it. I should be drunk next to a fire right now, not freezing my balls off. Does he at least speak a civilized tongue?"

"Aye, he speaks some. Siauakos, this is Lucius Silvanius Ferrata, leader of the Black Legion. Lucius, this is my cousin on my mother's side and leader of all the free Roxolani, Siauakos."

Lucius extended his arm and clasped hands with the barrel-chested man covered in full scale mail. "Would you mind sending a messenger to your people letting them know the young Caesar will depart shortly? For some reason, they don't feel safe."

Siauakos let out a bellow of a laugh as he turned, contemptuously eyeing the boy who would one day rule the Roman Empire. He whistled back toward his escort and barked his orders. Two riders took off back the way they came, cutting a wide path around Constantius's forces.

While Siauakos and Marpesia chatted, Lucius checked to make sure nothing was happening with Constantius's troops or with the boy currently pacing back and forth on the other side of the canopy. He looked like he was working himself up for something. His own officers seemed to ignore him, quietly going over their withdrawal from the debacle created by their young Caesar. Finally, he straightened his back and stalked toward Lucius, his jaw clenching and his hands trembling.

"I hereby banish you and your barbarian whore from the borders of the empire for all time! To violate my command is to sign your own death warrant!"

Marpesia scowled at his insult, translating for her cousin. He took a step forward, reaching for his sword. She put her hand on his forearm, forestalling him. She stepped toward Constantius and unleashed a lightning fast punch, busting his nose and knocking him to the ground, blood spilling onto his face.

Constantius struggled to his knees, his spatha halfway out of its scabbard. Lucius yanked his gladius free of its sheath, leveling the tip at Constantius's neck.

"It's not too late to find a box, boy." He looked toward the opposing officers, who were all studiously keeping their hands unmoving and far away from their weapons. "Get this arrogant pup out of my sight and get your men marching. If he even looks at me cross-eyed, I'll leave all your bodies for the carrion birds to pick over."

As one, they bowed to Lucius, two of them dragging the boy to his feet and pulling him back toward their line. Lucius lowered his sword, leaving it naked until they'd disappeared behind the first line of their legionnaires, then returned it to its scabbard.

Siauakos turned to Marpesia, nodding his head appreciatively toward Lucius. "I like him."

Lucius nodded at Siauakos then turned to see where his horse was. A young boy was standing just outside the canopy, respectfully holding the big, shiny Sogdian on a lead. The boy kept his eyes on the ground. He had the look of a German or maybe a Dacian; he lacked the olive or darker skin tones of the more southerly peoples. He reached up and stroked the cheek of the horse who pressed into his hand, enjoying the attention.

"Thanks for bringing my horse."

"Yes, sir," he said quietly.

"Are you a free man or a slave?"

"Sir?"

"Who do you belong to? Yourself or to someone else?"

"The Caesar, sir."

"Well, how would you like to be a free man?"

The boy looked back toward the legions of Flavius as they made ready to march then back toward Lucius. When he turned back, he lifted his head, making eye contact with Lucius as if checking to see what trap might be in store for him.

"I would like to not be owned by the Caesar, sir."

"Congratulations. You're now a free man. If you'd be so kind as to lead my horse over to the others?"

The boy nodded and started off.

"Wait. Where's my saddle?"

"Um, I couldn't find it. I think they threw it away, sir." He looked frightened, in case Lucius was going to blame him.

"Looks like I'll have to break in a new one." Lucius gestured with his head toward the cluster of Roxolani and Roman riders.

Pisakar walked up behind Lucius, grabbing his shoulder. "We should probably get out of here in case the little shit changes his mind and gets his men to listen to him. I don't want to be standing here without a legion around me."

Lucius nodded and walked over to Marpesia and her cousin. "Care to ride with me back to our lines?"

Marpesia nodded, turning back to her cousin. "Until later?"

"Aye, cousin, we'll share kumis and tell tales to the wind." He turned to Lucius, extending his arm.

Lucius clasped his hand and nodded. Together, they walked back to the cluster of banners and horses. Siauakos leapt onto his pony and pulled its head around, taking off to rejoin his forces and giving the legions of Flavius a wide berth. Pisakar relayed orders to everyone as he bounded onto the back of his pony. When Lucius approached his shimmering silver Sogdian, the boy knelt and offered his back for Lucius to step on to aid his mounting.

"Stand back, boy. This is how we mount a horse in the Black." He jumped up, planting his hands on the horse's back and pulled himself into position, grunting. He'd barely made it up after Flavius's harsh treatment. He leaned over offering his hand to the boy. "Ride behind me, we don't have time for you to run alongside."

The boy seemed unsure, but he took his hand and let Lucius pull him up. The boy settled in, wrapping his arms around Lucius's waist. They kicked the horses into a trot then into a ground-eating gallop that would deliver them to the safety of the Black Legion.

"Thanks for coming for me, Pisakar. I don't think my head was long for my body. The boy wanted to deliver it as a gift to his father," Lucius yelled over the thunder of hooves.

"Don't thank me, you fool. Thank Marpesia. If I hadn't brought the legion along, she'd have taken my head and brought them herself. She's a very strong-willed woman."

Lucius pulled his horse alongside Marpesia's golden mare. "Marpesia, thank you. For everything."

She made eye contact with him and nodded, turning her attention back to the approaching picket line. Pisakar called out the password as they slowed, a line opening up for them to ride through. As Lucius worked his way through, his men sent up a hearty cry of welcome, the nearest reaching out to pat his greaves and boots as he passed. As soon as he was through, the lines closed behind him.

When he pulled back on the reins, the boy slid off the horse. Lucius followed suit, tossing the reins to the boy. "Micipsa," he called, seeing his groom. "I got you an assistant. He's got a knack with this beast. See if you can find him some warmer clothes and some food. Oh, and see if you can find my old saddle. We're going to need to ride soon."

Marpesia and Pisakar followed him to the cluster of his other senior officers.

"Anything to report?" Lucius asked.

"Glad to have you back, Centurio. Nothing new to report." Tinkomaros extended his arm to Lucius.

"Alright, I don't think we'll have any problems, but let's swing the line so we can keep them facing Constantius's line as they withdraw. Send the Cavalry to the left wing." Turning to Marpesia, he continued, "Would you like to take your Wolves and swing behind them and cap off the valley?"

She nodded back, a stern look on her face. She crammed her helmet back on her head and leapt on her horse, taking off toward her people, her small retinue following. Lucius watched her ride off.

She had been quite tender with him, giving her cloak as he shivered in the cold and then again as she helped him put his armor on after it was returned. Since then, she'd hardly said a word to him, only replying with terse nods. He'd hoped time and being captured would have diminished some of the hurt he'd caused her by trying to end things. Pisakar snorted. Lucius turned toward his friend, an eyebrow raised.

"What?"

"Nothing we have time for now." Pisakar shook his head.

"Care to enlighten me?" Lucius asked.

"At the moment, I think we have other things to attend to. And I'm sure the chieftain will handle it."

"Right." He turned, looking for his secretary. "Martininius!"

He looked around for the young man, not finding him. A different young man in armor stepped forward.

"Oh…" He was reminded the young man had died trying to protect Lucius from being captured by Flavius. He sighed and turned to the man waiting for his orders.

"Centurio, I'm taking Martininius's duties until you can select his replacement."

Lucius nodded. "Thanks. See if you can find me something to eat, a focale, and armor padding."

The legionnaire saluted and took off to carry out his orders. Lucius watched his officers carry out his orders, shifting his lines. The legionnaire he'd sent off to fetch him food returned a while later with a warm bowl of porridge. Lucius absentmindedly spooned it into his mouth as he watched Flavius's forces march out at a quick pace, his officers wanting to get out of the way of Lucius's anger in case he decided to pursue them.

Looking across the valley, his eyes sought the shimmering gold mare of Marpesia that matched the glittering gold bronze and silver steel of her scale armor. He followed her progress as she wheeled her clan warriors through the valley, discouraging Flavius from changing his mind. Her horse warriors halted when they reached their line. Siauakos's heavy cavalry and archers filled the gap between their high ground and the right wing of Marpesia's horse archers.

Lucius's officers watched as Flavius disappeared over the horizon. Pisakar, sending out scouts to keep an eye on them, wanted to ensure no funny business. Pisakar and his officers had everything in hand while Lucius stared out over the valley, his eyes only for Marpesia.

"Centurio… Centurio…" one of his officers said, trying to get his attention.

"Lucius," Pisakar called, interrupting Lucius's reverie. "What are your orders?"

It took a moment for Lucius to pull his mind back to the moment. "Let's get the men moving northeast. I want to consult with Marpesia on a place to camp for tonight, but I want to put as much distance between us and Flavius as we can."

"Aye. Ah, looks like a delegation from the Wolves are on their way." Pisakar pointed to a handful of riders separating from the center of Marpesia's line and heading toward Lucius.

He didn't see Marpesia among them, keeping his gaze on her as he issued his orders, "Ready the scouts and get the reserves formed up to start their march. We'll thin our lines from the rear. Leave the First and the Eighth and my cavalry to screen our withdrawal. Have the camp ready for me when I arrive."

"Aye, Centurio," Pisakar barked, stalking off to carry out his Centurio's orders.

TWENTY-THREE

BY THE TIME LUCIUS, along with his cavalry and two cohorts, made it to the camp, it was turning from twilight to dusk as the bitter cold wind picked up, biting through armor and clothes. The Wolves, as had become their habit, had integrated their camp inside the wooden walls of the meticulously erected Roman fort. Marpesia's cousin had situated his camp further, his band of Roxolani too numerous to enclose in the Roman camp. Some of the wagons from the Wolves' extended clan were setting up near the fort, too big to pull inside the already tight confines of the walls.

The Primus Pilus of the I Cohort called the password, earning them entrance into the gates. Lucius didn't need to issue orders. His men knew their business. The centurions could take care of their own men. He rode toward the center of the camp, handing the silver Sogdian over to his groom. His valet had anticipated his arrival, preparing a bath. Lucius looked happily at the steaming water in the small camp bath. Flavius hadn't allowed him the courtesy of proper hygiene as a prisoner.

Lucius let his valet help him out of his armor, then halted his valet before he stepped out of the tent. "Will you see if Marpesia would like to join me for dinner?"

The valet nodded and disappeared to carry out Lucius's request and find his supper, allowing his commander to oil and scrape his skin before sinking into the warm water. He let its heat work out the cold and soreness of his time under Flavius's less than hospitable care. When his groom returned, Lucius was dressed in a fresh wool tunic and trousers—another set Marpesia had given him—his black legionary tunic covering the Sarmatian woolens.

Seeing only food for one, he raised his eyebrow. "Will Marpesia be joining me?"

"I'm sorry, sir. Aella says she has already eaten." He bowed. "Will there be anything else?"

He stared at the food on his camp table.

"Sir?" his valet asked.

"No, nothing else for tonight. Go find some wine and a fire."

"Thank you, sir."

Lucius stared at the food, lost in thought. He'd hoped he'd have an opportunity to apologize and fix his wrong, but it appeared that Marpesia wasn't going to let him. He mechanically scooped the food into his mouth until his spoon scraped the bottom of the bowl. He downed the watered wine and stood up, looking around for his cloak. His valet had left out a heavy cloak made from the fur of a brown bear, another gift from Marpesia. His black bear cloak needed a thorough cleaning.

He stepped into the cold night, looking up at the field of stars spreading from horizon to horizon, and marched toward the section of camp where Marpesia's wolves were quartered. Her tent was in the center. Walking through the field of tents, he stopped in front of hers. He could see movement inside, the light of their brazier creating silhouettes.

"Marpesia?" he whispered loudly enough to be heard inside, but not beyond. "Marpesia, please? Can we speak?"

He stepped back as he saw someone inside the tent walking toward him. A hand took hold of the flap and pushed it aside. His heart in this throat, he sank into himself when Aella stepped out, closing the flap behind her.

"My mistress is not feeling well and does not wish to be

disturbed, Primus Princeps Centurio." Aella sounded harsher than her face let on, her use of his full title telling him where he stood.

Lucius could see sympathy in her eyes along with a healthy dose of judgment directed at him for hurting her mistress, her lover. "Aella, please?"

Aella shook her head. Reaching out, she gripped his forearm, squeezing it. "She does not wish to entertain visitors at this time." She said it loud enough that Marpesia could easily hear it. Aella shook her head at herself, coming to a decision, and leaned in closer to Lucius, whispering, "Perhaps tomorrow, Lucius."

Aella let go of his arm and walked into the night on some errand for herself or her mistress. Lucius stood outside Marpesia's tent, warring with himself on what to do next.

"Marpesia?" He heard nothing except the wind crying in his ears. He sighed. "Sleep well."

He walked back to this tent, nodding politely at anyone who greeted him but ignoring anything more. Once he was back inside the sanctuary of his tent, he sank into his camp chair, his head falling into his hands, his elbows propping his arms up on his knees. His eyes burned as his chest constricted. A gust of wind bursting into his tent felt icy against the wet tracks running down from his eyes.

"Centurio?" called the deep voice of Pisakar.

Lucius didn't lift his head. "What, Pisakar?"

He heard his old friend enter the tent all the way, setting a camp chair down in front of Lucius.

"Lucius?"

Lifting his head, Lucius wiped the tears off his cheeks.

Pisakar sighed, extending his legs and slouching back into the chair, the wood of the chair groaning under the giant man. "Lucius, why are you doing this? There's nothing for you in the empire."

"There's nothing for me anywhere, Pisakar. Nothing but soulless demons."

"There's something for you here, if you're not too stupid to take it."

"I have nothing to offer but death. Death for monsters. Death for my enemies. Death for my friends."

Pisakar sat up, leaning forward, and captured Lucius's gaze. "Is that it? Is that the reason you're doing this?" He paused, pursing his lips. "I'm not just your Legatus, am I, Lucius?"

"No, I consider you my dearest friend, Pisakar."

"Will you mourn me when I die? When you outlive me?"

Lucius nodded, not breaking eye contact. "I've mourned all my friends. I still mourn them, holding them here." He tapped his chest over his heart.

Pisakar shook his head, sighing. "You're not afraid to bring more death to her. She's a warrior and a chieftain of her own clan of warriors. She knows death. You're afraid to bury her when you inevitably outlive her. You're afraid of the pain losing her will cause *you*. If you're both lucky, you'll have to watch her grow old. She'll fall to an enemy's axe, or to sickness, or to time at a ripe old age. You'll be there for all of it. Witness it, inviolate, as you witness every change of age taking her. You'll have to bury her. Say your farewells and send her on to her gods. That's the burden you'll have to take on to be with her. That's what you fear."

Pisakar paused for a moment, looking down at his own clasped hands. He'd seen through Lucius's excuses. "Lucius. I don't know if you've watched, but since we've kept a merged camp with the Roxolani after we left the empire, the women and men of Marpesia's Wolf Clan have visited many a tent of many a legionnaire. I've had my share of offers."

Lucius nodded. Normally, he'd demand more discipline of his men, but this deep beyond a border he was never crossing again, he couldn't bring himself to deny his men the affections of the free Roxolani interested in bedding the elite soldiers he led.

"I've seen a fair few Roxolani men and women eyeing you, sizing you up. Many like what they saw beyond your reputation. Do you know why not a one has approached you?"

Lucius shrugged. "I guess I didn't think about it. Why?"

"I asked Aella. It's the way of their people. They don't mate within the clan, although they're a newer clan formed from many peoples from the Sarmatian tribes. They seek lovers and mates outside their clan. Our men are prime candidates. Strong, elite soldiers. They won't couple with anyone they don't view as someone who can provide something to their clan—strong babies, strong warriors, good leaders."

Lucius nodded. "Marpesia and Aella told me a story like this when we were in Constantinopolis."

Pisakar smiled, giving a half chuckle. "You should be the first choice of every Roxolani woman trying to birth a strong baby. Do you know why not a one has even attempted to flirt with you?"

Lucius shook his head.

"Not a one of them will challenge their leader for the right to pursue you. When she knocked you down and then you returned the favor in that little duel, that was her testing you out as a potential mate. She marked you as hers then. She judged you her equal. When she beat you, then you put her on her ass, she proclaimed to every Roxolani that you were off limits to everyone but her."

"I didn't put the pieces together." Lucius bowed his head, looking at the ground. He lifted his head, making eye contact with Pisakar. "I didn't know…"

Pisakar shook his head, looking at Lucius sadly. "She knows who you are, Lucius. She knows what you are. She knows what a life with you might look like. She's seen pieces of it. She's not going into this blind and naïve. She's far too intelligent and wise to choose you without thinking of what it means. You're no ordinary man. And she's an extraordinary woman. You're robbing her of her choice. And worst of all, Lucius, you're robbing yourself of a life other than blood and monsters. You'd deny yourself waking up every day next to her, seeing that smile on her face—the one that makes you look like some giddy young man after the first time a beautiful woman seduced him into her bed. You'd deny yourself feeling the wind in your hair as your ride next to her."

A small smile tipped up the corners of Pisakar's lips. "I've seen the way you look at each other when you're on that Sogdian she gave you, riding next to her golden mare." Pisakar sighed, shaking his head. "You can't go through a life like yours avoiding inevitable pain, but you can choose to take happiness when it's before you."

Lucius's chin quivered, a fresh pool of tears forming in his eyes and leaking out. He nodded.

"Have you never been truly in love, Lucius? Body and soul, achingly in love?" Pisakar leaned closer to Lucius, staring into his eyes, filling them with sympathy.

"No."

Pisakar exhaled sharply, sounding exasperated. "You're a bigger fool than I thought if you think that's the truth."

"Have you?" Lucius wiped the tears from his cheeks again. "Been in love like that?"

"Once, when I was young, long before you and I met, before I decided to leave my home." Pisakar stood up. "Now, I'm going to return to my tent. There's a beautiful Roxolani woman waiting for me who said she'd like to have a handsome, strong baby to take back to her Wolf Clan. I aim to oblige her."

Pisakar reached his hand out and squeezed Lucius's shoulder and turned to leave. Putting his hand out to push his way out of Lucius's tent, he turned around. "Lucius? I don't want an answer to this question, but think about this. You'll outlive us all most likely. Me, Aella, Marpesia, everyone in this camp, *Nostrer Dominus* Constantius and all his whelps, all of us. You have to ask yourself—what do you want to carry forward with you for the rest of your long days? Regret at letting her ride out of your life? Or even just the possibility of one more day of pure joy with her?"

Pisakar stepped out of the tent and into the night. Lucius sighed, finding a cloth to wipe his face and nose clean. He found his bed, removing his black tunic but leaving the wool Marpesia had given him against his skin. He stared at the ceiling of his tent, Pisakar's words running through his head on an endless loop until he finally lost his battle with sleep and succumbed to its embrace.

LUCIUS WOKE, foggy and sandy-eyed after tossing and turning all night. When he peeked out of his tent, the camp was well into its morning activity. He'd been allowed to sleep late after his ordeal. His black bear cloak had been returned to his tent; his valet had finished brushing it clean. The armor, likewise, had been polished back to its high shine.

He pulled on the black wool trousers and tunic with white stars Marpesia had given him and added the black legionary tunic over it, leaving bands of stars on the black field visible on his arms and legs. Next, he added all his armor, finishing with the black bear cloak.

Taking a deep breath, he strode from his tent and headed toward the Sarmatian tents. Rounding the corner, he nearly fell over when he saw the open ground where their tents had been set up. He stared at the unoccupied space, lost to time until he was stirred back to the world by someone speaking to him.

"Centurio, can I help you with something?"

He turned to see one of the optios standing respectfully behind him. "Where are the Wolves?"

"They packed up and left just after sunup, sir. Last I heard, they were gathering upriver with the rest of their clan to march out."

"Fuck."

The optio shrank back slightly. "Were we supposed to stop them?"

"No, you weren't supposed to stop them. Damn it. Can you find my groom and have him saddle my horse?"

"Yes, Centurio." He saluted, looking happy to be sent somewhere besides Lucius's presence, and marched off to carry out his order.

Lucius walked briskly, nearly breaking into a low jog through the neat lines of tents back toward the center of the camp. He shoved his way into Pisakar's tent, not bothering to announce himself.

"Shit, sorry, Pisakar."

Pisakar wasn't alone. Lucius turned around, facing the wall of the tent. Apparently Aella was the beautiful Roxolani wanting Pisakar to sire a child with her. Lucius had caught them mid-attempt, Aella straddling the giant Kushite, a blanket wrapped around her hips and covering them both from the waist down. They had stopped moving.

"They're gone, Pisakar."

"Who?"

"The Wolves…"

"They're a free people. The reason for our alliance has ended. They're moving out."

"But…" Lucius sighed, his shoulders slumping and his head dropping. "Marpesia."

"They haven't left yet, and they won't be moving quickly with the wagons, not through this ground," Aella spoke up.

"It's too late. She probably won't even speak to me."

"I've never seen her more angry," Aella said. "You hurt her —badly."

"You'll never know if you don't try, Lucius," Pisakar added.

Lucius nodded to himself and took a deep breath, walking out of the tent. Aella was right. If she was still here, the Wolves couldn't be far. When he got back to his tent, he found his groom holding the big silver-gray Sogdian, saddled and ready to go. Looking at the horse, he made a snap decision, darted into his tent and grabbed his helmet, strapping it on. He stepped out of the tent and leapt into the saddle, taking the reins from his groom and trotting the horse through camp. When he approached the gate nearest to where the Wolves had been last seen, he called out the password and, as soon as he cleared the gate, kicked the horse into a gallop—the cold wind biting into his face, his black crest streaming out behind him. He wanted to urge the horse to go faster, but he was already pushing it in the rough ground torn up by feet and hooves.

When he crested the hill where the Sarmatians had been reported, he pulled up on his reins, slowing the horse and allowing her to catch a breather. The camp was abuzz with activity, like a kicked over ant mound. He trotted down the hill and into the camp, a few of the Sarmatians he recognized raising a hand or calling out a greeting as he weaved his way through the chaos of people going about their tasks.

Seeing a face with a name he remembered, he rode up, and called out in Sarmatian, "Where can I find Marpesia?"

"Last I saw, she was that way, in the center, directing things." He pointed toward the north and the mass of tents, horses, and wagons.

Lucius nodded his thanks and nudged his horse forward. When

he rounded a cluster of wagons, he saw the shimmer of her armor as she stood in a small clearing. Now that he was about to face her, he had no idea what he wanted to say. He'd traded words with some of the most powerful people in the Roman Empire only to be struck wordless at the sight of the Sarmatian woman.

He slid to the ground, giving the Sogdian a pat before stepping out of her shadow to approach Marpesia.

"What do you want Primus Princeps Centurio Ferrata? I thought I made it clear I didn't want to speak with you." Her stormy gray eyes, agate hard, bore down on him, her lips pinched and her brows furrowed.

"Marpesia, where are you going? I thought you were going to stick around a little longer."

"I see no reason to spend more time here. We're headed east and south to find warmer ground to ride out the rest of winter in." Her words were short and curt.

"Don't go. Stay."

"Why? Give me a reason why I should?"

He thought he saw a slight softening around her eyes, although she kept her tone angular and sharp. "I don't want you to leave." He knew it sounded childish, and his tone didn't help.

"Why, Lucius?" She closed the distance between them, her face still bearing her anger, but her eyes carried her vulnerability and a wary hope and question. "Tell me why I should stay."

Lucius opened his mouth and closed it several times, the words not coming.

Shaking her head, she looked down at the ground between, then looked up, making eye contact. She spoke lowly, "I will not beg…"

"Marpesia, I… Don't go."

Marpesia growled in exasperation and shoved Lucius in the shoulders, knocking him back. She spun to walk away but turned back to face Lucius. "You're a damned fool. I'm going to walk away, and you'll never see me again."

"Marpesia…" His knees trembled as his stomach churned.

She threw her hands up, turning around, and stalked away.

"Marpesia! Don't…" His legs gave out as he sank to the ground onto his knees. "I love you." He didn't know if she'd heard the last thing he said; he barely spoke it above a whisper.

She stopped, her shoulders rising and falling as her anger permeated her lungs. She turned and took a few angry steps toward Lucius. "What did you say?"

He lowered his eyelids, took a couple steadying breaths, and opened them, staring into Marpesia's stormy gray eyes. He switched to the Roxolani dialect he'd been learning whenever he had a moment. "Marpesia, I love you."

He untied his helmet and tossed it to the side. Taking another deep breath, he sat back on his heels and pushed himself back to a standing position. He unclipped the black cloak given to him by the emperor Marcus Aurelius and let it fall behind him. "I love you, Marpesia."

Next, he unbuckled his cingulum militare, dropping it, and took a step forward. He ducked his head under the baldric and dropped it along with his gladius, taking another step forward. "None of this means anything to me without you."

He reached down and untied the knot, and stripped out the leather thong holding his lorica together. He shrugged out of his armor, letting it clatter to the grounds. "The empire, my reputation, my legion, they've all been taken from me, but I'll not allow my own cowardice to take you away from me."

A crowd gathered around them as Lucius's voice grew stronger. A cold breeze carried an occasional murmur to his ear, but everyone was too transfixed on Lucius making a spectacle of himself for Marpesia to say much of anything. He took another couple steps toward Marpesia. The glint of a tear falling down her cheek caught his eye. Her fists flexed at her sides.

"What do you want, Lucius?" Her voice trembled.

"I want you! I've wanted you since the first moment I laid eyes on you sitting outside Constantius's throne room. I've wanted you every day since, and I'll want you every day forward. I want to love you every day until death parts us and beyond." Stepping close enough to touch her, he sank to his knees, raising his arms toward her. "I'm begging you, Marpesia. Don't make me live a life without you in it. I love you, and I promise I will love you from this day until I exhale my last breath."

The hardness had disappeared from Marpesia's face, tears falling freely from her eyes. Lucius stared up at her, his soul laid bare in his eyes. Every second she stood silent was an eternity over a bottomless chasm. He looked down, seeing her hands trembling; he reached out, his own hands unsteady, and took them in his.

"I am sorry for hurting you, for trying to take your choice away from you. I was wrong. You are a strong, powerful woman and capable of taking care of yourself." He tried to pour every bit of earnestness into his gaze. He'd hurt her deeply, and he owed her so much more than just an apology, yet he hoped she'd accept it. "If you will let me, I'll spend the rest of our time together making it up to you. Please. Let me stand by your side. Let us stand together."

The apology and the physical contact as he gently squeezed her hands pushed her to her knees as she sank into his arms. Flinging hers around his neck, she cried into his tunic. "That's all I wanted to hear, Lucius — that you loved me. That you wanted to be with me."

He cupped her nape and brought her lips to his. At first, their kiss was tentative, but as they assured each other of the reality of what had happened, it deepened until the sound of cheers and whis-tles pulled them back from each other.

Ignoring the noise, Lucius stroked her hair and rested his fore-head against hers. "I never want to be away from you. I will go where you lead. I will be your companion through good times or bad."

Marpesia pulled Lucius into a bone-crushing hug. "Lucius… You're shaking."

"I hadn't noticed, but it's a bit cold."

"You fool of a man." She shook her head, a chuckle in her words. Standing up, she offered him her hand. He took it and stood. She wound her fingers through his and walked away from the dissipating crowd. Catching the eye of someone, she called out, "Tell everyone we're holding camp for now. Prepare for a party. I feel like cele-brating."

"Aye, Marpesia."

"Also…" Marpesia gestured toward Lucius's effects strewn out on the ground. The man nodded.

Lucius, a giddy grin plastered to his face, laughed, feeling lighter than he'd felt in years. He had no idea what tomorrow held, but he knew that today he held Marpesia's hand as she led him to her wagon, her large felt tent set up next to it. Tucked away inside the cozy confines, they stripped quickly and slid into the luxurious pile of furs and blankets and made love.

After they'd finished, as they lay naked under the blankets in each other's, Marpesia's mess of curls spread out over his chest, she tipped her head back, kissing his chin. "I love you, Lucius."

"I love you too."

A gust of wind jolted them as someone poked their head through the tent's entrance. Aella smiled broadly. She pulled her head out of the tent, calling to someone outside with her, "I found them." She walked in, kneeling in one corner as another cold blast hit them. Pisakar blocked out the entrance, dwarfing everyone inside. He sat next to Aella.

Pisakar nodded at Lucius. "Good. You didn't fuck this up."

Everyone looked around the confined space at each other until Pisakar spoke up first, "Now what, Lucius?"

Lucius sighed, looking at his friend and squeezing Marpesia's shoulder. "Now, we pay out the men and bid the Black Legion good night."

EPILOGUE

LUCIUS RACED over the steppes on his blue-gray Sogdian, the tail of Marpesia's golden horse flying out in front of him. Occasionally, a few notes of her laughter would drift back on the wind to caress his ear, drawing a smile and laugh from his own lips. Ahead rose the hill Marpesia wanted to ascend to see what lay on the other side. Content to ride behind his beloved, he didn't force his long-legged mare into a full run. When he neared the top of the hill, he slowed Moonlight Dancing, allowing his loyal mare a breather and a chance to cool down after their dash across the summer grasses of the Sarmatian Steppes.

He rode next to Marpesia, letting his leg bump into hers as she stared over the eastern horizon. He reached out and grasped her hand, remembering a similar scene on the day he officially accepted his banishment from the empire and left its borders for the last time. Then, they were sitting on a pair of utilitarian ponies, Lucius staring at the death of his past as his legion marched across the bridge and out of Roma's borders, Marpesia staring at her future—and unbeknownst to Lucius at the time, his future too.

He turned his head, admiring the beauty and free spirit of his beloved, his mate, his wife. The stiff summer breeze tugged at her auburn curls, pulling them behind her as she squinted into the late morning sun, its light dancing across her locks. Marpesia and her love of her home, her steppes, had infected Lucius.

He'd never felt so free in his entire life, save for the times as a boy when he'd lay in fields of bluebells staring at the clouds. Feeling his eyes on her, Marpesia turned toward him, a joyous smile spreading across her face. She leaned forward. As Lucius responded, she took advantage of his proximity to wind her fingers through his long, shaggy hair to pull his face in for a kiss. When she let go of him, they sat straight in their saddles, looking to the eastern horizon.

"Where would you like to go next, my Pesi?" Lucius asked, not caring what the answer was as long as he could be by her side.

"I think I'd like to see what's on the backside of that hill over yonder." She lifted her arm, pointing to a distant hill.

"How long have you been riding over these steppes?"

"Since I was born," Marpesia replied.

"You've probably seen every hill there is to see," Lucius said, notes of teasing in his tone.

"Could be." She stared quietly toward the hill she'd pointed out. "But you never know until you see for sure."

Lucius laughed, turning in his saddle to look behind him. In the far distant, barely visible, a dark smudge moved toward them. The whole of Marpesia's Wolf Clan, along with the remainder of his legion—those who'd decided they'd rather stick with Lucius, and their new Roxolani lovers, in many cases—rode east in the wake of Lucius and Marpesia.

"It'll take a longtime for Pisakar and Aella to catch up with all the wagons…" Lucius left it hanging.

"Well, the grass is tall and makes for a lovely bed. I'm sure we can find something to do to occupy our time while we wait…"

Lucius laughed—a free sound filled with joy. He tugged lightly at Marpesia's hand, causing her to lean toward him. He caressed her cheek and pulled her gently into another kiss.

"I love you, Marpesia."

"I know you do, silly Roman. Now let's go see about the other side of that hill." She nudged her golden mare into a walk and started down the backside of the hill they'd just surveyed. Before she got too far, she turned to Lucius. "Are you coming?"

With a smile on his face, he nudged the mare into motion, settling into a gentle trot as he caught up to Marpesia and her mare. "I'll follow wherever you lead."

LEAVE A REVIEW

Reviews are the lifeblood of every indie author. Even a simple star rating means the world to us. If you enjoyed this book, please leave an honest review at Goodreads, BookBub, or your preferred online book retailer.

Would you like to join other readers who enjoyed this book? Join my Facebook Reader Group!

facebook.com/groups/CThomasLafolletteReaderGroup

Thank you!

C. Thomas Lafollette

NEWSLETTER

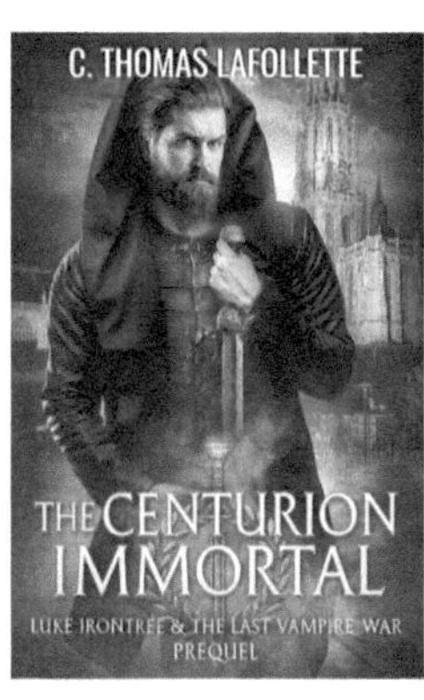

The Centurion Immortal is a Luke Irontree prequel novella and is exclusive to the Dispatches from C. Thomas Lafollette newsletter. Please sign up for your free copy and you'll also receive a twice-monthly newsletter with news, book updates, recipes, drinks tips, and other fun stuff. Your email will never be given out, rented, or sold.

CThomasLafollette.com/newsletter/

LUKE IRONTREE PREVIEWS

DARK FANGS RISING

LUKE IRONTREE & THE LAST VAMPIRE WAR - BOOK 1

An immortal vampire hunter has survived for almost two thousand years…

…yet he never suspected a rain-filled gutter in Portland, Oregon would be his grave.

When every advance ends in ambush, will allying himself with werewolves save the hunter from the trap the vampires have laid?

Former Roman legionnaire Luke Irontree stalks the dark, rainy streets of Portland to eliminate the vampires preying on his quiet city before they get out of hand. But when the streets run red with blood and the city's most vulnerable people start disappearing, he might be too late to stop the undead scourge — or even survive.

Suddenly hunted in his own town, Luke narrowly escapes when a werewolf and a human woman save him from the threshold of death, forging unexpected friendships in the process.

Can Luke protect his city and stay alive while training his allies, dodging hungry vamps, and recovering from grievous wounds? Will he uncover the sinister plan behind the disappearance of Portland's homeless population before the vampires can add him to their list of victims and end his undying life permanently?

You'll love this action-packed urban fantasy, because even a broken hero deserves a shot at redemption.

DARK FANGS RAGING

LUKE IRONTREE & THE LAST VAMPIRE WAR - BOOK 2

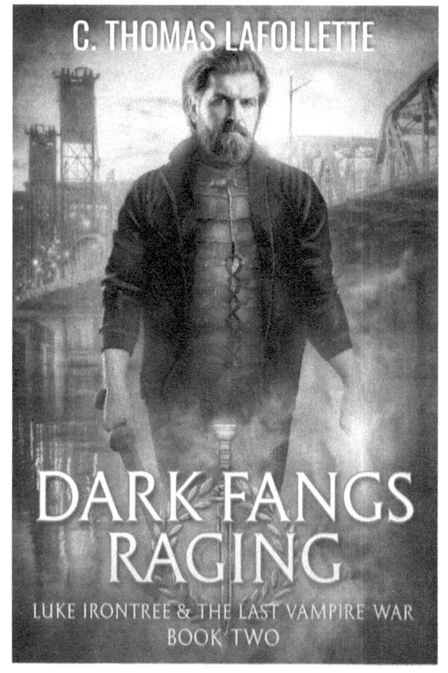

An old friend becomes a new enemy…

…and Luke is left playing catchup as the vampires turn up the heat.

Can Luke and the North Portland Werewolf Pack unravel the vamps' evil plan before it's too late?

Luke thought he knew what the vampires were up to. Same old enemy, same old tricks. But when a flood of heavily armed vampire mercenaries show up in Portland led by an old friend, Luke and his newly assembled crew of misfits are the ones left dodging bullets.

For Luke and his new friends, it's a race against time to stem the flow of heavy arms coming into Portland while also trying to find out how deep the connection goes between Portland's police and Luke's ancient enemy.

Will Luke get to the bottom of how the vampires are smuggling weapons into Portland? Or will the vampires finally eliminate their deadliest enemy?

You'll love this thrilling urban fantasy sequel because danger is better with friends.

DARK FANGS DESCENDING

LUKE IRONTREE & THE LAST VAMPIRE WAR - BOOK 3

Beware he who hunts the hunter…

…because the predator can become the prey.

When vampires infiltrate the police, will Luke and his ragtag band of werewolves survive as Portland's Most Wanted?

Trapped in a deadly game of cat and mouse, Luke and his growing werewolf army of vampire slayers are still a few steps behind the vamps and their vengeful leader, a man Luke once called a friend. This time, it's not only their fanged immortal enemies they're facing, but the very power structure of Portland itself.

Dodging cops and vampires makes for a lethal contest no one wanted to play and leaves all of Portland vulnerable as their invisible protectors are hunted by a corrupted government. Luke will be pushed to the very edge of his abilities with no guarantee of survival.

Can they escape the vampires' clutches yet another time? Or will Luke's luck finally run out?

You'll love the explosive conclusion to the Dark Fangs arc, because Luke isn't going down without a fight.

RISE OF THE CENTURIO IMMORTALIS

A LUKE IRONTREE HISTORICAL FANTASY ADVENTURE

It's dangerous business getting mixed up with gods…

…but a centurion always follow orders.

When blood sucking monsters attack, can even the gods protect a loyal soldier of Rome?

After three years campaigning in Armenia and Mesopotamia and a meteoric rise through the ranks of the legions, Lucius has been promoted to centurion and given a final mission from his dying emperor—go to Armenia to protect a remote temple dedicated to the god Mithras.

With a Parthian assassin on their trail and a ferocious Caucasus Mountains winter in front of them, Lucius and his men are running out of time. And with dark demons waiting for them at Mithras's temple, Lucius may be running out of luck.

Enemies—mortal and not—are dogging Lucius's every movement, and he isn't sure he'll be able complete his emperor's mission… or even make it out alive.

You'll love this blend of historical fantasy and vampires, because history is better with fangs.

ACKNOWLEDGMENTS

I'd like to thank all the people who made this book possible.

My production and editorial Team: Amy, C.D., Ravven, & Suzanne. Without you, this book wouldn't be as good as it is.

I want to give a special thanks to Nat of Reverend Nat's Hard Cider. Without your insights into kumis, one of the most pivotal scenes (and one of my favorite) wouldn't be as good as it is.

I also want to thank Adrienne Mayor and her research. Her book "The Amazons: Lives and Legends of Warrior Women across the World" was foundational for creating Marpesia and her clan of Roxolani Sarmatians.

To my critique group, thank you for all your hard work. Your eyes and efforts have made my writing better.

ABOUT THE AUTHOR

C. Thomas Lafollette is a writer of Urban Fantasy and Historical Fantasy and is the author of the forthcoming Luke Irontree novels. He earned a degree in Ancient History with a specialization in Classics at The College of Idaho. He's read poetry on stage with Yevgeny Yevtushenko* and dined with the Belgian Prime Minister**. C. Thomas has lived in Portland, Oregon for over Twenty years. He lives with his wife, fellow author Amy Cissell, his stepdaughter, and his three jerkface cats. He and Amy also run their own freelance editing business - Cissell Ink

*Yevtushenko was friends with a professor at C. Thomas's college. He was studying Russian at the time and Yevtushenko decided he wanted the Russian students to read with him on stage at his performance.

**This was purely coincidental. C. Thomas's host took him to dinner at a restaurant in Mons, which was Elio De Rupo's favorite spot. He'd had a pie thrown at him earlier that day and was having dinner with some friends. C. Thomas is still not sure what kind of pie it was though.

twitter.com/CTLafollette

facebook.com/CThomasLafollette

tiktok.com/@cthomaslafollette

instagram.com/CThomasLafollette

bookbub.com/authors/c-thomas-lafollette

amazon.com/C-Thomas-Lafollette/e/B09JMTR7W7

goodreads.com/cthomaslafollette

ALSO BY C. THOMAS LAFOLLETTE

Luke Irontree & The Last Vampire War

Book 0 - The Centurion Immortal

Book 1 - Dark Fangs Rising - March 22, 2022

Book 2 - Dark Fangs Raging - April 19, 2022

Book 3 - Dark Fangs Descending - May 17, 2022

Book 4 - Blood Empire Reborn* - August 23, 2022

Book 5 - Blood Empire Avenged* - September 20, 2022

Book 6 - Blood Empire Burning* - October 18, 2022

Book 7 - Blood Empire Collapsing* - November 15, 2022

Book 8 - Ancient Sword Falling* - February 7, 2023

Book 9 - Ancient Sword Unyielding* - March 7, 202

Book 10 - Ancient Sword Shattering* - May 9, 2023

The Luke Irontree Historical Adventures

Rise of the Centurio Immortalis - April 5, 2022

Fall of the Centurio Immortalis - May 31, 2022

The Moonlight Centurion* - December 27, 2022

The Highway Centurion* - April 11, 2023

*Forthcoming

Titles and release dates may be subject to change.

www.ingramcontent.com/pod-product-compliance
Lightning Source LLC
Chambersburg PA
CBHW050831190726

48286CB00007B/2050